THE VERY NEARLY HONORABLE
LEAGUE OF PIRATES

Magic Marks the Spot

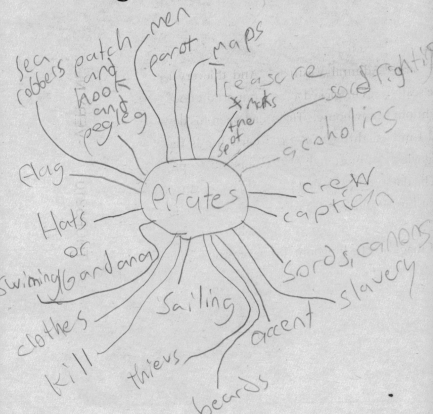

sea robbers · patch · men · parot · maps
and hook and pegleg
Treasure X Marks the spot
sord fighting
acaholics
flag
crew caption
Hats or Bandanas
Swiming
clothes
Sailing
sords, canons
slavery
kill
thievs
accent
beards

Pirates

CAROLINE CARLSON

THE VERY NEARLY HONORABLE LEAGUE OF PIRATES

Magic Marks the Spot

Illustrations by **DAVE PHILLIPS**

HARPER

An Imprint of HarperCollinsPublishers

The Very Nearly Honorable League of Pirates: Magic Marks the Spot
Text copyright © 2013 by Caroline Carlson
Illustrations copyright © 2013 by Dave Phillips
For information address HarperCollins Children's Books, a division of
HarperCollins Publishers, 195 Broadway, New York, NY 10007.
www.harpercollinschildrens.com

Library of Congress Cataloging-in-Publication Data
Carlson, Caroline.
   Magic marks the spot / by Caroline Carlson.
       pages   cm.— (The Very Nearly Honorable League of Pirates ; #1)
   Summary: "When Hilary Westfield escapes Miss Pim's finishing school to join a misfit
pirate crew, she embarks on an unexpectedly magical swashbuckling, plank-walking, sear-
faring journey"— Provided by publisher.
   ISBN 978-0-06-219435-0
   [1. Pirates—Fiction. 2. Adventure and adventurers—Fiction. 3. Magic—Fic-
tion. 4. Sex role—Fiction.]   I. Title.
PZ7.C21644Mag   2013   2013021822
[Fic]—dc23   CIP
                                                                                   AC

15 16 17 18   CG/OPM   10 9 8 7 6 5 4
❖
First paperback edition, 2014

For Zach, with love

AUGUSTA

HIGH
SEAS

SUMMERSTEAD

NORDHOLM

VNHLP
Headquarters

THE NORTHLANDS

HIGH
SEAS

GUNPOWDER
BAY

Town Square

GUNPOWDER
ISLAND

Gargoyle's quarry

MIDDLEBY

Scallywag's Den

HIGH
SEAS

THE SOUTHLANDS

OTTERPOOL

Royal
Dungeons

Miss Pimm's

Pemberton
Market

Queen's Palace

QUEENSPORT

Westfield House

PEMBERTON

WIMBLY-
ON-THE-MARSH

Queensport Harbor

Jasper's house

Claire's house

N
W   E
S

PEMBERTON
BAY

Little Herring
Cove

Royal Augusta
Water Ballet

THE VERY NEARLY HONORABLE LEAGUE OF PIRATES
Servin' the High Seas for 152 Years
MEMBERSHIP DIVISION

Master (Hilary) Westfield:

It is with great pleasure that the League accepts your application to our Piracy (Apprenticeship) Program. Welcome aboard!

Your application impressed our committee of (scourges) and (scallywags) with your remarkable knowledge of pirate lore, your knot-tying talents, and your reported ability to tread water for thirty-seven minutes. We look forward to observing your formidable skills in person when you join the VNHLP.

Today, you are a wide-eyed and innocent young man, but tomorrow—or, rather, at the end of our four-year training program—you will be a (swashbuckling), (grog-swilling), (timber-shivering buccaneer). If you would like to accept this offer of apprenticeship, and we hope you will, please mail a signed statement to VNHLP Headquarters at the following address:

16 Whiteknuckle Lane

Gunpowder Island

The Northlands

(Arr!) and best wishes,

One-Legged Jones

Membership Coordinator, VNHLP

Dear Mr. One-Legged Jones,

Thank you very much for your offer of admission to the Piracy Apprenticeship Program. I have dreamed of joining your organization all my life, and I am happy to accept a place as a pirate apprentice.

I have my own sword, but it is a bit rusty. Should I bring it with me, or will weapons be provided by the League?

I do feel I should mention that your information regarding my appearance is not entirely accurate. First, I am not wide-eyed: thanks to the (interminable) *unending* lessons delivered in a torturous monotone by my governess, my eyes are frequently closed. Second, I am not a young man, but a young woman. I would not want your committee of scourges and scallywags to be surprised when we meet in person.

Yours truly,

Miss Hilary Westfield
Pirate Apprentice

Miss Westfield:

We are pirates. We are not easily horrified. We have seen
shipwrecks. We have seen sword fights. We have seen men
eaten by crocodiles and crocodiles eaten by men. We have,
on occasion, hung skeletons from trees. None of these things
horrifies us in the least.

Your letter, however, is another matter.

We believe our rules are perfectly clear: No woman,
young or otherwise, may join our League. You may not set
foot on our ships, you may not retrieve our buried stashes of
magic coins, and you may not under any conditions hoist the
skull and crossbones. ~~raise the pirate flag~~

In fact, we are not sure you should even be reading this
letter. We will send a copy to your father at once. Admiral
Westfield is no friend to pirates, but if there is one thing
upon which the VNHLP and the Royal Navy can agree, it
is this: permitting girls to prance about on the High Seas
would be entirely undignified.

Under normal circumstances we would, of course, require you to walk the plank. However, our Code of Piracy does not permit us to treat young women in such a fashion, so we will be generous: with your father's permission, we will forward your application to Miss Pimm's Finishing School for Delicate Ladies.

With shock and consternation,

One-Legged Jones

Membership Coordinator, VNHLP

Special

Mr. Jones: ④ School where girls go

Don't you dare listen to a word my father says.
He may believe that the only proper place for a
young girl is (finishing school,) but he also believes
that the only proper place for pirates is the Royal
Dungeons, and I am quite certain he is wrong
about both of these things. I assure you that I will
walk the plank a thousand times, into cold and
shark-infested waters, before I will attend Miss
Pimm's.

I remain,

Hilary Westfield

Really Quite Furious with You

Miss Pimm's Finishing School for Delicate Ladies

Where Virtue Blossoms
OFFICE OF THE HEADMISTRESS

Dear Miss Westfield,

We would like to extend a warm welcome to you as you prepare to join the Miss Pimm's community. It is highly unusual for Miss Pimm's to accept a new student so close to the beginning of term, but you are clearly talented: our games mistress is eager to recruit you for our water ballet team, and your interest in knot tying will serve you well in our beginners' macramé course.

We have received a generous sum from your father, so no further payment is required. Enclosed in this package you will find:

> Two (2) green cardigan sweaters embroidered with our dancing-sheep logo,
>
> Two (2) gray woolen dresses (petticoats not provided).
>
> One (1) gray woolen bathing costume,
>
> One (1) white bathing cap with green chin strap,

⑤ girl underwear

One (1) copy of the textbook _A Young Lady's Guide to Augustan Society,_

One (1) copy of the pamphlet _Waltzing for the Eager Novice,_ and

One (1) sterling silver crochet hook engraved with your initials.

Please bring these items with you when you report for the start of summer term next Saturday.

Be well, and remember: "A Miss Pimm's girl is a virtuous girl!"

Sincerely,

Eugenia Pimm

Headmistress

CHAPTER ONE

EVER SINCE THE letter had arrived from Miss Pimm's, Hilary had spent more and more time talking to the gargoyle.

Her parents disapproved, she knew perfectly well, but she much preferred the gargoyle's company to theirs. Hilary and the gargoyle did not always see eye to eye, but she found his opinion of finishing school to be thoroughly refreshing.

"A bathing cap!" said the gargoyle as Hilary packed the clothing from Miss Pimm's in the gold-plated traveling trunk her mother had dragged out from some attic or another. "No self-respecting pirate would be caught dead in a bathing cap."

"I know," said Hilary. "And look what Mother's done to it." She held up the bathing cap so the gargoyle could see her name embroidered in golden thread around the edge. "She says it's fashionable."

"Fashion!" said the gargoyle. "Pirates don't care about fashion! Although," he added after a moment's thought, "I've always wanted one of those pointy black hats—you know, the kind with a feather coming out the top. . . ."

Hilary closed her trunk and climbed on top of it to reach the gargoyle, who was carved into the stonework over her bedroom door. Before he could protest, she draped the embroidered bathing cap—very fashionably, she thought—over his stone ears.

"But you're not a pirate," she reminded him, "and I have a horrible feeling that I won't get to be one either."

"Don't say that." The gargoyle squirmed and wiggled his ears but couldn't manage to free himself from the bathing cap. "Just because that dumb One-Legged Who-ever said—could you get this thing *off* me?" The gargoyle sighed. "I wish I had hands."

"Oh, all right," said Hilary. "But you do look awfully dashing." She plucked the bathing cap from the gargoyle's ears and tossed it onto her bed, where it landed on top of the seven white eyelet nightgowns and twenty pairs of gray stockings her mother had picked up in town that morning. "You're lucky, gargoyle. No one can make you do anything you don't want to do."

"Ha!" said the gargoyle. "And I suppose you think protecting Westfield House is all sunshine and spider legs? Living on a wall for two hundred years isn't all it's cracked up to be, you know. How would you like it if people kept leaping up to grab your snout and ordering you to protect them?"

Hilary had to admit that she wouldn't like it one bit. "I suppose neither of us likes being ordered about," she said. "At least Father hasn't ordered you off to finishing school."

"And he'd better not try," the gargoyle said darkly. "I'd bite him."

Hilary's father was an ~~admiral~~ comander in the Augusta Royal Navy, which meant, as far as Hilary could tell, that he was required to eat every Sunday dinner with the queen and spend the rest of his time in his study at Westfield House, tossing out sharp and hurried orders at any captains or commodores who happened to be visiting. Even though he hardly ever went to sea anymore, Hilary saw her father rarely and spoke to him even less. Half of the time, when Hilary was dressed in old uniforms handed down from former naval apprentices, her father would mistake her for a staff member and urge her to "fetch me the Northlands file" or "polish that sextant and be quick about it!" The other half of the time, when someone had been nimble enough to lace Hilary into a dress, her father would kiss her on the forehead and say, "Run along and be a good little girl." Hilary intended to be a

(handwritten margin notes) comander · ① navigational tool for the water

great many things, and a good little girl was not one of them, but she had not quite worked up the courage to tell this to Admiral Westfield.

Hilary's room was practically bare now—most of her things had been packed in the golden trunk or sent off to Miss Pimm's by train, as Hilary herself would be the next morning. She was not looking forward to the journey. "Six hours in a private compartment with a governess," she said to the gargoyle as she folded the dancing-sheep cardigans, "and I'm sure Miss Greyson will make me do lessons the entire time. And she'll pack those little sandwiches without crusts that young ladies are supposed to eat, and she won't let me look out the window because young ladies aren't supposed to smudge the glass."

"Yes, yes, that's all very sad," said the gargoyle. "Little sandwiches, et cetera. But let's focus on the real tragedy here."

"The VNHLP *is* being terribly unreasonable," said Hilary, "and as for Father——"

The gargoyle sighed. "I was talking about *me*! What's going to happen to me when you're gone? Who will read me *Treasure Island*? What if your parents host noble guests in this room? What if the guests don't want to talk to me? Or what if there are no guests at all, ever again, and I get cobwebs in my ears? Oh, Hilary," said the gargoyle, "what if I'm *renovated*?"

The gargoyle looked so earnest that Hilary could tell

he was really concerned. "You mustn't worry," she said. "I'll come home and visit you between terms; I won't let anything bad happen to you. You know I'd take you with me if I could."

The gargoyle wrinkled his nose and let out a noise halfway between a sneeze and a landslide. "I don't think I'd enjoy that," he said. "The pirates in *Treasure Island* didn't have to go to finishing school, did they?"

"No," said Hilary, "they most certainly didn't."

"Then I'm not interested," said the gargoyle. "And if you really want to be a pirate, you shouldn't go, either."

Hilary sat down hard on top of her traveling trunk. "Of course I want to be a pirate," she said. "I've wanted it all my life." And why shouldn't she be a pirate? She was already a better sailor than most of the boys in her father's Royal Navy, and she cared far more about sword fights and treasure than she did about stitching petticoats and minding her manners. Surely even Admiral Westfield could see that finishing school was no place for her. He disapproved quite heartily of piracy, of course, but perhaps if she had a word with him—if he could only see how fine a pirate she'd be—he might be impressed. He might even convince the VNHLP to reconsider.

"Oh, good, you're all packed up." Hilary's mother poked her head through the doorway. "*Must* you wear those wretched cabin-boy clothes? They're far too large for you, and that shade of blue does nothing for your eyes.

Something in green, perhaps; a nice new dress—"

"I can't climb ship's rigging in a dress, Mother," Hilary said, "and you *know* I hate green. Besides, two horrid woolen dresses from Miss Pimm's ought to be enough for anyone."

"Mrs. Westfield," said the gargoyle, bending his head over the door frame to address her upside down, "when Hilary's at school, do you intend to dust me?"

Mrs. Westfield flicked her hand through the air as though she were swatting away a small and persistent fly. "Ship's rigging!" she said to Hilary. "I've never heard such nonsense. They shall teach you how to dress properly at Miss Pimm's, and perhaps they'll take your hair out of that silly braid once and for all." She patted her own carefully sculpted curls.

"Ahem," said the gargoyle, who was still hanging upside down. "About the dusting . . ."

But Mrs. Westfield charged on. "I always dreamed of being a Miss Pimm's girl myself, you know. Miss Pimm is quite choosy about her students. You'd do well to remember that not every girl is as lucky as you."

"If being sent to Miss Pimm's is lucky," Hilary said, "then I don't much care for luck."

But her mother just laughed. "Don't be a silly goose," she said. "It's very generous of your father to give you this experience."

Hilary sighed; there was no point in arguing any

further. "Do you know if Father's busy right now?" When Admiral Westfield wasn't in town on naval errands, he was locked away in meetings; the question hardly seemed worth asking. "There's something I need to discuss with him—something important."

Mrs. Westfield looked down the hall. "You know your father can't abide discussions, dear, but his study door is open. If you hurry, you just might catch him."

Hilary waited until her mother had wandered away, no doubt searching every inch of Westfield House for a servant to pester. Then she reached under her bed, grabbed her sword, and strapped it to her waist.

"Planning to run your father through?" asked the gargoyle. "It's certainly a traditional solution, but I wouldn't recommend it." The gargoyle swished his tail. "It makes an awful mess."

"Don't be silly," said Hilary. "I don't want to run anyone through." Although she wasn't about to admit it to the gargoyle, carrying the sword made her feel a little bit braver, and walking into Admiral Westfield's study required every ounce of bravery she could gather. Father?

EVEN WALKING DOWN the main hall of Westfield House was a fairly grand and intimidating experience. The hall was lined on both sides with elaborate stained-glass windows depicting the great heroes of history. Good King Albert, Augusta's first ruler, peered out from the window nearest Admiral Westfield's study, looking noticeably more emerald green and rose pink than he had in real life. King Albert's neighbor in the next window over was Simon Westfield, a long-ago ancestor who had explored the kingdom in his hot-air balloon, and his across-the-hall companion was the Enchantress of the Northlands.

The Enchantress had ruled over the kingdom's magic ages ago, when magical objects were as common as cooking pots in the households of Augusta. In fact, the gargoyle was fond of telling anyone who would listen that he had been carved by the Enchantress herself. In her window, she wore a long gown and a small, amused smile, though Hilary had always thought the window maker had gotten that part wrong: after all, the Enchantress was holding a heavy-looking wooden chest filled to the brim with magic golden coins, and Hilary suspected she should look less amused and more exhausted. But her window was Hilary's favorite, swirling with oranges and golds like a furious sunset. Admiral Westfield, on the other hand, referred to the Enchantress as That Meddling Old Biddy and kept threatening to have her window removed.

As Hilary passed by the Enchantress's window, a tall boy in a blue naval-apprentice uniform stepped out of her father's study and blocked her way. He glanced down at Hilary and sneered, although because he was the sort of person who sneered at everything, it was hard to tell whether this particular sneer had been created especially for her.

"Hello, Oliver," said Hilary. "Are you feeling all right now?" The last time she had seen him, he'd been dangling upside down from a navy ship's rigging. It was entirely his fault, of course: he'd proclaimed that no girl could tie a knot he couldn't undo, and surely no one could have blamed Hilary for tying two such knots around his ankles. She had finally cut him free with her sword, although she'd genuinely regretted having to do it. On the bright side, she had discovered the interesting, hollow sort of noise that a forehead makes when it connects with a boat deck.

"I'm perfectly fine, no thanks to you." Oliver brushed his hair forward to cover the purple lump above his eye. "What do you want?"

"I want to speak to my father."

(5) Victorioos

"Can't." Oliver's sneer looked triumphant. "He's busy."

"No, he's not." Over Oliver's shoulder, Hilary could see Admiral Westfield tying bits of rope into intricate sailor's knots.

(6) detailed

Oliver shrugged. "Sorry. Can't help you."

Hilary was a good deal shorter than Oliver, but she stood up as straight as she could. Miss Greyson would have been pleased, she thought. "Please move aside, Mr. Sanderson," she said, brushing by him and rapping her knuckles on the open door.

Admiral Westfield glanced up. "Ah, Hilary." He brushed the bits of rope into a desk drawer. "Please, my dear, come in."

"That's *Lieutenant* Sanderson," Oliver said, but Hilary pretended not to hear him as she let the door slam shut between them.

"Good fellow, that Oliver," said Admiral Westfield, putting his boots up on his desk. "Like the son I never had. A fine sailor, too, of course." He glanced up at Hilary, as though he expected a reply.

"Of course," Hilary murmured. It was difficult to speak loudly enough in the admiral's study, where thick woven carpets from the far side of the kingdom covered the floor, and any noise that didn't soak into the carpet was bound to be muffled by the ticking rows of nautical instruments that lined the walls. Carved into the wall behind Admiral Westfield's desk was a row of porthole-shaped windows; after so many years at sea, the admiral claimed that windows of any other shape made him feel uneasy. Books also made him uneasy, because they were generally unavailable at sea and because he considered most of them to be impertinent. As a result, books of all sorts were strictly forbidden within the study, but drawers upon drawers of maps and charts took up the space that bookcases might otherwise have occupied. A globe spun slowly in its wooden frame beside the desk, and a telescope stood at attention next to one of the portholes. In fact, everything stood at attention, including Hilary, because other than Admiral Westfield's desk chair, there was no place to sit. The whole effect made Hilary feel slightly seasick.

"Now then, Hilary," said Admiral Westfield. He beamed at her, and her legs went wobbly. First he'd called her by name—by her *correct* name, no less—and now he was smiling! Hilary wondered if he was feeling entirely well. "What can I do for my Miss Pimm's girl?"

Oh dear. That explained it. "Actually," she said, "it's about Miss Pimm's." She stared firmly at the porthole above her father's head. "I don't want to go."

"I'm sorry, my dear," said Admiral Westfield. "I can't hear you; you'll have to speak up."

Hilary took a deep breath. "I don't want to go to Miss Pimm's."

"But *every* girl wants to go to Miss Pimm's."

"Not me, Father. I want to be a pirate."

"Oh, yes." The admiral picked up a new bit of rope and started tying a half hitch. "That was quite an impertinent prank, my dear, and your mother tells me she's already scolded you for it. But I'm afraid I can't play games just now. I'm planning an important voyage, and time is of the essence."

Hilary's legs swayed beneath her, and the sword in its scabbard bounced against the side of her knee. "It's not a prank or a game," she said. "I'm a good sailor—heaps better than Oliver, in fact."

Admiral Westfield opened his mouth, but Hilary hurried on before he could protest that such a thing simply wasn't possible. "I know you've never seen me sail, but I've been practicing for years. I can row just as fast as your apprentices can, and I know what to do when a storm comes up or a scallywag attacks. I'd be a terrible schoolgirl, Father, but I think I'd be a very good pirate." She hesitated. "If you'd just come down to the harbor with me—just for a few moments—perhaps I could show you."

Admiral Westfield sucked in his breath and released it in a tremendous gust. "My dear," he said, "there's no need to do anything rash. Let me be clear: You are a young lady. Moreover, you are a Westfield. You will not tell silly tales, you will not ruin your prospects in High Society, and you will never be a pirate."

"But Father—"

"You know perfectly well that piracy is disgraceful," Admiral Westfield continued. "Sailing off on adventures at a moment's notice, digging up treasure without turning it over to the queen, ignoring *my* orders—why, the kingdom would be far better off without all those pirates sailing through it." He slammed his boots against the desktop. "Whyever would you want to be one? Is this that governess's influence, or that wretched gargoyle's? Is this something you've read about in *books?*"

Hilary enjoyed a good pirate yarn as much as the gargoyle did, but she'd wanted to be a pirate for as long as she could remember—well, nearly as long. She had one bright, long-ago memory of taking her mother's hand, walking down the cobblestone streets to the Queensport docks, and waving good-bye to the billowing canvas sails of her father's fleet as he set off on a grand adventure. She'd told her mother then and there that she wanted to join the navy when she was old enough, to sail the High Seas on grand adventures of her own. But her mother had only smiled and laughed. She'd told her father, too, when he'd returned from his voyage, but he'd looked very serious and informed her that the navy was no place for little girls, and certainly no place for a daughter of his.

And perhaps Admiral Westfield had been right after all, for a career in the navy, with its tedious rules and dull assignments, was hardly as interesting as life on a pirate ship. On a pirate ship, Hilary could have all the grand adventures she pleased. She'd set navy boys like Oliver shivering in their fine leather boots, and her father would finally be able to see what a daughter of his could do. She'd be the most fearsome pirate on the High Seas, no matter what One-Legged Jones and Admiral Westfield had to say about it.

Admiral Westfield, however, did not have much more to say to Hilary about anything. "Now," he said, getting up from his desk, "let's have no more of this nonsense. I don't believe they tolerate nonsense at Miss Pimm's. Or in the VNHLP, for that matter—they were quite right to turn you down." He put his hands on Hilary's shoulders and brushed a hurried kiss across her forehead. "Run along now, and be a good little girl."

Hilary didn't budge. Instead, she stared at the wall beyond her father's head. Then she rubbed her eyes and stared again, just to be sure she wasn't mistaken.

Admiral Westfield cleared his throat. "Run along," he said again, a bit more loudly, "and be——"

"Father," said Hilary, "you'd better turn around. Something very odd is happening to your window."

As they watched, one of the porthole windows behind Admiral Westfield's desk was growing larger and larger. It swallowed up the surrounding windows and half the wall besides. The admiral's nautical instruments were knocked off their pegs, and his charts of the High Seas fluttered to the floor, but the window appeared determined to continue growing until it had reached the fringe of carpet below. Hilary had never seen anything like it. She hurried to the window and tried to press her hand against it, but her fingers slipped straight through the frame.

"The glass——it's vanished somehow." Hilary poked at the window frame with the tip of her sword. "And I think the frame is still growing." She turned around to stare at her father. "I don't understand. Do your windows normally move about by themselves?"

"Stand back, my dear," said Admiral Westfield, "and for goodness' sake, put that ridiculous weapon away. I'll take

14

care of this." He tugged Hilary out of the way and marched up to the wall, which was now more air than stone. "Look here, window!" he cried. "I'll have none of this impertinence. I am in charge of this house, and I demand that you shrink yourself at once!"

Hilary rubbed her arm where Admiral Westfield had tugged at it. She was rather pleased to see that unlike most everything else in the kingdom, the window refused to obey her father's orders. It only stretched farther to reveal two figures standing on the lawn outside Westfield House. They were too far away for Hilary to make out properly, but they seemed to be dressed entirely in black, with black masks around their eyes and black gloves around their fists. Hilary swallowed hard and pointed her sword in their direction.

The window hesitated for a moment, as though it were worried that growing much larger would be rude. It wobbled from side to side. Then, all at once, every drawer in the admiral's study flew open, and every door burst from its hinges. Hilary yelped and held up her sword to fend off the cabinet doors that swung wildly over her head. Admiral Westfield let loose a barrage of nautical-sounding curses as his desk drawer hit him in the stomach and knocked him to the floor.

A scroll of paper flew out of the open desk and sailed over Admiral Westfield's head. He snatched at the scroll, but it darted past his fingers, and before Hilary could run over to help, the scroll had traveled out the enormous window and into the waiting, black-gloved hand of the tall person on the lawn.

"Stop, you scoundrels!" cried Admiral Westfield, but the tall person merely gave a cheerful wave. Then, with a great shudder, the porthole window collapsed back to its proper size, and all the drawers and cabinet doors slammed shut.

Hilary hurried to Admiral Westfield's side and helped him up from the floor. "Are you all right?" she said. Her father looked a little red, but then again, he always did. "What in the world just happened?"

"Magic!" cried Admiral Westfield. "And thievery to boot. Those scallywags magicked a most important document straight out of my house!" He pulled open his desk drawer and fumbled through it. "And what use is that blasted gargoyle?" he muttered. "He's supposed to protect us, but he doesn't do a blessed thing unless we run to him and beg him—and I refuse to beg that creature for anything. How the Westfields got stuck with the most useless piece of magic in the kingdom, I'll never know." The admiral cursed under his breath and shut the desk drawer with a bang. Then he looked up at Hilary. "Terribly sorry you had to witness all this, my dear. Getting mixed up in magic hardly improves a young lady's reputation. You'd better hurry back to your room at once while I sort out this mess."

Hilary frowned. Surely a true pirate wouldn't hide in her room after a battle. No, a true pirate would pursue the enemy, no matter what her father had to say about it. "But I can chase after the thieves," she protested. "I might not be able to catch them, but surely I can find out where they've gone."

"No, my dear, don't be ridiculous. There's nothing you could possibly do. And wherever did you get that sword?"

Hilary had, in fact, swiped the sword from a suit of armor on display in the Westfield House ballroom, assuming that she could get more use out of it than the suit of armor could—but now was hardly the time to explain this to her father. "Tell me what I can do to help," she said, "and I'll do it."

"You can help," said Admiral Westfield, "by not breathing a word of this to anyone. The sooner you're safely off at Miss Pimm's, the better. By the way, my dear, this type of scandalous behavior is exactly what one might expect to find on board a *pirate ship*." He spit the words out onto the carpet. "Shocking, isn't it?"

Actually, Hilary had found it all rather thrilling, but Admiral Westfield didn't leave her any time to answer. "Now if you'll excuse me, I've got to call a few of my men together and set them on the trail of those rapscallions." He turned back to Hilary. "And for heaven's sake, give me that sword. It's dangerous, and you certainly won't be needing it at Miss Pimm's."

He reached out for the sword, but Hilary pulled it away. "I think I'll hold on to it, Father, if you don't mind," she said. "I hear the girls at Miss Pimm's can be quite vicious."

"Hilary, I don't have time for this nonsense. Sword or no sword, all I ask is that you are safely on the train to Miss Pimm's at ten o'clock tomorrow morning."

Hilary tried to look solemn. "Yes, Father," she said. "I promise I'll get on the train."

Admiral Westfield nodded and dismissed Hilary from his study. At least he had not made her promise to *stay* on the train all the way to Miss Pimm's, for that was a promise she did not intend to keep.

HILARY HURRIED DOWN the corridor, past the kings and the explorers and all the other stained-glass heroes trapped forever in the halls of Westfield House. When she reached her bedroom at last, she slammed the door behind her.

"So," said the gargoyle, "did you run your father through after all? You can't say I didn't warn you about the mess. . . . Hey! What are you doing with that thing?"

"I," said Hilary as she chipped away at the stones around the gargoyle with the point of her sword, "am taking you with me. I'm sure Father won't miss you one bit."

"What?" The gargoyle squirmed, and small chunks of doorway fell to the floor. "Are you crazy? I don't want to go to finishing school! You can't make me go! I won't learn water ballet, and that's final!"

"Hush, don't worry. We're not going to finishing school."

The gargoyle's ears perked up. "We're not?"

"No," said Hilary. "We're going to sea."

From Newspaper

The Illustrated Queensport Gazette
YOUR GATEWAY TO THE CIVILIZED WORLD!

MISSING * MISSING * MISSING

One important and valuable DOCUMENT from the personal files of ADMIRAL JAMES WESTFIELD. Two feet in length and width, rolled into a SCROLL, and tied with RED RIBBON. Last seen in the NEFARIOUS GRIP of two MASKED INTRUDERS clad all in black. Contains SECRETS of importance to the ENTIRE KINGDOM! (If discovered, please do not read.)

Please return said document to Admiral Westfield at Westfield House, Queensport, AT ONCE! Simultaneous delivery of MASKED INTRUDERS preferred if possible. Needless to say, successful return of document and/or intruders will earn a significant and generous

REWARD.

= Evil

NORTHLANDS MINING EXPEDITION A COMPLETE AND UTTER FAILURE

NORDHOLM, AUGUSTA—In a development that should surprise absolutely no one with an ounce of common sense, the royal expedition to search for unmined magic in the Northlands Hills has failed, just as ninety-four previous expeditions have done.

"We thought we'd found an untapped source of magic ore," said expedition leader Sir Archibald Trout, "but once we started digging, we discovered that the material we'd spotted was only gold. Better luck next time, eh?"

No new magic ore has been mined from any location in Augusta for over two hundred years, and experts believe that this once-valuable natural resource has been completely exhausted. "Every ounce of magic in the kingdom's been dug up," Nordholm University scholar Salima Svensson confirmed today. "If the queen is looking for magic, she'd be better off searching for a pirate's treasure chest." Ms. Svensson hastened to add that she was not seriously recommending that the queen attempt to recover one of the stashes of magic rumored to be buried around the country. "Many of us have been living without magic for generations now," said Ms. Svensson, "and we've made some remarkable technological discoveries as a result. Just the other day, I used the woodstove in my kitchen to warm an entire plate of biscuits. Isn't it time to give up on the search for magic and start living sensibly?"

The queen and her royal advisers could not be reached for comment.

CHAPTER TWO

"I THOUGHT," SAID the gargoyle faintly from inside the canvas bag, "we were going to sea."

Hilary reached inside the bag and clapped her hand over the gargoyle's snout. "What did I tell you?" she whispered.

"You told me not to move and not to make a sound." It was hard to make out his muffled response, but at least he sounded suitably apologetic.

Hilary glanced across the train compartment at her governess, who was still absorbed in her newspaper. As far as Hilary could tell, Miss Greyson did not plan to move from her seat until she had read every last article, and Miss Greyson was a very thorough reader. Behind her left ear was tucked a single sharp pencil, which she used to make notes in the margins of her paper from time to time, and she was forever quizzing Hilary about the news of the day. "A lady must always be aware of current events," she liked to say. Hilary didn't dare sneak out of the compartment for fear that Miss Greyson would suddenly lift her head and ask Hilary's opinion of mining operations in the Northlands, or of the latest theft from one of Augusta's grand mansions.

"You'll just have to wait a little longer," Hilary murmured into the bag. "She'll have to get up eventually, and that's when we'll make our move." Running away to sea hadn't seemed like a difficult plan at first, but Hilary had forgotten to take her governess into account.

"If you are going to chat with that gargoyle," said Miss Greyson without glancing up from her newspaper, "you might as well do so in a proper conversational tone, so the rest of us can join in if we have something to contribute."

The gargoyle poked his head out of the bag. "You weren't supposed to know I was here!"

"You should have kept still, then," said Miss Greyson. "Your ears wiggle."

Hilary and the gargoyle looked at each other in dismay. "They went all tingly," the gargoyle said, "and I thought that maybe if I gave them a good shake . . ."

"Honestly," said Miss Greyson, "you look like a pair of wet hens." She folded up her newspaper. "Don't worry, Hilary; I won't make you send the gargoyle back. I know the first few weeks at finishing school can be lonely, and it will be pleasant for you to have a friend."

"I am *not* a hen," announced the gargoyle, "and I am *not* going to finishi— hey, cut that out!" Hilary had poked him in the place where she thought his ribs might be.

"But you must take care to keep the gargoyle out of sight, especially on the train," Miss Greyson continued. "All sorts of people travel on trains, you know." She said the word *people* in a way that suggested she really meant scoundrels. "You wouldn't want your gargoyle to be stolen, would you?"

"No, Miss Greyson."

"In fact, there's been another theft from a High Society household just this morning." Miss Greyson tapped her newspaper with the delicate golden crochet hook she always carried. "Twelve entire place settings of magic cutlery—including dessert spoons! Then again, the Grimshaws have always been far too bold with their magic. When one regularly transforms one's good linen napkins into flocks of turtledoves, one can't be too surprised by thievery."

"How sad for the Grimshaws." Hilary kicked her heels against the bottom of her seat, knowing Miss Greyson would disapprove. "I'm sure their dinner parties will be utterly dull from now on."

"What I mean to say, Hilary, is that thieves can be quite

unscrupulous. Especially when it comes to magic." Miss Greyson lowered her voice and glanced from side to side. "If a teaspoon of magic can turn a napkin into a turtledove, imagine what a thief could do if he got his hands on the gargoyle."

"Just let a thief try!" said the gargoyle. "I'm much more fearsome than a teaspoon, Miss Greyson. And I don't like to be used; it makes my heart go fluttery." He grimaced at the thought. "Besides, I'm not allowed to turn things into birds. The Enchantress told me so when she carved me."

"Really?" said Miss Greyson. "How very specific of her."

The gargoyle hesitated. "Well, she didn't say that *exactly*. But she did say my magic could only be used for protection. Isn't that right, Hilary? A thief couldn't make me turn things into birds, could he?" He shuddered. "I don't like birds."

"Oh, gargoyle, don't worry." Hilary patted his small stone wings until they stopped fluttering. "I promise I won't let anyone use you, and I'll keep you safe from anyone who looks even slightly unscrupulous."

"Much appreciated," said the gargoyle.

Miss Greyson nodded. "Very good. Now, I suspect"—she consulted her pocket watch—"yes, it's nearly lunchtime." She reached into her enormous carpetbag and produced a handful of rectangular packets wrapped in wax-coated paper. "I've brought sandwiches if you'd like them. Cucumber or egg?"

"Neither, thank you," said the gargoyle. "Do you have any spiders?"

Upon learning that Miss Greyson did not, in fact, have spiders, the gargoyle burrowed deeper into his bag, and Hilary wished she could join him there. A true pirate would never eat tiny sandwiches; would Miss Greyson never leave? "Egg, please," she said at last. Miss Greyson passed her one of the packets and tried to fasten her carpetbag, but the clasps wouldn't come together.

"Oh dear," said Miss Greyson. "I always overpack on train journeys. I do so like to be comfortable—and if our train gets delayed, I've brought enough supplies to keep us warm and snug in this little compartment for at least a week!" She laughed, and Hilary did her best to join in, but the situation was hardly funny: it appeared that Miss Greyson had no intention of leaving the compartment anytime soon, or perhaps ever again. Outside, along the edge of the tracks, fir trees and wildflowers slipped away into the distance as the train raced toward Miss Pimm's.

Hilary looked down at the egg sandwich. Then she looked at the gargoyle, who had snuggled down next to her battered copy of *Treasure Island*. "I'm sorry, Miss Greyson," she said, tucking the sandwich into her bag, "but I've got to leave."

"Leave?" Miss Greyson's carpetbag snapped shut. "Whatever do you mean?"

"Just to use the washroom," said Hilary quickly.

Miss Greyson started to rise from her seat. "Of course. I'll accompany you."

"Oh, I'm sure that's not necessary. I'll only be gone a few moments." Hilary stood up and slung the canvas bag over her shoulder. "Besides, I'll have the gargoyle with me."

The gargoyle gave Miss Greyson his most charming grin, and she sighed. "He's hardly a proper chaperone, but very well. You must hurry directly back, though. You are a young lady, not a royal explorer."

"Please don't worry, Miss Greyson." Hilary opened the compartment door, and for a moment she thought she'd caught the faint scent of the sea, though it was quickly overpowered by the scent of egg sandwiches. "If I meet any unscrupulous people, I'll be sure to let you know."

IF IT HADN'T been speeding quite so determinedly toward Miss Pimm's, Hilary thought she would have enjoyed being on the train. She didn't often get to travel on trains—because they were not boats, her father disapproved of them—and this one was particularly elegant, with velvet carpeting on the floors and gold-painted flourishes on the wall panels. Hilary wouldn't have been surprised to spot the queen herself in one of the compartments, although all she saw as she walked down the corridor were small knots of gentlemen in dark suits, along with the occasional sticky-faced child pursued at high speeds by a nanny.

"Are we really going to the washroom?" the gargoyle asked from inside the canvas bag. "Are you going to scrub behind my ears?"

Hilary clutched the bag to her chest and smiled at the two gentlemen who were approaching her from the other end of the carriage. "Of course not," she whispered into the bag once the gentlemen had passed. "We're escaping! We'll leave the train at the next stop, wherever that is." Hilary hadn't managed to sneak a look at the train timetable stowed away in Miss Greyson's carpetbag, but she knew the tracks from Queensport to Pemberton followed the curve of the coastline. Wherever they ended up, the sea wouldn't be too far away, and wherever there was sea, could pirates be far behind?

"Oh," said the gargoyle. "Well, that's all right, then. Let me know when we get to the sea."

Hilary hurried through the train until she felt sure that she was a safe distance from Miss Greyson. She found a comfortable bit of wall to lean against near the carriage door, and she set her bag down on the floor beside her. She was happy to have the gargoyle as a traveling companion, but he did grow awfully heavy after a while.

To pass the time while they waited for the train to stop, Hilary read to the gargoyle from *Treasure Island*. "'Though I had lived by the shore all my life,'" she read, "'I seemed never to have been near the sea till then. The smell of tar and salt was something new. I saw the most wonderful figureheads, that had all been far over the ocean.'" She glanced up to make sure Miss Greyson wasn't approaching. "'And I was going to sea myself; to sea in a schooner . . . bound for an unknown island, and to seek for buried treasures!'"

The carriage door swung open. Hilary stuffed the book in her bag and pulled the canvas over the gargoyle's ears as the two gentlemen who had passed her before entered the corridor. They were elegantly dressed, as though they had set out for the opera and accidentally boarded a train instead. Hilary guessed they were members of High Society, though one of the gentlemen—really more of a boy, now that Hilary got a better look at him—kept tripping over his trousers, which covered his feet and a good deal of the floor below. His black hair fell nearly to his collar, and he looked about as comfortable in his suit as Hilary felt in her uniform from Miss Pimm's.

The other gentleman looked a bit older and didn't trip nearly as often. He carried a narrow black case under one arm, and he flipped a coin in the air as he walked, catching it again in his gloved hand after every toss. He nodded to Hilary. Then he paused for a moment, and the coin fell to the floor.

"Excuse me," said the elegant gentleman, "but have we met before?"

Hilary shook her head. Maybe this man had attended a ball at Westfield House—her mother was always planning the next ball or cleaning up from the last one—but Hilary made a point of avoiding her parents' social events whenever she could. "I'm sorry," she said, trying desperately to remember the guidelines for discouraging unwanted company in *A Young Lady's Guide to Augustan Society*. "I don't believe I know you."

"Well, thank goodness we've met at last." The man bowed low to retrieve his coin, tucked it away in his pocket, and stuck out a gloved hand. "It's a pleasure. The name's Smith. And this"—he gestured to the boy—"is my ward, Charlie."

Hilary shook Mr. Smith's hand as quickly as possible. She tried to shake the boy's hand, too, but he hung back behind Mr. Smith. "It's nice to meet you both," she said.

She hoped that that would be the end of it—that Mr. Smith and his ward would return to their compartment and discuss lawn bowling, or top hats, or whatever it was that elegant gentlemen discussed—but they seemed intent on staying exactly where they were. The boy named Charlie studied Hilary for a moment; then his eyes grew wide, and he elbowed Mr. Smith. "I think she's a finishing-school girl," he said. He did not sound at all pleased about it. "Just look at her cardigan." sweater ③

Hilary sighed and picked up her bag. If the elegant gentlemen were going to insist on standing in her way, perhaps they could make themselves useful. "Can you tell me where this train stops next? I don't want to miss my station."

"Oh, you needn't worry about that," said Mr. Smith. "We're on a direct route, you see. Queensport to Pemberton, with no stops in between. We'll be in Pemberton soon enough, I expect."

Hilary stared at him. "But I've got to get off the train! I can't go to Pemberton!" Pemberton meant Miss Pimm's, and Miss Pimm's meant bars on the windows, wrought-iron fences, and a whole minefield of governesses. Whatever Miss Pimm's girls did all day, they certainly didn't escape.

The corners of Mr. Smith's mouth twitched into a smile. "As it happens," he said, "we're not too keen on going to Pemberton, either. We're in a bit of a tight spot, and if you're in a tight spot as well, we might be able to assist each other. Only if you're willing, of course."

Behind Mr. Smith, Charlie sucked in his breath. "You can't possibly be asking *her*," he said. "She'll never agree."

"And why shouldn't I agree to help people?" Hilary met Charlie's stare until he looked down at his trouser legs. "I'm not as horrid as all that, you know. And I don't care for this cardigan any more than you do."

Mr. Smith leaned forward. "So you'll help us, then?"

Hilary hesitated. Despite their tailcoats and clean white gloves, something about Mr. Smith and his ward seemed quite unscrupulous indeed. But a true pirate wouldn't be afraid of these gentlemen, and a true pirate would do whatever it took to avoid Miss Pimm's. "I could certainly use some help," said Hilary, "but I'm not sure what I can give you in return." She thought for a moment. "Do you like egg sandwiches?"

Mr. Smith looked almost embarrassed. "Actually," he said, "we're both rather exhausted, and we hoped you might help us with some magic."

Inside the canvas bag, the gargoyle began to tremble, and Hilary held him close. As if being shipped off to finishing school were not infuriating enough! If Mr. Smith thought he could lay a single gloved finger on the gargoyle's granite ears, he was terribly mistaken. "Do you think I am the Enchantress of the Northlands, Mr. Smith?" she said. "I haven't got any magic, not an ounce. And I don't know the first thing about using it."

Mr. Smith fumbled in his pocket. "I think you misunderstand—"

"I understand perfectly. If you're trying to steal magic from me, you're wasting your time."

"I knew it," said Charlie. "We'd better find someone else to ask before she calls the guards on us." He looked straight at Hilary. "You High Society girls are all the same, aren't you?"

Before Hilary could reply that she was not a High Society girl but a pirate—or very nearly a pirate, at any rate—a great screeching noise filled the carriage, and the train rattled to a stop. Hilary was almost thrown to the floor, but Mr. Smith reached out with an elegant arm and steadied her.

"That's odd," he said, once the screeching noise had died away. "We can't have reached Pemberton yet." He walked briskly to a window and peered out. "Ah. That explains it. Magic or not, my lad, I believe this is our stop."

The train had come to a halt in the middle of a meadow. There was no station in sight, and Hilary couldn't even make out any towns in the distance. Along the train tracks, however, stood a row of stern-faced men dressed identically in red jackets and gray trousers. A mud-splashed carriage painted with the queen's emblem waited behind them.

Hilary stared at Mr. Smith. "Whatever are the queen's inspectors doing here?"

"Did I mention," said Mr. Smith, "that we were in a bit of a tight spot? Yes, I'm fairly sure I did. I rather hoped we'd be magicked away before they caught up to us." He put his arm around Charlie's shoulder. "But now I'm afraid we must rely on our manners."

With a great deal of boot stomping, the queen's inspectors filed into the carriage. They hardly bothered to look at Hilary, but they paused when they caught sight of Mr. Smith.

"Sorry to disturb you gentlemen," said the inspector at the front of the line, "but we're searching for thieves, and we think they may have hopped this train in Queensport."

"Dressed all in black?" said Mr. Smith. "Wearing masks? Acting terribly suspicious?"

"Yes, that's right. You've seen them, then?"

cuse

Mr. Smith smiled. "I have indeed. They ran that way"—he pointed down the corridor—"not more than five minutes ago."

"Hmm," said the inspector. He jotted something down on his notepad. Then, quite unexpectedly, he turned to Hilary. "And how about you, little girl? Did you see anything suspicious?"

Across the corridor, Charlie slumped against the wall and pressed his white-gloved hands over his eyes. Hilary frowned at him. Then she straightened her dancing-sheep cardigan and nodded to the inspector. "The gentleman is right, sir," she said—too loudly, perhaps, but the inspector didn't seem to notice. Charlie lowered his hands and blinked at her. "Two men dressed in black dashed straight through this carriage. If you hurry, I'm sure you'll catch them."

"Very good," said the inspector. "You've all been a great help." He strode off in the direction Mr. Smith had pointed, and all the other inspectors tipped their hats and followed.

When the last inspector had left, Mr. Smith turned to Hilary. "I'm sorry to run without a proper good-bye," he said, "but we really must be off." He gestured to the open door where the inspectors had boarded. "If you still need to leave the train, I recommend doing so before those gentlemen in red jackets return. They're sure to be in a foul temper." And with that, he slipped out the door and disappeared into the tall grass.

Charlie followed him, but halfway out the door he paused, and Hilary was almost sure she saw him smile. "By the way," he said, "it was decent of you not to rat us out." (6) snitch telling

Hilary nodded. "Not all High Society folk are the same, you know," she said—but she needn't have bothered, for he was already gone.

Through the open doorway, Hilary could just make out a faint blue strip of ocean shining beyond the meadow grass. She unfastened the clasp on her bag, and the gargoyle poked his head out. "Are the scallywags gone?" he whispered.

"Yes," said Hilary, "they're gone."

"Thank you for protecting me."

"I promised you I would."

"I wasn't scared, you know," said the gargoyle. "Pirates are never scared."

"It's very lucky that we're going to be pirates, then," said Hilary. "What do you think? Shall we escape to sea?"

Just then, the carriage door crashed open. Miss Greyson flew in with a gaggle of queen's inspectors at her heels.

"Hilary Westfield!" Miss Greyson cried, waving her crochet hook in the air as though it were a cutlass. "What in the world are you doing? Get away from that door at once!"

Hilary gulped. "I'm sorry! I needed some fresh air, and

I thought . . ." But it was no use trying to pull wool, or any other sort of fabric, over Miss Greyson's eyes. Miss Greyson crossed her arms, tapped her foot, and sighed. This was exactly the pose that governesses were supposed to strike when they dealt with disobedient charges, and Miss Greyson had gotten a good deal of practice.

"I can handle this, thank you, inspectors," she said with such authority that the inspectors could do nothing but nod and scurry away. Then she turned back to Hilary. "I can't think of a single young lady who needs a term at Miss Pimm's as much as you do. Honestly! Were you aware that there were *thieves* on this train? You could have been in grave danger. And escaping to sea, of all the foolish ideas—it simply can't be tolerated." Miss Greyson took Hilary firmly by the shoulders and marched her back to their compartment. "What would your father say if he knew what you've been up to? Just imagine how disappointed he'd be."

It wasn't difficult for Hilary to imagine her father frowning at her and sighing in exasperation—but didn't Admiral Westfield admire daring deeds? Didn't he often escape from perilous situations himself when he was out on the High Seas? He had no love for pirates, of course, but Hilary hoped that when she became a true pirate at last, Admiral Westfield wouldn't be disappointed. He might even be impressed.

WHERE HIGH SOCIETY TURNS FOR SCANDAL

Beloved Scuttlebutt readers, guard your valuables!

The band of thieves looting High Society households is still at large, and they appear to be targeting magical items. The Grimshaws' magic cutlery, the Feverfews' magic paperweights, and Mr. Thaddeus Wembley's magic coin collection have all been stolen this week, and it's rumored that even the magic in the Royal Treasury is in danger. But who is responsible for this thievery? The queen's inspectors haven't got a clue, but the Scuttlebutt has a hunch: whispers of <u>piracy</u> have landed upon our delicate ears.

The queen assured this reporter that her inspectors have the matter well in hand. We hear, however, that these same inspectors were foolish enough to lose the thieves' trail on the Pemberton train. Until the villains are captured, the Scuttlebutt urges caution and advises its readers to avoid the company of masked figures dressed all in black.

WE ASKED, YOU ANSWERED:
Do you think pirates are responsible for the recent string of thefts?

"If they are, I must admit I'm grateful to them for taking all that magic out of High Society's hands. The rest of us have hardly a magic coin to our names, you know."
—L. REDFERN, PEMBERTON

"The whole affair certainly reeks of piracy. Can't say I'm surprised, though. As a victim of theft myself, my thoughts are with those brave individuals who have suffered at the hands of these villains."—J. WESTFIELD, QUEENSPORT

"I can't think why pirates would need to steal magic from High Society households. Can't they sail off and dig up some treasure chest or another? Or have those run dry as well?"
—T. GARCIA, SUMMERSTEAD

"I shall be guarding my antique magic shoehorn very closely from now on. It once belonged to my great-grandmother, and no pirate shall get his grubby hands on it. I hear that life without magic is terribly dull and common, and I don't care to experience it."—G. TILBURY, NORDHOLM

"I don't have magic and never did, but if I were a fancy High Society fellow, I wouldn't be careless enough to lose my magic in the first place. If the thieves are reading this, I hope they'll bring their loot to my place. There's plenty I could do with a magic coin or two."—W. PIPPIN, OTTERPOOL

"I'm sure I don't know a thing about it. You can't possibly expect me to comment on such a scandalous topic."
—E. PIMM, PEMBERTON

various extracts

From

A Young Lady's Guide to Augustan Society

* * * * * * * * * * * * * * * *

A few words about the ENCHANTRESS:

An Enchantress is a highly trained and powerful magic user appointed by the crown to distribute magic within the kingdom and ensure its proper use. The Enchantress must have good sense, strong morals, and a natural talent for the use of magic. However, there has not been an Enchantress in Augusta for nearly two hundred years, since the Enchantress of the Northlands proved herself to be both irresponsible and impolite by vanishing without appointing a successor. This guide would like to point out that such a shocking event would not have taken place if the Enchantress of the Northlands had paid more attention to her manners.

A few words about MAGIC:

Magic is a substance with certain peculiar properties, discovered in the hills of Augusta many centuries ago. Although its appearance is similar to gold, its behavior is quite different: when a piece of magic is held in the hand, it obeys the holder's spoken requests. It is said to draw its power from the magic user herself, and only a few individuals are powerful enough to use it in great quantities without becoming faint or fatigued. However, with proper training and practice, all persons are capable of using magic to some degree.

In the past, the government mined magic ore from the hills, minted it into coins and various other objects, and oversaw its distribution to all Augustan citizens. These citizens used magic to perform appropriate everyday tasks such as bread baking, sock mending, and maintenance of public roadways.

The use of magic was governed by an

Enchantress, who punished any citizen who used his magic improperly or impolitely. This guide regrets to say, however, that many citizens actually preferred impoliteness, and they were not at all fond of the Enchantress. After enduring a number of magical attacks, the Enchantress of the Northlands took her revenge: she collected nearly all the magic in the kingdom and hid it away. The Enchantress herself disappeared soon afterward, and her hidden magic has never been recovered.

Several High Society families still own magical items that the Enchantress did not manage to collect, and it is rumored that a few magic coins are buried throughout the kingdom in pirates' treasure chests. Most citizens, however, have no magic at all, and recent attempts to retrieve additional magic ore from the hills of Augusta have been unsuccessful.

Readers of this guide, being young ladies of quality, are likely to encounter magic in their travels through High Society, but they must take care not to offend commoners by waving their magic about or by mentioning it too often. (Commoners, in this guide's experience, are quite easily offended.) Therefore, it is best to discuss magic in low voices in High Society sitting rooms. Remember: a polite magic user does not draw attention to herself and does not cause a ruckus. (12) *Disturbance*

A few words about PIRACY:

This guide is shocked—simply shocked!—that a young lady of quality would consult it on such a scandalous topic. This guide politely requests that the reader close its covers and place it gently on a nearby shelf before it falls into a swoon.

* * * * * * * * * * * * * * * *

(13) *Faint*

CHAPTER THREE

①Bold

THE REST OF the afternoon was filled almost entirely with frowning. Miss Greyson frowned at Hilary across the train compartment, and Hilary frowned into the (haughty) pages of *A Young Lady's Guide to Augustan Society,* which she felt sure were frowning right back at her. After the train, there was a carriage pulled by a gloomy-looking horse and barely large enough to accommodate all the frowns. The driver stacked Hilary's luggage behind the hard wooden seat, but Hilary insisted on keeping her canvas bag on her lap. Soft, pebbly snores escaped through the seams.

Finally, as the carriage clopped along Pemberton's winding main street, Miss Greyson's frown dismissed itself.

"I really do think you'll enjoy school," said Miss Greyson, "if you'll only give it a chance. Did you know I attended Miss Pimm's myself?"

Poor Miss Greyson. Hilary wondered what she had been like as a young girl, before finishing school had gotten to her. "No, I didn't know."

"It wasn't so very long ago. I didn't particularly want to go either, but one can't say no to that sort of opportunity." Miss Greyson tucked her crochet hook into her hair bun. "And in the end, I was quite glad I went. Miss Pimm is a wise woman."

"She seems awfully fond of dancing sheep," said Hilary, glancing doubtfully down at her cardigan.

Miss Greyson laughed. "That's true enough. But her deportment classes are not to be missed. You'll get started with those in your second year."

The thought of a second year at Miss Pimm's, or even a second day, was more than Hilary could bear. "Does every girl at Miss Pimm's become a governess?"

"Some do." Miss Greyson paused. "You know, Hilary, I don't intend to be a governess forever. In fact, I've just given your mother my notice."

Hilary sat upright and studied Miss Greyson's expression; she didn't look like she was joking. She had a very governess-like face, with sharp blue eyes that saw too much and severe silver glasses that rested on the tip of her proper, intelligent nose. It certainly wasn't a face that could belong to a tightrope walker, or a botanist, or whatever Miss Greyson intended to be instead of a governess. "But what will you do instead?"

"I'm going to open a bookshop by the harbor. I'll have all the local papers available, of course, and tea and chocolate to drink, and comfortable armchairs for reading in." For what might have been the first time in her life, Miss Greyson smiled. "I think your father will absolutely hate it."

Hilary smiled back. "I'm sure he will." Admiral Westfield disliked chocolate almost as much as he disliked books, and Hilary quite admired Miss Greyson for daring to fill a shop with things that would send the admiral into a rage. "But I think you'll do wonderfully well, choosing books for people and telling them all about the news of the day." It seemed just right somehow—much more appropriate than tightrope walking, in any case. "Will you put in a section for pirate yarns? So the gargoyle and I can read them when we come to visit?"

"And romances," the gargoyle mumbled sleepily inside his bag. "Don't forget the romances."

"Of course there shall be romances, and pirate yarns as well." The carriage came to a halt, and Miss Greyson bent down to adjust Hilary's skirts. "For the next ten minutes, however, I am still your governess, and I won't have you looking like a ruffian on your first day at Miss Pimm's." She sighed. "After that, I'm afraid I won't be able to control it."

The carriage door swung open, and the driver offered his arm to Miss Greyson. "Here we are, miss," he said. "If you'll just come with me."

Miss Greyson took the driver's arm and stepped gracefully out of the carriage, but Hilary climbed down herself, managing to get a stripe of grease on her new stockings along the way. Thankfully, Miss Greyson pretended not to notice. Instead, she reached for Hilary's hand and led her into the dark, vast shadow of Miss Pimm's.

The building was gray and heavy as the sky. In front of it stood a cold iron fence, punctuated every few feet with no-nonsense spikes that might once have displayed the heads of disobedient schoolgirls. The air hung thick with smoke, and Hilary wished she could cough. She gripped her bag tighter as Miss Greyson guided her through the iron gate, pulled her up several stone steps, took hold of the heavy-looking door knocker, and rapped three times.

"A pirate is never scared," Hilary whispered to herself as the door creaked open in front of her. If only her sword weren't hidden away under layers of petticoats at the bottom of her traveling trunk. "A pirate is never scared." She squeezed Miss Greyson's hand despite herself. the Overthrow the caption ④

A pirate might not be scared of cannon fire or mutiny, but the glare on the face of the girl who opened the door was fierce enough to strike terror into the breast of One-Legged Jones himself. "Welcome to Miss Pimm's," the girl said flatly. She looked Hilary up and down, ran her fingers through her long blond hair, and wrinkled her nose. "Are you Hilary Westfield?" She sounded like she hoped it wasn't the case.

Hilary nodded.

"Oh. Well, I'm Philomena. I have to show you to your room."

Hilary looked wildly at Miss Greyson. "I'm Miss Westfield's governess," Miss Greyson said, to Hilary's relief. Maybe talking politely to people like Philomena was something you learned at Miss Pimm's, or maybe getting past Philomena was a sort of entrance exam. "Is there any chance we could see Miss Pimm? We're old acquaintances. I used to go to school here, you see." ⑤ Friends

Miss Greyson smiled for the second time that day—the world was getting stranger and stranger by the minute— but Philomena didn't smile back. "I'm terribly sorry," said Philomena, "but Miss Pimm doesn't receive visitors. You can leave Miss Westfield with me, and the porter will collect Miss Westfield's bags." She raised her eyebrows as the carriage driver deposited the golden traveling trunk on the doorstep. "I hope you have another pair of stockings in there."

"I do." Hilary met Philomena's stare. "I have nineteen pairs, in fact. And a sword."

Miss Greyson groaned and put her hand to her forehead.

"Excuse me?" said Philomena.

"I'm afraid Miss Westfield is prone to fits of imagination," Miss Greyson said quickly.

Philomena's eyebrows retreated. "I understand completely," she said. "Well, you have nothing to worry about. Miss Pimm's will cure her of that nasty habit soon enough. Now, Miss Westfield, please come along with me."

Hilary and Miss Greyson started to follow Philomena inside. "Only students and instructors are permitted inside the school building," said Philomena to Miss Greyson. "With all the thefts breaking out in the kingdom these days, one really can't be too careful. But you're perfectly welcome to say your good-byes outside."

Miss Greyson agreed and knelt down in front of Hilary. "A *sword*?" she whispered.

"I'm sorry, Miss Greyson."

"All I ask is that you take care not to carve up your classmates. If I were not a governess, however, I might mention that the lovely Philomena is in need of a haircut."

Hilary nearly laughed, but she suspected it might be against the rules to laugh on the grounds of Miss Pimm's, so she gave Miss Greyson her most solemn nod instead.

"Now," said Miss Greyson, "you must promise to write. You must keep up with the news of the day and tell me all about it in your letters. And you'll come and visit me in my bookshop at the end of the term, won't you?"

"Of course." Hilary's stomach was starting to feel very strange, and she didn't trust herself to say more than a few words at a time. This couldn't be right; pirates were hardly ever sentimental. Then again, neither was Miss Greyson. Yet here she was, leaning forward to hug Hilary, and Hilary found herself hugging Miss Greyson back. "Please don't tell me to be a good little girl," she said.

Miss Greyson sniffed and stood up. "My dear," she said, "I would never dream of it." She gave Hilary's canvas bag an affectionate pat, nodded politely to Philomena, and walked down the steps and through the gate, back to the waiting carriage.

"Come along," said Philomena, picking up the lightest of Hilary's bags. "And please don't dawdle. I have lessons to finish."

⑦ Lingre (Follow behind)

HILARY FOLLOWED PHILOMENA through a maze of dark stone walls and high archways. From the inside, the building seemed more like a fortress than a school, with small slits for windows and halls branching in every direction. "That's the library," said Philomena, waving a hand toward one archway, "and that's the refectory. We eat all our meals together here." She waved at an identical archway on the other side of the hall. All the rooms soon muddled together in Hilary's mind, but with any luck she wouldn't be at Miss Pimm's long enough to get lost.

At the end of the hall, Philomena made a sudden sharp turn and opened a small wooden door. Hilary followed her up a set of endless stairs. Every so often, the stairs paused for a while to make a landing, with another wooden door opening off of it. Unlike the other rooms Hilary had seen, these rooms were labeled with name plaques. "This is the dormitory staircase," Philomena explained. "Most of us have been here for ages already. You and your roommate are the only two girls starting in the summer." Hilary gathered from Philomena's expression that starting at Miss Pimm's in the summer was only slightly more socially acceptable than robbing the Royal Treasury.

"I didn't know I'd have a roommate," said Hilary. With any luck, her roommate would want to escape from Miss Pimm's as badly as she did, but the only luck she'd had for the past few days had been the disastrous kind.

"Oh, yes." Philomena stopped outside a door labeled "Miss Westfield & Miss Dupree." "I had to move her in, too"—Philomena gave her hair an irritated flick—"and I think the two of you will get along perfectly."

HILARY'S ROOMMATE'S NAME was Claire, and she was thirteen years old, fourteen in November, and she had an older sister named Violet and a younger brother named Tuck and two very large brown dogs, and she loved climbing trees and hated boiled beans and had just arrived—only two hours ago!—from Wimbly-on-the-Marsh, which was quite close to Pemberton but not nearly as nice. "And I am so thrilled that I'm finally here," Claire concluded, flopping down on her bed and taking a breath at last. "Now that you're here, too, everything will be perfect."

"It's very nice to meet you," said Hilary, and it was, especially compared to Philomena. After the porter had brought up the rest of Hilary's luggage, Philomena had disappeared, leaving only a vague warning that she might be back later.

"That girl's horrid, don't you think?" said Claire. "Old Philodendron, I mean. I hope the other senior girls aren't much like her. *I* certainly don't intend to be like her. I'm going to be a great actress someday." She sat up on her bed and struck a dramatic pose for half a second. "Oh, would you like help unpacking? I've done all my bags already, so I can help with yours if you'd like."

Hilary hadn't quite decided what to do about her luggage. Unpacking all her belongings seemed an awful lot like the first step toward staying at Miss Pimm's forever. Then again, she certainly wouldn't be dragging her woolen bathing costumes and dancing-sheep cardigans off to sea; those, at least, could safely be left in the dormitory wardrobe. "I'd love some help," she said, dragging her trunk across the floor and flipping its latches. "That is, if you really don't mind."

Claire stared at the gold-plated trunk and whistled. "Is your family very rich?" she asked. Then she clapped her hands over her mouth. "I'm sorry," she said; "I know that wasn't ladylike. Oh, I've already gotten off on the wrong foot!" She hopped from one foot to the other a few times, and Hilary wondered which was the wrong one.

Hilary rolled up a woolen bathing costume and shoved it in a drawer. "Please don't feel bad," she said to Claire; "I promise I don't care a bit. And my family isn't *very* rich—at least, I don't think they are." She had never really thought about it before, but it had to be quite expensive for her parents to employ all the cooks and servants and stained-glass-window cleaners, not to mention Miss Greyson. She blushed. "I don't really know. My father works for the queen."

"Oh, he's not *Admiral* Westfield?" Claire dropped the petticoat she was holding. "He's always on the front page of the papers. We try not to wrap fish in him." She picked up the petticoat and dusted it off. "My parents sell fish, and I help at the market most days. Or I did, until now. My parents are very excited for me; they say that once I leave Miss Pimm's, I'll be able to enter High Society and never wrap fish again." She sighed and placed the petticoat in a drawer much more neatly and tenderly than Hilary had done. "But you're probably used to much grander sorts of people."

"Grand people," said Hilary, "are mostly horrid, and I can't stand High Society. At least fish are friendly."

"I suppose they are," said Claire, "when they're not dead. But if you don't want to be in High Society, what *do* you want to do?"

"Actually," said Hilary, "I'm going to be a pirate."

"Oh, that's brilliant!" Claire hopped up and down again. "It sounds so thrilling. And you could meet all sorts of dashing sailors."

Hilary squirmed. The only sailor she knew particularly well was Oliver, and he was only dashing in the sense that whenever she was near him, she wished he would dash away as quickly as possible.

"And there's treasure, of course," Claire continued. "But girls aren't allowed to be pirates, are they?"

"Apparently not." Hilary tried to close the drawer, but it had been stuffed too full of stockings and petticoats. It would just have to stay open. "I'll find a way, though." She wished she felt as sure as she sounded.

"That explains the sword, then," said Claire cheerfully. She pulled Hilary's sword from the bottom of the trunk. "I'm afraid I don't know where this goes."

"It should be safe in the wardrobe. You don't think they come around and inspect our rooms here, do you?"

Claire shuddered. "I hope not. I absolutely cannot *stand* making my bed. It's too similar to wrapping a fish."

"Maybe we'll have to take bed-making classes here. Or petticoat-folding classes."

"Ugh." Claire closed the lid of the traveling trunk and sat down on it. "I'm awfully glad you're not one of those stuck-up girls. I had nightmare visions of being the most awkward young lady at school. Oh, goodness, not that I mean—" She clapped her hands over her mouth again.

"I'm so sorry. My sister, Violet, says I don't think before I speak, and you know what, she may be right. She was a student here, too, before she entered High Society. She's more or less perfect." Claire kicked the thing nearest to her foot, which happened to be Hilary's canvas bag.

"Hey!" the gargoyle yelled as the bag skidded across the floor. "What do you think you're doing?"

Both Claire and Hilary leaped up at once, and Claire turned pale. "I think," she said, "your bag just spoke to me."

Hilary rushed to the bag and snatched it up. "It's—well—"

"It's *me*!" cried the gargoyle. "The gargoyle! And," he added, "I do *not* enjoy being kicked."

Hilary sighed and unfastened the bag. "Now you've done it," she said to the gargoyle. "Have you already forgotten what Miss Greyson said about unscrupulous people?"

"Claire doesn't look unscrupulous," said the gargoyle, blinking a few times in the sunlight and grinning at Claire, showing off his sharp stone teeth. "But she did kick me. Shall we run the scallywag through?"

Claire gave a little shriek and backed up against the wall.

Hilary clamped her hand around the gargoyle's snout. "Behave yourself," she told him. Then she turned to Claire. "I promise he's not dangerous; he's just had a long journey. He's usually very pleasant."

Claire didn't unpeel herself from the wall. "I'm so

sorry," she said, "but I didn't expect you'd have magic." She tugged on her hair ribbon. "He *is* magic, isn't he?"

Hilary nodded. "He used to be part of our house."

The gargoyle cleared his throat. "Don't forget to tell her about the Enchantress," he said through Hilary's fingers.

"Oh, very well," said Hilary. "He wants you to know that he was carved by the Enchantress of the Northlands herself. She fell in love with some long-ago Westfield, and she gave him the gargoyle as a gift—or that's what the gargoyle says, at any rate. He's quite fond of storytelling."

"How romantic!" said Claire. "Is your house absolutely full of magic, then? I hear some High Society houses are."

"Ours isn't," said Hilary, "and Father complains about it constantly." According to Admiral Westfield, Westfield House had been rather packed with magic long ago, before the Enchantress came along and took away his family's entire stash of coins, cuff links, and goblets. She hadn't taken the gargoyle, though, and no one knew exactly why. Hilary thought it was because the Enchantress was too polite to take back a gift she'd given, while the admiral swore she'd only left the gargoyle behind to annoy future generations of Westfields.

"My father complains, too. We've never owned a single piece of magic in our lives." Claire took a few cautious steps toward the gargoyle. "May I talk to him? I've never met a gargoyle before."

Hilary removed her hand from the gargoyle's snout.

"Hello," said the gargoyle. "How do you do?"

"Hello," said Claire. "May I pat you on the head?"

"I don't think that would be appropriate," said the gargoyle. "Would you pat a human acquaintance?"

But Claire had already begun to scratch behind his ears. "Oh," he said. "Well, now. In that case." He closed his eyes and leaned into the scratch.

"You're not quite as—well, as *golden* as I thought you would be," said Claire after a while. "Aren't you made of magic?"

"Certainly not!" the gargoyle said. "No self-respecting gargoyle would go about looking all polished and shiny. I'm Southlands granite from snout to tail—except for my heart. That's the magic bit, if you must know."

"I see," said Claire. "So you grant wishes, then?"

The gargoyle drew back in horror. "Wishes!" he said. "If I could grant wishes, I'd have a heaping plate of spiders in front of me right now. *And*," he added, "I'd be wearing a pirate hat."

"He's only for protection," Hilary explained, "and he doesn't like being used. It makes his heart go all fluttery."

"That's a shame," said Claire. "Protecting people is a very kind thing to do."

"It can be," said the gargoyle. "It depends on who's asking. Thank you for the scratch." He hopped over to Hilary. "Now, if you don't mind, I'm ready to go on my wall."

There wasn't a slot for a gargoyle above the door, so Hilary balanced him on the bookshelf above her bed. The gargoyle seemed particularly happy about this arrangement because he was in charge of propping up *Treasure Island*. "Maybe finishing school isn't so bad after all," he said as he curled up next to the soft leather cover. "It's making my ears feel awfully tingly, though."

The gargoyle swished his tail in Hilary's direction, and she patted it. "Perhaps you're allergic to finishing school. Curtsying and minding one's manners are enough to make anyone itch."

There was a sharp knock at the door, and Philomena entered without waiting to be invited. "How rude!" Claire mouthed to Hilary.

"Come along, both of you," said Philomena. "You really should brush your hair, but there's no time. We're going to be late enough as it is."

"Late for what?"

Philomena rolled her eyes at Hilary. "For your meeting with Miss Pimm."

HILARY AND CLAIRE followed Philomena through the stone halls, taking care to stay a few steps behind her so they wouldn't be hit in the face by her bouncing hair. Miss Pimm's office was as far away from the dormitory wing as it was possible to be without ending up in the next town over, and Hilary thought this showed surprisingly good sense on Miss Pimm's part. As they walked, Claire chattered away, telling Hilary everything she'd heard about Miss Pimm from her sister, Violet. Violet said Miss Pimm had once been a great beauty, and quite important in High Society besides. It was rumored that she'd even been friendly with the queen. But she fell in love with an aeronaut, who plummeted over the side of his balloon basket during a terrible storm. After his death, Miss Pimm was so distraught that she abandoned her family and her High Society duties to follow her heart's desire: establishing a school for young ladies of quality. Hilary couldn't imagine how opening a finishing school could be anyone's heart's desire, but clearly it had been Miss Pimm's, and Hilary very nearly admired her for it. Running away and pursuing one's dream was quite a piratical thing to do.

By the time they reached a doorway marked simply with the image of a dancing sheep, Claire was nearly out of breath from storytelling. Philomena opened the door and curtsied to a woman sitting behind an ornately carved desk. "The new girls," she murmured.

"Thank you, Miss Tilbury. You may go."

Philomena swished her hair and walked away, leaving Hilary and Claire standing in the doorway.

"Miss Westfield and Miss Dupree?"

Hilary nodded, and Claire attempted a wobbly curtsy.

"I am Miss Pimm." The woman rose from the desk and pulled two chairs away from the wall. "Please take a seat."

Behind Hilary, the heavy door slammed shut.

Miss Pimm was very tall, taller than Hilary's father. She had a pleasant face—to Hilary's surprise, she was actually smiling—and a braid of snow-white hair wrapped around her head like a crown. On the collar of her purple silk jacket, she wore a silver dancing-sheep pin. All in all, she looked like she might be someone's beloved great-aunt, the kind who gives wonderful presents and is always a bit of a bother when she comes to visit. Her desk was a jumble of papers, punctuated by the occasional fountain pen, and on the edge of the desk nearest Hilary, an ink sketch of an old-fashioned gentleman in a balloon basket smiled out from a silver frame.

Claire nudged Hilary with her elbow and nodded at the picture frame. "Her lost love!" she whispered, and clutched her hands to her chest with a sigh.

Thankfully, Miss Pimm did not seem to notice. "Welcome, girls," she said, beaming first at Claire, then at Hilary. "I'm so glad you could join us for our summer session. I have already heard so much about both of you."

Oh, no. What had she heard about Hilary? Considering that her application had been forwarded to Miss Pimm's by a committee of scourges and scallywags, it probably wasn't anything flattering.

"I do like to make an effort to get to know all my girls personally," Miss Pimm continued, "and I hope we'll become fast friends by the end of our time together."

"I'm sure we will!" cried Claire, who was leaning so far forward in her chair that Hilary worried she'd topple out of it.

"Very good. Now, you're most likely wondering what you'll be up to this term." Miss Pimm shuffled through a pile of papers. "I have your class schedules here, and I thought I'd run through them with you in case you have any questions. In the mornings, you'll have handwriting, current affairs, embroidery, etiquette, and fainting. Our more active classes are scheduled after lunch. Those are dancing, water ballet, and archery—a most graceful sport, if one can manage to fire one's arrows without perspiring. . . ."

Miss Pimm's litany of classes went on and on. How many different things did a young lady have to know about? Archery sounded vaguely useful, but when would a pirate ever need to perform a perfect waltz step, or faint on command? Worst of all, it seemed that every second of every day was scheduled. Even if Hilary could find a free moment to run away to sea, she'd probably be too tired from all the horseback riding and soufflé baking to manage an escape.

The walls of Miss Pimm's office were decorated with plaques and awards that Miss Pimm had won from groups like the Delicate Ladies' Society, the Eligible Bachelors' Club, and the Coalition of Overprotective Mothers. Among the awards were a number of framed embroidery samplers emblazoned with tasteful mottoes. *Beware the dangers of reverie,* proclaimed the sampler behind Miss Pimm's left ear, while the sampler by the window reminded its audience that *A lady never shrieks.* Hilary decided that the worst of all was the sampler directly over Miss Pimm's head, which read, in badly embroidered rhyme, *The greatest treasure in all the land—the delicate touch of a lady's hand.*

"Hilary?" Miss Pimm sounded concerned. "You look a bit green. Are you feeling well?"

Hilary jumped. "Yes, Miss Pimm. I'm fine. Thank you."

"You're welcome, my dear. As I was saying, you'll have every Wednesday afternoon and Saturday morning free to do as you like, though we ask that you stay in Pemberton. Some girls like to visit relatives during these free periods, but you must alert a teacher to your plans if you wish to leave town."

Hilary leaned forward almost as far as Claire. "Excuse me, Miss Pimm. Does that mean our first free afternoon is this Wednesday?"

"It does, though I hope you're not already tired of school."

"No, Miss Pimm. I'm just excited to explore Pemberton." Wednesday was only four days away. Surely it was possible to survive four days at finishing school. Four days of bathing costumes and history lessons, and then— somehow—freedom.

"The city is a wonderful place," said Miss Pimm, "and so is this school. I hope you'll learn a great deal during your time here. I look forward to handing you your golden crochet hook at the start of your second year as a symbol of all the progress you've made."

"Violet never lets me touch her golden crochet hook," Claire told Hilary. "It's a huge honor to switch from silver to gold."

"It is indeed." Miss Pimm smiled and handed them their schedules. "Please don't hesitate to stop by in the future if there's anything you need. Miss Dupree, Philomena should be waiting outside to show you back to your room. And Miss Westfield . . ." Miss Pimm turned her gaze toward Hilary. She didn't smile. "May I speak to you privately for a few moments?"

It was one of those questions that was really an order. Claire slipped Hilary a smile and left the room. Miss Pimm leaned across her desk, so close that Hilary could smell her rose-scented perfume.

"You are James Westfield's daughter, are you not?"

Hilary swallowed hard. "Yes. I am."

"I'm quite fond of your family. The Westfields and I are old friends—but that's neither here nor there." Miss Pimm settled back in her chair. "I have been trying to get in touch with your father for some time. Do you know where he is?"

"He's at home, Miss Pimm. At Westfield House. I'm sure you could schedule an appointment. If you wanted to see him, I mean."

"No, I don't think that will be necessary." Miss Pimm paused. "So he hasn't been away from home lately?"

"I think he goes into Queensport sometimes." It probably wasn't very ladylike to lose track of one's own father. "To be honest, Miss Pimm, I don't see him much. He's usually in his study with the door shut."

"I see. And do you know if he is planning any trips? Perhaps an errand for the queen?"

"I honestly have no idea." Even when Admiral Westfield did have plans, he rarely shared them with Hilary. "We talked yesterday, and I think he did mention something about an important voyage. But I don't know if it's for the queen or not."

"No matter," said Miss Pimm. "I'm sure I'll manage to contact him somehow. But please do let me know if you have any news from him."

Hilary almost laughed. "I'm sure he won't be writing me."

"But if he does."

"Yes, Miss Pimm. Of course."

"Thank you." Miss Pimm smiled. "You may return to your room, Miss Westfield. I look forward to getting to know you better."

Miss Pimm sounded so earnest that Hilary almost felt sorry for her. After all, if she did not get to know Hilary better by Wednesday afternoon, there was a very good chance that Miss Pimm would never see her again.

Dear Hilary,

(12) Emotionally upset

I hope you will forgive my eagerness to write, but I have just
arrived back at Westfield House, and I feel rather at
a loss without you. I am hurrying to collect my things, and
I should like to move into my bookshop as soon as possible,
because I'm afraid the atmosphere here has become quite
tense. I have no doubt that your parents are devastated now
that you are gone, but that is no excuse for their behavior.

(13)

Honesty

Your father has been acting—please excuse my
frankness—very strangely since he found himself burgled. I
cannot blame him for stationing a fleet of guards at
his office door, but your mother and I both feel that
surrounding Westfield House with cannons is a bit much.
One cannot come home from the market without feeling as if
one is under siege, and the milk delivery boy is too terrified
to come near our kitchen door. But I fear we shall have
to go without milk for as long as Admiral Westfield's
paranoia persists. To make matters worse, your mother has
become convinced that another attack on Westfield House
is imminent, and she refuses to leave her chambers. She is
supposed to host a ball at the weekend, but I wonder what

sort of ball it will be if the hostess has locked herself in her wardrobe.

In addition to this strangeness, I discovered upon my return that Admiral Westfield's favorite apprentice, young Lieutenant Sanderson, has been dismissed for no reason whatever. The household is shocked by this turn of events, and many of the naval officers now fear for their livelihoods. As I recall, you and Lieutenant Sanderson were not always the closest of acquaintances, so perhaps this item of news will bring a smile to your face.

I hope you are enjoying Miss Pimm's, or at least finding it not quite as terrible as you anticipated. Have you met Miss Pimm herself? Have you been keeping up with all the newspapers? The ongoing thefts from High Society households have become quite a nuisance indeed. I trust you are being cautious and keeping a healthy distance from all unscrupulous persons.

I look forward to hearing all about your adventures at Miss Pimm's. Until then, I remain

Your

Eloise Greyson

Postscript: Please give my love to the gargoyle.
P.S.

CHAPTER FOUR

Golden hook
crochet

BY WEDNESDAY AFTERNOON, Hilary had embroidered six pot holders, broken two archer's bows, trodden deliberately on Philomena's foot seventeen times, and set the school record for treading water. At times she had nearly enjoyed herself, but not even the satisfaction of hearing Philomena shriek could keep Hilary at finishing school an instant longer than necessary. It was time to escape from Miss Pimm's.

But escape was proving to be more difficult than Hilary had expected. She'd intended to leave directly after Wednesday's fainting class, but Claire caught her arm on the way out of the classroom. "You'll come to lunch with me, won't you?" she said. "Oh, good; I knew you would. I can't stand walking into that horrid refectory alone. There are never any seats, and I'm sure we're already late. We practiced that simple swoon for *hours*." Claire poked at her scraped elbow and winced. "Honestly, I don't believe young ladies of quality are supposed to have quite so many bruises."

"Maybe not," said Hilary as Claire dragged her toward the refectory, "but I hear bruises are awfully respectable in the pirate community. I'm sure that purple one on your knee would be the envy of the High Seas."

By the time they reached the refectory, servants in starched white aprons were already walking along the rows of long tables, passing out plates of food. Claire pulled Hilary toward the last two empty chairs in the room, then stopped so suddenly that Hilary nearly crashed into her.

"Oh, drat," Claire whispered. Just across from the empty chairs sat Philomena. "Perhaps no one will notice if we hide under the tablecloth."

"Don't be silly," said Hilary. "A good pirate doesn't run away from nefarious scoundrels—she confronts them."

Claire protested that she was not a pirate of any sort, but Hilary marched up to the chair directly across from Philomena and sat down in a most unladylike fashion. Claire hesitated, and for a moment Hilary thought she really *would* dive under the tablecloth.

"Miss Dupree," said Philomena, "please sit down. Or are you one of the serving girls today? I'm simply dying for some water. Would you fetch the pitcher for me?"

Claire flushed and slipped into the empty chair. Hilary

smiled at her and turned back to Philomena. "I'd be happy to fetch that water for you," she said, "but you must let me know where you'd prefer me to pour it. Down your back? Into your lap? Your schoolbooks are looking rather parched these days; perhaps they'd welcome a drink."

Philomena sat up even straighter than she usually did. "If you don't mind, Miss Westfield," she said, "I'd prefer to eat in silence." Philomena unfolded her napkin and frowned at Claire, who slapped a hand over her mouth to stifle her giggles.

The luncheon plates arrived at the table, bringing with them a smell that reminded Hilary of Queensport Harbor. Some girls recoiled from their plates, and there was a great deal of handkerchief waving and nose holding all along the table.

①Something to hate

"Fish sticks again? How loathsome!" Philomena poked at the breaded fish with her fork. "Surely we won't encounter fish sticks after we enter High Society."

Claire shrugged. "I don't think they're all that horrid," she said. She cut into her fish, took an experimental bite, and nodded. "They're very fresh, actually."

Philomena's mouth twitched into something resembling a smile. "So you're a fish expert, Miss Dupree? How fascinating."

"Well, I'm not exactly an *expert*," said Claire, "but I grew up selling fish—my parents are fishmongers, you see—and it's easy to learn a bit about fish when you're around them every day. They're really not so bad once you get used to the smell."

Philomena tapped her fork against her plate. "Your family sells fish? Isn't that a job for commoners?"

The other girls at the table stopped talking. Some of them stared down at their plates; others stared at Philomena. Claire had gone all rigid and pale, and Hilary dearly wished she had brought her sword to lunch. "Don't you dare speak to Claire that way," she said. "She's done nothing to you, and she's the kindest girl here."

Philomena sniffed. "Really, Miss Westfield," she said, "I can't believe your parents would encourage you to associate with fishmongers' daughters." She took a dainty sip of water. "I wonder whatever possessed Miss Pimm to let Miss Dupree enroll here. After all, this is a school for young ladies of quality, and it's clear she'll never be anything but a fishwife."

Claire gasped and dropped the bit of fish stick she'd been holding.

Hilary leaned across the table and fixed her most fearsome stare on Philomena. "If you say another word," she said, "I'll see to it that you're strapped to a ship's mast and sent off to a deserted island where you can't be cruel to anyone. I'll tie you up myself; don't think I won't." Hilary looked over at Claire and smiled. "I hear that horrid girls on deserted islands don't often get invited to High Society balls."

Claire bit her lip. Then she smiled back at Hilary.

"Perhaps," she said in a small voice, "if Philomena is very lucky, a fish might ask her for a waltz."

For a moment, the entire table fell silent. Then, very quietly, the girl next to Claire began to laugh. Claire laughed, too. Even Philomena's glare wasn't strong enough to stop the laughter from spreading, and soon enough, all the girls at the table were giggling over their fish sticks.

Philomena, however, was perfectly silent. Her knuckles turned white around her fork. Then, to Hilary's amazement, she placed the fork primly on the tablecloth and smiled. She reached under her seat for her schoolbag and fumbled inside for a moment until she found a small, gleaming object, which she clasped in her fists so quickly that Hilary couldn't make out its shape. Then she murmured a few small words and looked up at Claire.

The fish sticks on Claire's plate started to wobble. They squirmed about until they were standing upright on the plate, and after a moment's hesitation, they formed a rather tidy line. Hilary stared at the regiment of fish sticks in horror as, one by one, they leaped off the plate and smacked themselves against Claire's forehead.

Claire shrieked and grabbed her knife, but the fish sticks dodged her swipes. Even when Hilary had gathered her senses enough to overturn the plate, the remaining fish sticks wriggled out from underneath it and dove into Claire's lap as fast as they could manage. By the time the assault reached its end, Claire was dripping with crumbs and smelling quite a bit like Queensport Harbor herself.

Hilary pushed back her chair and stood up. "I can't imagine," she said to Philomena, "that Miss Pimm tolerates any sort of bullying at her school, let alone the magical kind. She'll have you expelled when I tell her what you've done."

"Magic?" Philomena blinked at Hilary. "Whatever do you mean?"

"You know perfectly well that those fish sticks didn't leap about by themselves."

Philomena looked up and down the table at the other girls. None of them was laughing anymore. "Poor Claire overturned her plate, and her lunch flew everywhere. It was rather clumsy of her, don't you all agree?" Some of the girls nodded. "Miss Westfield, I'm sure Miss Pimm has no time for silly stories. And what could possibly possess her to take your word over mine?"

"She's right, you know." Claire wiped at her dress miserably with a handkerchief. "Please, Hilary, don't waste your time on my account."

"But it wouldn't be a waste. . . ."

Claire stood up and let fish sticks fall from her skirts. "Hilary," she said quietly, "would you be good enough to accompany me to our room? I believe I've lost my appetite."

CLAIRE HURRIED UP the dormitory staircase without saying a word, and Hilary could hardly keep up with her. As soon as they'd reached their room, Claire slammed the door behind them, threw herself onto her bed, and covered herself in blankets.

The gargoyle looked up from the pages of *Treasure Island*. "Oh, good," he said; "you're back. Is it time to go to sea?"

Under the blankets, the lump that was Claire let out a great and tragic wail.

Hilary shook her head at the gargoyle and ran to Claire's bedside. "Let me take care of Philomena," she said. "If Miss Pimm only knew how horrid she was, she wouldn't stand for it."

The lump sniffled. "It was my fault," it said. "I shouldn't have laughed. Oh dear!" Then the lump gave a great heave and resumed wailing.

"You didn't do a thing wrong," said Hilary, patting the lump where she thought Claire's back might be. "You defended your honor like a true pirate. But Philomena's got magic somehow, and she's even more awful with it than without it. We've got to do something!"

The lump writhed about as Claire attempted to untangle herself from her blankets. She sat up at last and blew her nose on the handkerchief Hilary offered her. "You don't understand," she said. "There's nothing to be done. It's not only Philomena who acts that way—who uses magic to be nasty, I mean. You should see them at the fishmonger's. All sorts of grand High Society gentlemen come in with magic coins, enchanting extra trout into their parcels. They don't pay for them, of course." Claire tugged at her blankets. "They do laugh quite a bit, though."

"But that's terrible!" If a grand gentleman ever tried something of the sort on Hilary, he'd quickly find a cutlass pressed against his linen-ruffled throat. "Can't you do anything to stop them?"

Claire laughed, but she didn't sound happy. "I don't have a gargoyle to protect me, and I'm not a pirate like you. I thought things would be better at Miss Pimm's—I thought no one would dare use magic on a High Society girl." She pulled her bedding back over her head. "Now, if you don't mind, I'm going to spend the rest of my life under these blankets."

"Oh, Claire, I *do* mind. You can't stay a lump forever. How will you go to class?"

"Lumps don't need to go to class," said Claire from under the blanket.

"Well, then, you'll need to eat."

Claire shuddered. "I'm never eating again! What if it's *fish sticks*?"

After a few minutes, she poked her head out of the blankets. "I guess I am a little hungry, though. I hardly got any lunch."

"You could go to the market," Hilary said. "You're allowed to go into town this afternoon. And I'm sure they won't have fish sticks."

Claire sat up and sniffed. "That sounds nice." She wiped her wet cheeks. "Will you come with me? Oh, unless you have other plans, of course . . . I don't want to be a bother. . . ."

Up on his shelf, the gargoyle groaned. "We're not supposed to go to the market!" he said. "We're supposed to be like the pirates in *Treasure Island*, exploring the High Seas and watching handsome sailors fall in love with golden-haired maidens!"

Hilary rolled her eyes. "You know perfectly well that's not what happens in *Treasure Island*."

"It is when I read it," said the gargoyle. "Now, are we going to sea or not?"

Hilary looked toward the wardrobe, where her sword rested under a pile of petticoats. "I'm sorry, gargoyle," she said at last, "but a pirate simply can't abandon her friends." She turned back to Claire. "Of course I'll come with you."

THE PEMBERTON MARKET was a bustling rectangle of stalls set up every morning in the town square. Behind the stalls were farmers and butchers and chefs selling every type of food imaginable; jellies and marmalades glowed like jewels amid stacks of frilly greens and slabs of smoked meats. Claire's eyes lit up at the sight of roast chicken legs, and Hilary bought one for each of them, along with little cups of custard for dessert. They walked through the market as they ate, watching customers haggle and listening to a street musician endeavor to play the bagpipes.

Claire had stopped wailing, though she still wasn't

talking nearly as much as she usually did. She caught sight of a woman selling brightly dyed embroidery threads and ran over to purchase some for class, while Hilary waited for her in front of the town message board. People had posted all sorts of announcements on the board: On one flyer, a gentleman announced a great reward for the return of his beloved pet rabbit. On another flyer, a traveling illusionist ⑤ announced that he had found an unfamiliar rabbit inside Magtian his top hat and wished to return it to its rightful owner. Colorful posters advertised country dances, and a grimy scrap of paper gave an address near Pemberton Bay where one could purchase small quantities of magic. In fact, the message board was so overflowing with information that Hilary nearly missed the small advertisement printed on smudged and tattered paper:

✪ WANTED: PIRATE CREW ✪

Established, respected freelance pirate seeking experienced crew members for upcoming voyage. Must be able to swashbuckle, swab decks, swill grog, fire cannons, and climb to the crow's nest. Successful applicants will sign contract for one round-trip voyage, with opportunity for further collaboration if merited. Voyage details to be divulged upon acceptance. Applicants trained in treasure location are of particular interest. Please apply in person to 25 Little Herring Cove, Wimbly-on-the-Marsh, at ten o'clock on Saturday morning.

Eye patches and hooks OK.

Please—no parrots.

Hilary tore the paper from the message board and ran over to Claire, who was carrying an armload of thread. "Look!" she said. "Read this!"

Claire promptly dropped the thread and skimmed the advertisement. "Hilary," she said solemnly, "you have to apply. Little Herring Cove is only a few miles from here."

"I don't know how to do half the things they ask for—I mean, I've never even tried to look for treasure—but . . ."

"It's your destiny." Claire handed the advertisement back to Hilary. "I'm sure you'll be a natural at swabbing grog, and climbing the cannons, and everything else."

"And it doesn't say anything about having to be a boy, so perhaps I have a chance."

Claire nodded, but her lip was starting to wobble again. Hilary's stomach twitched the way it had when she'd said good-bye to Miss Greyson.

"It's possible," she said, "that the freelance pirate won't want to take me on. I'm sure I'll come back to Pemberton on Saturday afternoon, and we'll be roommates, and nothing will have changed at all."

"Don't be ridiculous," said Claire, collecting her embroidery thread from the ground. "You are going to be a pirate, and I am going to help you."

"Really?"

"Of course. When Miss Pimm asks me where you've gone, I'll have a chance to practice my acting skills."

"And when I'm a famous pirate, I'll come back to school and tell Philomena that if she's horrible to anyone ever again, I'll make her walk the plank."

"That," said Claire, "sounds absolutely wonderful."

Miss Pimm's Finishing School for Delicate Ladies

Where Virtue Blossoms

Dear Miss Greyson,

(It feels so awkward to call you Eloise. I will have to keep calling you Miss Greyson for the time being. Is that all right?)

Thank you for the news of my family. If you can manage to slip my mother some food—perhaps something flat?—under the wardrobe door, I'm sure she would appreciate it. If I were you, however, I would get out of Westfield House as quickly as possible.

Your news about Oliver was the most thrilling

thing I've heard all day. I hope that sea monsters truly do exist, so he can be eaten by one.

I have met Miss Pimm, and she reminds me a little of you, only much older and more terrifying. She seems very interested in Father's affairs. Do you know if she has a penchant for sea captains? So many older ladies seem to. I don't suppose Father has asked after me. Has he?

So far, Miss Pimm's is not quite as horrible as being eaten by a sea monster. My roommate, Claire, is wonderful. Do you remember that girl Philomena? She has been making Claire's life a misery ever since she found out that Claire is not from a High Society family, but Claire stands her ground valiantly and takes out a large portion of her aggression during archery class. (Frustratingly, we are only allowed to aim our bows and arrows at turnips, but piercing the heart of a villainous vegetable is still quite satisfying.) When she is not busy being nasty to Claire, Philomena mocks me for wearing my hair in a braid and for falling down during curtsying lessons, but ~~pirat~~ proper young ladies can't waste too much time worrying about these things. You will probably be shocked to hear that I am at the top of my class in waltzing, but you will be less shocked by my difficulty with penmanship. I hope you are able to read this letter. My knuckles have been rapped upon so many times by the handwriting mistress that I worry they will stage a rebellion and escape from my hand in the dead of night.

The gargoyle wanted to send you a pressed spider as a token of his affection, but I encouraged him to send pleasant words instead. He declined, arguing that spiders are easier to catch. But I am sure he sends his love.

We are so very busy here that I may not have time to write back to you after this Saturday. Whatever else you may hear from Miss Pimm's, please know that I am thinking of you, and I promise to visit you in your new bookshop when I return to Queensport.

Love,
Hilary

CHAPTER FIVE

ATURDAY DAWNED WARM and bright, with just a hint of thunderclouds at the edges of the sky. A perfect day, Hilary thought, for piracy.

She packed all her most important possessions—her secondhand shirts and trousers, *Treasure Island*, and the gargoyle—in her canvas bag. Then she pulled on her scuffed sailor's boots and strapped her sword over her gray school dress. Claire had promised to look after the rest of her things while she was away, and truthfully, Hilary was relieved to be free of the gold-plated traveling trunk at last. It had given her far too many stubbed toes during her week at Miss Pimm's.

Claire, still in her nightgown and bare feet, came

downstairs with Hilary to say good-bye. "Remember," she whispered, "it's a right at the big oak tree, then a left at the bridge, then follow the stream for half a mile and you're there." She reached inside Hilary's bag and gave the gargoyle a good thorough scratch behind the ears. "I'll miss you both."

"Avast, me hearties," the gargoyle said sleepily.

"I think he means he'll miss you, too. And so will I." Hilary gave Claire a hug. "Thank you for everything."

"You have to let me know if you meet any (dashing) sailors." (7) Handsome

"Oh, of course. I'll be sure to send them right along to Miss Pimm's."

Claire laughed. "And I'll try to keep Miss Pimm off your track for as long as I can. Are you ready?"

"I think so."

"All right." Claire raised her voice so it echoed through the stone hall, turning the heads of the maids who were bustling through on their way to prepare the refectory breakfast. "I hope you have a wonderful time visiting your elderly relative in Pemberton, Miss Westfield! It's such a shame that your elderly relative, who lives quite nearby, is feeling ill! I am sure you will be a great comfort to him or her!"

The maids gave Hilary sympathetic smiles. Hilary smiled back and tried to keep her sword well out of view as she opened the front door. "Thank you for your kind words, Miss Dupree."

"I am saddened to hear that you may have to stay to look after your relative for several days! Maybe even months!" Claire put her hand to her forehead and tried to look distressed. "Good luck," she whispered.

Hilary waved, and the gargoyle flicked his tail goodbye, and then they were through the gate, away from Miss Pimm's, and off to sea.

IT WAS AN hour's walk to Little Herring Cove, and Hilary sang sea chanteys nearly the whole way. Once the gargoyle had woken up a bit more, he joined in occasionally on the harmonies. Hilary had the road to herself, and soon enough, the pavement below her feet turned to gravel and then to dirt. She plucked a buttercup from the grass along the roadside, remembered with a start that she was going to be a pirate, and hid the buttercup away in her bag, where the gargoyle declared it to be surprisingly tasty.

Hilary took a right at the big oak tree and a left at the bridge. She walked a little more slowly along the stream— she did not want to miss the freelance pirate's house, and she especially did not want to arrive early. Punctuality, she had heard, was not greatly appreciated in the pirate community, and most pirates arrived for treasure hunts and mutinies fashionably late.

It turned out, however, that she'd worried for nothing. When she reached 25 Little Herring Cove, she could tell she'd arrived at the right address not because of the number on the falling-down mailbox but because of the long and winding line of pirates waiting outside the door.

Hilary had not expected there would be so many of them. There were one-eyed pirates and no-eyed pirates, fancy pirates with billowing sleeves and shabby pirates with patched-up knees. They had pointed beards and pointed hats, curly mustaches and curly hooks, peg legs and real legs. They had golden teeth and golden earrings and gold doubloons sparkling in their mouths and ears and pockets. On their shoulders perched monkeys and toucans and tortoises, all seemingly named Polly. Shouts of "Arr!" and "Blast!" filled the air whenever a pirate swung his sword too close to his neighbor or tried to cut in line.

Hilary waited at the end of the line behind a large, bald pirate with an eye patch, a hook, and a peg leg. His name, he said, was Cannonball Jack. "And what be yer name, laddie?" he asked.

"Hilary," said Hilary.

"And why be ye wearin' those strange skirts, Hilary?"

"It's my school uniform," Hilary explained. "I'm a girl, you know." Her hair hung in a long dark-brown braid down her back, as usual, and she'd put on her best hoop earrings, but neither of these things set her apart from most of the other pirates in line.

Cannonball Jack laughed and slapped her on the back with the hand that wasn't a hook. "Arr, a jokester! That be a good one, lad. 'Tis a good thing to have a sense of humor if you wish to be a pirate. 'Twill serve you well during the sword fights and typhoons."

Hilary rolled her eyes. The other pirates didn't sound half as silly as Cannonball Jack; he had to be even more nervous than she was. "Do you know anything about this freelance pirate?" she asked.

"Very secretive, he be. Said to be the Terror of the Southlands, and a fearsome cruel captain."

"Cruel?" After spending a week with Philomena, Hilary had had quite enough of cruelty.

"Aye. 'Tis said that even uttering his name will bring his wrath upon ye." (4) Anger

"That hardly sounds like a practical response. What's his name, anyway?"

Cannonball Jack glanced from side to side and cupped a hand around his mouth. "Jasper," he whispered.

No sooner had the name left his lips than the door of 25 Little Herring Cove creaked open. A masked man wearing a red brocade doublet and a black three-cornered hat appeared in the doorway, and the crowd of pirates went utterly silent.

"Curses!" said Cannonball Jack. "He's heard me utter his name. I'm doomed for sure."

"I don't know," said Hilary. "He looks a bit short to be the Terror of the Southlands."

The masked man—Jasper, Hilary supposed—wandered

up and down the line of pirates, casting his gaze over every scarred and suntanned face. "Too old," he said to a wizened pirate leaning on a cane. "Too scary," he said to an alarmingly fierce-looking pirate. "I'm sorry," he said to a muscular young man with a kitten on his shoulder, "but I'm allergic to cats. You'll have to go."

"See?" said Cannonball Jack. "He's ruthless."

Jasper drew closer to the end of the line, dismissing pirate after disappointed pirate. To some pirates, he simply nodded. "Those applicants whom I do not dismiss," he announced, "may remain in line for a personal interview." Cannonball Jack mopped his brow with a ragged bandanna.

The gargoyle poked Hilary in the side. "What's going on now? I can't see anything in this ridiculous bag."

"He's coming toward us," said Hilary, "and you'd better keep quiet for the next few minutes." The last thing she wanted was for Jasper to proclaim her "too friendly to gargoyles." Even without the gargoyle's antics, she was sure she'd be marked "too young," "too female," or both.

Jasper drew level with Cannonball Jack and looked him up and down. "Too stereotypical," he declared at last. "Sorry." ⑤ Predicting and assuming

Cannonball Jack hung his head and trudged away as Jasper approached Hilary. Up close, Jasper looked a few inches taller and a few inches more fearsome than he'd seemed from a distance. He stared straight at Hilary.

Hilary stared back. His eyes narrowed, and the corners of his mouth twitched up into a smile.

"A fascinating turn of events," said Jasper. He clapped his hand on Hilary's shoulder. "This way, please. I hope you're prepared for your interview."

HILARY FOLLOWED JASPER past the line of grumbling pirates, several of whom tried to trip her with their peg legs. "For heaven's sake, there's no need to be nasty," said Jasper. "If this one doesn't work out, I'll send her off the plank and call the next applicant in." Some of the pirates chortled approvingly. (6) Laugh

Jasper led Hilary inside the ramshackle house, which smelled not unpleasantly of seaweed and leather. The front door opened directly into what Hilary guessed was a sitting room, although it did not look at all like any other sitting room she'd ever seen. Instead of chairs or velvet couches, a few well-worn rope hammocks hung from hooks drilled into the rafters. Standing in for a table was an old wooden box that looked suspiciously like a treasure chest. The room's only decoration was a gleaming wire cage containing a small bright-green bird. The bird croaked grumpily when it saw Hilary.

"Welcome to my salon," said Jasper. "Can I get you anything? Grog?"

"No, thank you." Grog at ten o'clock in the morning— Miss Greyson would have been horrified.

"Just for me, then." Jasper picked up a mug and took a long sip. "Please take a seat, any seat."

Hilary balanced herself in the hammock farthest away from the bird. "I thought your advertisement said parrots weren't allowed."

"Ah, but Fitzwilliam here is a budgerigar. That's a very special kind of parrot, and a parrot for which I make exceptions." Jasper removed his hat and started to untie his mask. "Besides, Fitzwilliam himself insisted on the no-parrot rule. He simply can't abide competition." He laid his hat and mask on the floor and looked up at Hilary. "It's a pleasure to see you again, by the way. And I must apologize—when last we met, I'm afraid I was in a bit of a hurry."

Hilary nearly fell out of her hammock. There, across from her, sat Mr. Smith. He looked quite different without the tailcoat, but now that his mask no longer hid half his face, there could be no mistaking it: he was the very same elegant gentleman she'd met on the train.

"I'm sorry, Mr. Smith," she said, once she'd caught her breath. "I didn't recognize you."

"That's the whole idea behind a disguise," said Jasper. "The name was a disguise, too, I'm afraid. I'm really Jasper Fletcher."

"And you're really a pirate?"

"Naturally." Jasper grinned, flipped a gold coin out of his hand, and caught it again. "Even pirates must travel by train every so often, I'm sorry to say."

Of course. No wonder he'd been wandering the train corridors looking for magic to steal—and no wonder he'd dashed away when the queen's inspectors had arrived. Being unscrupulous was all part of his profession.

"Now," said Jasper, "I believe it's my turn to ask a question. Who are you?"

"I'm Hilary," said Hilary. Should she have given herself some sort of fancy pirate nickname? The way things had gone for Cannonball Jack, it was probably safest to keep things simple.

Jasper pulled out a notepad and started scribbling. "And do you have a last name, Hilary?"

Hilary opened her mouth, then closed it again. The navy and the pirate league were not on good terms, and Jasper Fletcher could hardly be expected to hire the admiral's daughter for his crew. He might be more inclined to take her hostage, and she would almost prefer Miss Pimm's to that.

"Smith," she said. "My last name is Smith."

Jasper smiled. "Very well; that's a game I can appreciate." He looked up. "Ah, here's my first mate. Perhaps he'd like to ask you some questions as well. Charlie, come and join us."

The boy from the train hesitated in the doorway. He wore torn-up work clothes splattered with paint, and he held a half-eaten cinnamon bun in one hand. "That's that finishing-school girl," he said, pointing the cinnamon bun at Hilary. "What's she doing here?"

"Her name is Hilary," said Jasper, "and she's hoping to be my apprentice. Hilary, this is my ward, Charlie—though of course the two of you have already met."

"You want to be a pirate, do you?" Charlie took a bite of the cinnamon bun. "I didn't think you High Society types cared much for piracy."

"Well," said Hilary, "I do." She gave him the same fearsome look she'd practiced on Philomena, though she was not sure how well it would work on an actual pirate.

To her relief, Charlie simply shrugged and settled down into an empty hammock. Perhaps she wouldn't need to be quite so fearsome after all. "Is your name really Charlie, then?" she asked. ⑧ Picture on doc

"It is. I'm not famous enough for an alias—not like our Mr. Smith here." Charlie jabbed a thumb in Jasper's direction. "He's the Terror of the Southlands, you see. Quite well known in certain circles."

"It's a difficult burden," said Jasper, "but someone must be the most fearsome pirate on the High Seas, and I'm happy to oblige. Now, Hilary." He turned back to her and flipped to a new page in his notepad. "If you truly want to be a pirate, whatever were you doing at finishing school?"

Hilary took a deep breath. "I applied to the Very Nearly

Honorable League of Pirates, but they rejected me because I'm a girl—"

"A frightfully stupid reason," Jasper cut in. "Of course, frightful stupidity is a hallmark of the VNHLP."

Hilary beamed. "They were wrong, don't you think?" she said. "And I tried to tell them exactly that, but they wouldn't listen, and I got sent off to Miss Pimm's. I've only just managed to run away."

Jasper scribbled more notes. "And is there any good reason," he said mildly, "why I shouldn't send you back to Miss Pimm's right now?"

Hilary stared at him in horror. "You can't send me back there! My handwriting's atrocious, and I'm not a proper young lady, and I don't intend to be one!" Hilary unsheathed her sword, and Jasper swung back in his hammock. Charlie nearly dropped his cinnamon bun. "I can sail and row, and I can swim a mile without stopping. I can tie all the knots that have been invented, and a few that haven't been. I can climb, I can read a map, and I'm willing to fight. I've spent my whole life dreaming of being a pirate, and I'll do whatever it takes, I swear."

Jasper wrote "PASSION" in large letters on his notepad and underlined it twice.

After a moment, Charlie set down his cinnamon bun. "You're serious, aren't you?"

"Of course," said Hilary. "A pirate is always serious."

"It's just that most of you lot want nothing to do with

pirates, and I thought . . ." Charlie shifted uncomfortably in his hammock.

"It's all right," said Hilary. "I've met some thoroughly nasty High Society folks myself. I can't say I'm sorry you're stealing their magic."

Jasper furrowed his brow. "Pardon me?"

"You *are* the ones behind those magic thefts, aren't you?"

"Thefts!" cried Jasper, leaping up from his hammock. "Do you take us for common criminals? We are pirates! We may plunder a few things here and there, but I assure you, we're not thieves."

"But weren't you escaping from the queen's inspectors? They came after you on the train!"

Jasper sighed. "As it happens," he said, "we'd picked up a certain item in Queensport, and the inspectors were under the impression that it didn't belong to us. If they'd caught us, they certainly would have drawn the same conclusion you did—that we'd been stealing magic from High Society for weeks. It's not true, of course, but I doubt the queen's inspectors would have believed me."

Hilary frowned. Jasper seemed honest enough, but pirates were hardly known for being trustworthy. And the masked figures she'd seen outside Westfield House might have been Jasper and Charlie—though they'd been so far away that they might have been anyone else, too. "Do you mean to say there's a second pair of unscrupulous gentlemen traveling around Augusta and stealing things?"

"That is exactly what I mean to say." Jasper returned to his hammock. "And I do wish they'd stop, whoever they are; they're becoming a terrible nuisance." He flipped his coin in the air once more. "But you've got nothing to worry about. If we take you on our crew, your magic piece will be safe with us."

Hilary froze. "I don't have a magic piece! I told you on the train; I swear I don't have magic!"

"There's no need to look so terrified." Jasper held the coin out in his palm; it wasn't a doubloon. It was imprinted on both sides—a crown on one side, a figure eight on the other—and Hilary knew without asking that it was very old. "I've got a magic piece here myself, and I certainly don't need anyone else's."

"Most pirates have a bit of magic, once they've dug up a treasure or two," Charlie added. "Not me, though; I can't stand to use the stuff. Which means that when Jasper here uses his coin to magic up some fancy clothes for the two of us, he exhausts himself making silk handkerchiefs and leather gloves and enormous trousers. Soon enough he's too tired to conjure up anything larger than a cufflink, and we've got to find another magic user to help us vanish off a train." Charlie shook his head. "Jasper gets a bit carried away with disguises."

"But it all worked out in the end, didn't it?" said Jasper. "Even though Hilary here refused to magic us away?"

"I suppose so," said Charlie. "Next time, though, I'd like some trousers that fit properly."

In Jasper's palm, the magic piece jumped.

"Ah," said Jasper. "I thought so." He turned to Hilary. "Did you know that magic vibrates when it senses more magic nearby?"

Hilary shook her head.

"Well, it does. And you apparently have such a large chunk of magic, it's got this coin jumping about all over the place. It happened on the train, and it's happening now." Jasper waved the coin at Hilary's face, but it didn't move. As he brought it closer to her bag, however, the coin started to jitter uncontrollably. So did the bag. "Very curious," said Jasper. "Will you tell me what you've got in there, or shall I take a look for myself?" 9) Sick to your stomach

Hilary felt queasy, but she knew the pirate meant business. She reached into her bag and pulled out the gargoyle, whose ears were shaking as furiously as Jasper's coin. "If you hurt him," she said, holding him tight against her chest, "I'll slice you from port to starboard."

"And I'll bite you," said the gargoyle. "Would you put down that dratted coin? It's making my ears tingle, and I'd rather not lose them. I'm missing enough limbs as it is."

Jasper burst out laughing. "I'm not sure what I was

expecting," he said once he'd recovered his composure. "A bag of magic coin, perhaps, or a magic bracelet. But certainly not that."

"I am not a *that*," said the gargoyle. "I am a gargoyle. And a pirate," he added after a few moments' thought.

Jasper leaned forward. "If you had a hand," he said, "I would shake it. How did you come to be a pirate, might I ask?"

"I came to be a pirate in Hilary's bag," said the gargoyle. "Obviously. Wimbly-on-the-Marsh is a long way to hop."

Jasper laughed again, and Charlie knelt down to introduce himself to the gargoyle, who immediately requested a scratch behind the ears. Overhead, Fitzwilliam the budgerigar gave out an annoyed sort of tweet.

"He doesn't like you," Jasper explained to the gargoyle. "But I do. In fact, I like both of you very much." He put down his notepad. "What do you think, Charlie?"

"She's survived finishing school, so we know she's brave," said Charlie, "and she helped us escape from those inspectors on the train. I say we take her on."

"A good argument," said Jasper. He turned back to Hilary. "You've got more wits about you than all those blustering idiots out there combined. And I think your friend here could be a useful addition to our crew." He nodded at the gargoyle, who glanced modestly down at his tail. "Still, you're not a League member, you've got no real experience, and you are"—he lowered his voice—"a girl."

The gargoyle's ears flopped, and Hilary's heart flopped right along with them.

"There are a lot of pirates right outside this door who'd want to run me through for hiring a schoolgirl over them, you understand. And I have to maintain my reputation. Terror of the Southlands and all that."

"I understand," Hilary whispered. Her hammock swayed from side to side, making the floorboards lurch beneath her feet.

"However," said Jasper, "I'm willing to cut you a deal. You might as well know that Charlie and I are on the search for treasure. I'll offer you a spot on our crew, and if you find that treasure for me, I'll tug a few strings, make sure you're established in the League, a full-fledged pirate, et cetera. Sound fair?"

"Yes! Yes, it does." Miss Greyson had often reminded Hilary that jumping up and down was not ladylike, and she suspected it wasn't particularly piratical, either, so she tried very hard not to bounce in her hammock. "Thank you so much," she said. "I swear you won't be sorry."

"Please, don't thank me yet. If you don't get me that treasure, I don't care how fast you can fire a cannon, or how sharp your sword is—it's back to Miss Pimm's for you, and you'll never be able to show your face on a pirate ship again." He lifted his mug and took a swig of grog. "I'm very good at blackening people's names, you know."

"I'm sure you are," said Hilary quickly. Jasper seemed pleasant enough, but she had no desire to end up on the wrong end of his sword—especially on her first day as a pirate.

"Right." Jasper smiled at her. "Do we have a deal?"

He extended his hand, and Hilary shook it.

"I'll find that treasure for you, sir," she said. "My governess would throw a fit if my name were blackened."

"Then we're settled," said Jasper. "Welcome to the crew."

From the Humble Pen of
ELOISE GREYSON

Hilary Westfield!
What are you up to?
Get back here right now!

POSTAL COURIER COULD NOT DELIVER
REASON: COULD NOT FIND
MISS WESTFIELD ANYWHERE.
SORRY.

From

Treasure Hunting for Beginners:
THE OFFICIAL VNHLP GUIDE

A BRIEF INTRODUCTION TO **TREASURE:**

If you are a pirate who does not know what treasure is, you are sure to be laughed out of every groggery in Augusta. In fact, you may be laughed straight out of your own ship by schools of small, disdainful fish. But fear not: this guide is here to save you from that wretched fate. You are a beginner, after all, and we at the VNHLP are not entirely heartless.

Although you may think highly of your best pirate jacket, your parrot-feather collection, or your hundred-year-old bottle of grog, *these things are not treasure.* We assure you that any pirate who opened a treasure chest containing these items would be sorely disappointed. Nor should any decent treasure chest contain gold, rubies, emeralds, diamonds, or other useless stones. High Society folks may have use for such baubles, but pirates do not! Have you ever seen a pirate pacing the deck of his galleon in a diamond tiara? We did not think so.

Real pirate treasure consists of one thing, and one thing only: magic ore. After the ore is smelted to produce pure magic, that magic is traditionally formed into gold-colored coins, but other tools and figures made of magic are not uncommon discoveries in a pirate's treasure chest. Indeed, a scallywag by the name of Blackjaw Hawkins once buried a treasure chest packed from top to bottom with magic toothbrushes. You may scoff at the notion of tooth brushing—you are a pirate, after all—but remember: treasure is powerful stuff, and it must not be scoffed at.

CONCERNING FAME AND FORTUNE:

Small treasure troves hidden by previous generations of pirates can be found on deserted islands and rocky outcroppings throughout the kingdom. However, many a pirate has tried to make his name on the High Seas by searching for famous, long-lost treasures. These include the fabled wreck of the good ship *Petunia*, the infamous magic stash of the Enchantress of the Northlands, and, of course, the toothbrush collection of Blackjaw Hawkins. Although several pirates have set out in search of these treasures, none have been successful, and more than a few have perished in the attempt. If you seek such a treasure, beware! The VNHLP takes no responsibility for the foolish actions of overeager young pirates, although we will most likely declare a half holiday on the High Seas when you perish.

*Ships must be capitalieized and must be italics.

Chapter Six

THE DAYS THAT followed were a flurry of plans and preparations. Jasper's small pirate ship was moored in the cove behind his house, and there was a galley to stock, a deck to swab, a mainsail to mend, and a badly damaged Jolly Roger to repair. "Just a cannonball wound," said Jasper, looking at Hilary through the giant hole in the skull and crossbones. "Nothing to worry about, really."

The only thing Jasper was worrying about at the moment, it seemed, was finding the final two members of his pirate crew. He'd spent the rest of Saturday interviewing the pirates who remained in line, and all of Sunday with an entirely new batch of scourges and scallywags, but each one was unsuitable in some way. By Monday evening,

he had reached the depths of despair. "I have never," he shouted, "met so many ill-behaved people in my life! They're all as greedy as thieves, and twice as traitorous." He paced the length of his salon. "Perhaps my luck's run out at last."

And perhaps it had, because on Tuesday, Jasper hired Oliver.

Hilary and Charlie were stocking the ship with cannonballs when Jasper appeared on the dock with Oliver at his side. "Young Oliver here knows more about ship repair than I do myself," said Jasper, "and he's smarter than you might think from looking at him. He was first in line this morning and far more polite than the usual rapscallions—so I signed him up."

"Happy to be aboard, sir," said Oliver, giving Jasper a small salute. He'd scuffed up his good boots, and he'd traded in his naval uniform for a well-worn set of pirate clothes, but not even the threadbare jacket and faded eye patch could disguise his familiar sneer. Jasper hurried back to the bungalow to interview the next pirate in line, and Hilary and Oliver stared at each other in horror.

"It's a good thing you're here," said Charlie. "We've still got loads of work to do. The mainsail needs stitching up; you could start with that."

"Stitching?" Oliver flicked a bit of dust from his jacket and sneered at Hilary. "If it's all the same to you, I'd prefer not to do girls' work."

"Would you prefer it, then," said Hilary, "if I dropped this cannonball on your foot?" She took aim at his toes, but to her great annoyance, Charlie stepped in and blocked her path.

"All work on this ship is pirates' work," he said to Oliver, "and we're all pirates here. You'd do well to follow my orders when Jasper's not around." Then Charlie turned to Hilary. "He may be as miserable as a dishrag," he said, "but he'll be no help to us at all with a broken foot."

Hilary sighed. She didn't care to admit that Charlie was right, but at least he disliked Oliver as much as she did. "All right," she said as she handed Charlie the cannonball. "Perhaps I'd better have a few words with him." She grabbed Oliver by the elbow and dragged him down the deck until she was sure they were out of Charlie's earshot. "What are you doing here?" she whispered.

Oliver shrugged. "Same thing you are."

"But you can't possibly want to be a pirate."

"Of course not." Oliver lifted his eye patch. "I'm getting revenge on your father. When I couldn't chase down those thieves who broke into Westfield House, he yelled at me for half a day. Then he dismissed me from the navy—for good, he said." Oliver's sneer deepened. "Not that I'd go back there. I was out of a job, so I thought I'd join up with some pirates. Maybe I'll let slip a few navy secrets, attack a few of Her Majesty's ships . . . it doesn't matter to me, as long as it makes Westfield squirm. Isn't that what you're doing as well?"

"Oh, you toad!" Hilary wished she had broken his foot after all. "That is *not* why I'm here."

"Say what you like," said Oliver. "Anyway, I don't intend to lose this job. If you tell a soul where I've come from, I'll have you flapping from the mast like a flag, you understand?"

"Fine, but you'd better keep quiet yourself. Tell them who my father is, and you'll think the skull and cross-bones is a self-portrait. As far as I'm concerned, we're total strangers."

"Suits me." Oliver snapped his eye patch back into place, turned on his heel, and began to mend the mainsail in silence.

OLIVER WAS POLITE enough when Jasper was around, and after the mainsail-stitching affair he always did as he was told, but as the days wore on, the mood inside 25 Little Herring Cove turned black. Jasper couldn't find one last suitable pirate for his crew; Oliver and Hilary went out of their way to avoid each other; Fitzwilliam had taken a tremendous dislike to the gargoyle, which he expressed by decorating the gargoyle's head with bird droppings; and all of them were furious because Jasper refused to tell them about the treasure they were going to search for, or even where they'd be sailing, until they were safely at sea.

Charlie, at least, was a bit more helpful: he loaned Hilary a book called *Treasure Hunting for Beginners*, which he'd been given during his VNHLP training, and she read passages aloud to the gargoyle every day before dinner.

"This bit's about the tools a pirate needs for treasure hunting," she told the gargoyle one dreary evening. "Let's see—you need a map, of course, and a compass to guide your way. And once you've found treasure, you'll need a spade to dig it up."

"And a rope," the gargoyle added, "for climbing into towers and rescuing damsels in distress." He fluttered his wings happily. "Damsels in distress are *very* romantic."

Hilary set down the treasure-hunting guide as Charlie came into the room and slumped into a hammock. "Any news from Jasper?" she asked. They'd finished the final repairs to the ship earlier in the day, but Jasper showed no signs of setting sail anytime soon.

Charlie shook his head. "He just dismissed another batch of pirates. Sent them all home without an interview."

"But he's being ridiculous," Hilary said. "How am I supposed to find this treasure for him if he won't even tell me what it is?"

"Or if we never go to sea?" Charlie swung back and forth in his hammock. "I don't know what's gotten into him; he's never been this picky about his crew before. This must be an important voyage."

"If it's so important, shouldn't we begin the piracy as soon as possible?"

"Yes," said the gargoyle, "we should." He'd climbed into Hilary's lap and was hiding under her arm to shield his head from Fitzwilliam. "In *Treasure Island*, there's none of this sitting around."

Jasper and Oliver came in from the kitchen with bowls of stew for everyone, and Jasper looked around the room. "What are you all doing?"

"Sitting around," said the gargoyle. "Feeling glum."

"Ah," said Jasper, and they all sat around feeling glum together, frowning into their bowls of stew.

A sharp rap on the door cut through the glumness. "I demand," called a voice, "that you let me in at once!"

"Coming, coming." Jasper pulled himself out of his hammock. "If you want an interview, I'm afraid you'll have to come back tomorrow."

He opened the door. There, on his front step, stood Miss Greyson. Her hat was sliding off the side of her head, her skirts were splattered with mud, and she had pulled the crochet hook out of her windblown hair, making her look rather like an ancient Augustan warrior queen. The expression of fury on her face, however, was all too familiar to Hilary.

Jasper stared at Miss Greyson as though he had never seen a governess before. Then he took off his hat and bowed. "To what do I owe this pleasure, madam?" he asked, extending his hand. "Please come inside."

Miss Greyson ignored his hand and stepped past him into the house, setting her carpetbag down in front of her. "Hilary," she said, "who is this overdressed person? What are you doing here? Never mind; I don't even want to know. Just get your things and come with me at once. They're absolutely frantic at Miss Pimm's."

"Miss Greyson!" Hilary leaped up, sending the gargoyle tumbling into the hammock. "How did you know I was here?" Even though Miss Greyson had a habit of being everywhere at once, her arrival in Wimbly-on-the-Marsh was still faintly remarkable.

But Miss Greyson wouldn't be badgered. "Governesses have their ways," she said. "Even former governesses." She brushed her hands together, and that was that.

Jasper cleared his throat. He'd sat back down in his hammock, but he hadn't stopped staring at Miss Greyson. "Er, Hilary," he said, "would you mind introducing us?"

Apparently, Miss Greyson's mere presence had brought on a fit of etiquette. "This is Miss Eloise Greyson," Hilary said in her best finishing-school voice. "She used to be my governess. Miss Greyson, this is Jasper Fletcher. He's a pirate."

"A *freelance* pirate," Jasper corrected.

"Sorry, a freelance pirate. The gentleman next to Jasper is his first mate, Charlie, and next to Charlie is someone

(2) Good Manners

who is a complete stranger to both of us." Hilary nodded at Oliver, who looked as though he might lose his stew at any moment.

"My goodness," said Miss Greyson; "isn't that—?"

Hilary gave Miss Greyson a quelling look. "His name is Oliver, and you've never met him before in your life."

"I see." Miss Greyson pursed her lips. "This is all quite fascinating."

"Up there is Fitzwilliam the budgerigar. That's a kind of parrot. And I believe you already know the gargoyle."

"Enchanted," said the gargoyle, bowing in Miss Greyson's direction.

Jasper rose from his hammock again. "Eloise," he said, "may I offer you some stew?"

"It's Miss Greyson, if you please. And I really don't think stew is necessary. We're about to be on our way, aren't we, Hilary?"

"I'm not going back to Miss Pimm's," said Hilary. "Besides, I'm Jasper's employee now."

"And what, may I ask, has he employed you to do?"

"Swashbuckling, grog swilling, mast climbing, and treasure hunting, for the most part," said Jasper, delivering a bowl of stew into Miss Greyson's hands. He steered her toward an empty hammock. "In short, piracy."

Miss Greyson sank into the hammock. "Oh dear," she said. "It's worse than I thought. Mr. Fletcher, I simply cannot let Hilary sail with you and your crew. She is supposed to be in finishing school, and running away with a gang of pirates would be terribly improper."

"I'm sorry to hear that," said Jasper, "because it puts me in an awkward situation. I'm afraid Hilary has given me her word that she'll sail with me, and any pirate who breaks her word must walk the plank."

"He's just making that up," Charlie whispered to Hilary. "Pirates break their word fifteen times a day."

Miss Greyson's knuckles had turned white around her bowl of stew. "If you make my charge walk the plank," she said, standing up again, "I'll see to it personally that a sea monster dines on you for dessert." Her nose was nearly level with Jasper's. "Don't think I can't do it. I am a governess, after all."

Jasper stammered something about being terribly sorry and backed away.

"Now, Hilary." Miss Greyson turned to her. "It's a long walk back to Miss Pimm's, and we're not going to find a carriage at this hour—"

"Miss Greyson, please. I'm happy here."

"In a pirates' den?"

"It's more of a bungalow, really," said Jasper.

"And it's much nicer than Miss Pimm's. I can use my sword here, and I don't have to embroider anything! And Jasper's lovely—I mean, he's obviously the Terror of the Southlands, but otherwise he's very nice. Besides," said Hilary, "I'm not your charge anymore." She stared down at her boots to avoid meeting Miss Greyson's eyes.

"No, I suppose you're not." Miss Greyson frowned. "But honestly! Associating with ruffians and rapscallions? Putting your very reputation at risk? Whatever would your father say?"

Oliver nearly choked on a carrot.

"My father has nothing to do with this," Hilary said quickly, "and neither does my reputation. You've always taught me to honor my promises, and now that I've made a promise to Jasper, I don't intend to break it. I'm a pirate now, Miss Greyson, and that's final."

Behind her, Charlie applauded and the gargoyle cheered. Even Jasper put his arm around her.

"You see," he said, "she's one of us."

Miss Greyson tapped her foot as she waited for the cheering to die down. "Oh, very well," she said at last. "If you've truly been careless enough to give these ruffians your word, it would be quite improper to go back on it now. I suppose there's only one thing to do." She put down her bowl of stew and untied her hat. "Now, when do we leave for sea?"

Everyone stared at her.

"I'm sorry," said Jasper. "Do you intend to join us?"

"Of course." Miss Greyson peeled off her cream-colored gloves one at a time and tucked them inside her hat. "If you think I'm going to let Hilary run about on the High Seas without proper supervision, I don't mind asking you to think again."

Hilary had seen that firm, fierce spark in Miss Greyson's eyes hundreds of times before. Each time the spark appeared, Miss Greyson got her way. "But what about your bookshop?"

"Unless it's grown feet I don't know about, it won't run off while I'm gone."

Oliver glared at Hilary. "Now look what you've done," he whispered.

"Oh, hush. She's not that bad. Besides, Jasper will never let her come along."

But Jasper was staring at Miss Greyson with a strange look on his face, a look Hilary didn't think was at all appropriate for pirates. "It will be an honor to have you on our ship, Miss Greyson," he said.

Oliver groaned and buried his head in his hands. Charlie didn't look much happier—Hilary supposed his distrust of finishing-school girls extended to governesses—but after a few moments, he began to smile. "Say, Jasper," he said, "now that you've hired this governess, can we finally go to sea?"

The strange look departed from Jasper's face, and Jasper stood up straight. "Yes," he said, "I believe we can. Our crew is complete. Enjoy your stew, my friends, for it'll be hardtack and grog from-here on out." He grinned, as though this thought cheered him immensely. "We set sail in the morning."

KINGDOM OF AUGUSTA
OFFICE OF THE ROYAL RECORDS KEEPER

FORM 118M: INTENTION TO SET SAIL
INSTRUCTIONS: Please write legibly in ink.
Forms completed in blood will be rejected upon
receipt. All questions are mandatory.

NAME OF CAPTAIN: *Jasper Fletcher*
NAME OF VESSEL: *The Pigeon*
TYPE OF VESSEL: *Pirate ship (small)*
HOME PORT: *Wimbly-on-the-Marsh, The Southlands*
DESTINATION: *Gunpowder Island, The Northlands*

GENERAL PURPOSE OF VOYAGE
(please check one):
☐ BUSINESS ☐ PLEASURE ☒ PIRACY

If PIRACY is checked, the Kingdom of Augusta
reserves the right to send the Royal Navy to attack
your vessel if necessary. Do you accept these terms?
Do I have a choice?

NUMBER OF CREW MEMBERS: *4 human, 2 other*

NAMES OF CREW MEMBERS (please list):

Charlie Dove   *Eloise Greyson*

Oliver Sanderson   *Fitzwilliam Fletcher*

Hilary Smith   *The Gargoyle*

PRIMARY OBJECTIVE OF VOYAGE: *If you must know, we're looking for treasure. Does that satisfy your endless curiosity, you* impertinent *form?*

③ Disagreeable and disrespectful!

NUMBER OF FLOTATION DEVICES ON BOARD:
I think we have a few somewhere.

NUMBER OF WEAPONS ON BOARD:
Definitely more than the flotation devices.

If you PERISH AT SEA, would you like a MEMORIAL PLAQUE installed in your honor at the Royal Palace?
☐ YES   ☒ NO

Thank you for complying with the rules and regulations of the Kingdom of Augusta, and enjoy your voyage!

Miss Pimm's Finishing School for Delicate Ladies

Where Virtue Blossoms

Dear Hilary,

I hope this letter finds its way to you. I have addressed it to "Pirate Hilary, The High Seas," just as you told me to. Do you think there is more than one Pirate Hilary? Oh, I hope you are the proper Hilary. If you are not the Hilary you are supposed to be, and you are reading this letter, please stop right away. It's not polite to read someone else's mail. If you had gone to finishing school, you would know this, although since you are a pirate, I'm not sure what sort of education you've had. If you are the proper Hilary, you are allowed to keep reading, and I'm very sorry for the delay.

Oh, Hilary, Miss Pimm's is dreadful without you. I think my acting fooled everyone at least through Sunday evening, and the dance mistress said she hoped your sick relative would feel better soon so you could come back and demonstrate the waltz step for those of us who have two left feet (she meant me). But on Monday, Philomena asked where you were, and she said she didn't think you had a sick relative at all! I'm afraid I dissolved in a sea of tears, or at least a largish puddle, and of course that rat Philomena went straight to Miss Pimm to raise the alarm.

Now they are all out looking for you, and I think they are going to print your picture in the paper, the way they do for Wanted Criminals. It must be ever so glamorous to be a Wanted Criminal! Not that you are a criminal, of course, and I haven't told anyone that you are a pirate, but I wanted to let you know that people will be looking for you in case you want to wear a disguise. I have enclosed a false beard that I crocheted in class today. I know your hair is not bright purple, but I couldn't find any dark brown yarn, and I do have an uncle whose beard is a different color from his hair, so it must not be entirely impossible. The beard hooks around your ears, by the way, and I hope it fits. Please pardon the dropped stitches, as I was working very quickly to finish the sideburns before the postal courier came.

I hope you are having fun on the High Seas. Is it very similar to the way they describe it in books? Have you met any dashing sailors yet? Have you gotten in any sword fights? I should think sword fighting would be very similar to waltzing, only less romantic and with a more gruesome conclusion. I am sure you are brilliant at it. Please write if you get a chance in between all the cannon swabbing and scoundrel fighting. Your news is sure to brighten up the gloom of Miss Pimm's.

Your friend,
Claire

ON **TREASURE MAPS**, AND HOW TO **READ** THEM:

If you are reading this official guide, you are undoubtedly eager to set off on your first treasure hunt. Do not sail away in haste, however: it is the height of recklessness to search for treasure without first obtaining a map to guide you to its location.

A good treasure map is handcrafted by a worthy pirate and stamped with the skull-and-crossbones seal of the VNHLP. You can recognize a reputable treasure map by looking for a few telltale signs:

No matter how old it may be, a treasure map should look ancient and on the verge of crumbling to bits. It may be torn or water stained, and it should be a pleasing shade of brown. Scorch marks around the edges of the map are preferred.

A treasure map should have an atmospheric title, such as "Map to the Buried Fortune of a Fearsome Pirate." Drawings of monstrous beasts, whirlpools, and other dangers of the sea may also lend the map an atmosphere of vague foreboding.

To guide future pirates, a treasure map must include a dotted line indicating the best route to the treasure. Obstacles along the route (such as crocodile dens, hanging skeletons, et cetera) should also be noted on the map. The route must end in a large X to mark the spot where the treasure is buried.

Along the edges of the map, pirates who wish to give treasure hunters more of a challenge may include tantalizing but mysterious clues to the treasure's location.

If you are in possession of such a map, congratulations! You are well on your way to finding treasure. Simply follow the clues and the dotted line provided on the map, taking great care to avoid traps and obstacles. When you reach the location marked by an X, you need only dig beneath your feet to reveal a wealth of riches—assuming, of course, that no other pirate has beaten you to the spot. Even if you uncover an empty treasure chest, you may pride yourself on your excellent map-reading skills.

If you do not possess a VNHLP-approved treasure map, abandon the quest for treasure at once! Without proper maps, pirates would wander aimlessly through the kingdom digging holes in the ground at random, causing disruption and potential injury to citizens who do not watch their step. If you still wish to search for treasure, you may purchase copies of certified treasure maps, which are kept on file at the VNHLP's Gunpowder Island headquarters.

Chapter Seven

"ARE YOU SURE," said the gargoyle, "that this whole thing is the sea?"

"Of course!" Hilary tightened another knot around the gargoyle's middle.

"Even the bumpy bits?"

"Those are waves," said Hilary. "Don't worry; they're completely normal."

"They're moving awfully fast." The gargoyle leaned forward as far as the knots would allow. "And they're very far down."

Hilary scratched the gargoyle behind his ears—not quite as expertly as Claire, he had informed her earlier, but good enough in a pinch. "You know," she said, "you don't have to be the figurehead if you don't want to."

"And let some no-good mermaid get the job? I think not!" He nudged his ears against Hilary's fingers. "A little to the left, please."

With Charlie's help, Hilary had fashioned a sort of basket for the gargoyle on the bow of the *Pigeon*, and she was pleased to see that it neither bounced nor swayed as the boat sailed out of Little Herring Cove. "I like it," said the gargoyle, letting his tail hang through the small hole in the bottom of the basket that Charlie had cut for just this purpose. "I'll call it the Gargoyle's Nest."

"A very seaworthy name," said Hilary. "Now, let's review. What do you say if you see land on the horizon?"

"Land ho!" cried the gargoyle.

"And what if you see other pirates approaching?"

"Shiver me timbers, there be buccaneers ahead!"

"Very good. And what if you spot a sea monster?"

The gargoyle considered for a moment. "Help?" he said at last.

"Good enough." A warm breeze brushed past them, carrying with it the scent of salt and the sound of someone calling Hilary's name. "Oh, bother. That'll be Miss Greyson."

"You'd better go see what she wants," Jasper called from behind the ship's wheel. He looked every inch the dashing pirate, with his second-best coat billowing in the wind and Fitzwilliam perched on his shoulder. His hat sat confidently atop his head, and the sword at his side glinted in the sun. "I'll look after the gargoyle for you."

"I do *not* need looking after," the gargoyle called across the ship. "Say, Jasper, can I borrow your hat?"

Hilary scrambled up the deck, saluting Jasper as she passed him. "Good luck, Captain," she said. "You may need it."

THE ROOM HILARY shared with Miss Greyson was small—hardly more than a cubbyhole, really, with a single round window that reminded Hilary of the ones in her father's study. Through the window, Hilary watched the cheery houses that dotted the coastline bob past like smears of paint or bits of stained glass. Jasper's bungalow was quickly becoming a faint yellow blob amid a blur of forest-colored blobs. "I don't know, Miss Greyson," she said. "I don't think pirates unpack."

"Oh, I'm afraid there's no doubt." Miss Greyson pulled a blue cotton dress from her carpetbag, followed quickly by an iron, a folding ironing board, and three sweet-smelling oranges. She really did pack for every possible situation. At least the oranges might come in handy for preventing scurvy, or firing out of cannons, but if Miss Greyson expected Hilary to spend her days on a pirate ship *ironing*— well, it was too terrible to consider. "If you poke your head in next door, I believe you'll find that Charlie and Oliver are unpacking as we speak."

Hilary poked her head in next door. To her great dismay, Miss Greyson was right.

"Now," said Miss Greyson when Hilary had returned, "you really must explain to me what's going on with Oliver." She tucked a pair of fuzzy slippers under her bunk. "The two of you didn't"—she paused and cleared her throat—"well, you didn't *run away together*, did you?"

"Miss Greyson!"

"Oh, don't stamp your foot like that, Hilary; you'll bust a hole straight through to the bilge."

"I assure you," said Hilary, "that I have no desire to run anywhere with Oliver, but we seem to be stuck with each other for the time being. He says he's getting revenge on Father." Hilary shrugged and balanced *Treasure Island* on the ledge under the porthole. "By the way, Miss Greyson, please don't mention Father to anyone. I don't think Jasper cares much for the navy, and it would be a shame if he decided to toss us overboard."

"Understood," said Miss Greyson. "You may consider my lips sealed."

"Of course, if you did fall overboard, Jasper would probably swoop to your rescue."

"That's quite enough of that," Miss Greyson said tightly, but Hilary noted with interest that she did not stamp her foot. Instead, she fiddled about in her bag until she located her crochet hook, a great many knitting needles, and a ball of green yarn. She placed the needles and yarn next to her slippers, tucked the crochet hook into her bun, and nodded approvingly.

"Is that from Miss Pimm's?" Hilary asked. "The crochet hook, I mean?"

"Indeed it is. It's a very great honor to receive one's golden crochet hook, you know."

"Yes, I've heard." Hilary gave up folding her spare clothes neatly and shoved them under her bunk when Miss Greyson wasn't looking. "My friend Claire can hardly wait to get hers. But I suppose I'll have to make do with silver."

Miss Greyson sighed. "At least it matches your sword. I've put a message through to Miss Pimm's, by the way, and another one to your mother, telling them not to worry. But I did have to take great care not to divulge any details. My reputation can tolerate a bit of scandal, but yours—honestly, Hilary, stockings are not to be rolled into little balls!"

Hilary worried Miss Greyson might fall into a faint right there in the cubbyhole, but the sound of a bell ringing at the front of the ship interrupted her swoon. "All hands on deck!" Jasper bellowed. "Yes, gargoyle, that means you, too. We've got important matters to discuss."

DURING THE YEARS of interminable geography lessons with Miss Greyson, Hilary had made a point of paying attention during the bits about the sea. According to her atlas, Little Herring Cove opened out into a much larger gulf of water, Pemberton Bay, which in turn spilled into the High Seas that spanned the globe. Hilary was glad to see that, so far, the atlas appeared to be trustworthy: The *Pigeon* had just entered the bay, where a wooden sign bobbing on a buoy proclaimed:

Welcome to Pemberton Bay!
HOME OF THE
Royal Augusta Water Ballet
ONLY 10 LEAGUES TO THE HIGH SEAS

The vast, empty bay stretched ahead of them beyond the sign, and Jasper must have decided that it was safe to abandon the wheel for the moment, because he knelt on the deck, unrolling a thick sheet of paper and pinning down its corners with rocks. This proved to be no easy task, even for the Terror of the Southlands, and Jasper muttered salty swears each time the bottom left corner flew loose and slapped him on the chin. Hilary could have watched this performance for hours, but Charlie took pity on Jasper at last and rolled a cannonball on top of the loose corner.

"Thank you," said Jasper, touching his chin tenderly. "Now, everyone, gather round."

They gathered. Hilary held the gargoyle in her arms to give him a better view.

"Who can tell me what sort of document lies in front of us?" asked Jasper.

Hilary wondered if this was one of those trick questions

Miss Greyson was so fond of. "It's a map," she said cautiously. In fact, it looked a good deal like the maps Admiral Westfield stored in his office, but she certainly couldn't say such a thing to Jasper.

"Precisely. Gold star for Hilary." Jasper grinned, and Miss Greyson gave the sort of sniff that suggested Jasper was not cut out to be a governess. "Furthermore, it's a very *old* map. A map of Gunpowder Island."

A thrill skittered down Hilary's spine, and she felt the gargoyle tense in her arms. Gunpowder Island simply wasn't talked about in High Society, unless it was discussed in echoing whispers in the halls of Westfield House. Most of the history books declined to mention it, and even Hilary's atlas included a lengthy note of apology for acknowledging its existence. A good Miss Pimm's girl would never have heard of such a place, and if she did accidentally overhear its name, the very sound was likely to reduce her to tears.

Hilary wanted to go there at once.

"Do you mean to suggest," said Miss Greyson, "that we are traveling to a known pirate stronghold?"

"Of course," said Jasper.

"Filled with villains and Northerners?"

"Naturally," said Jasper. "It's really quite beautiful in the summer. Roses climbing up the crumbling stone walls, picturesque sunsets over the rooftops—the ones that haven't been set on fire, of course—anyway, you'll love it." He sat back on his heels. "But this isn't a pleasure cruise. In addition to being a very old map of a very interesting location, this map"—he stabbed his finger in its direction—"is a treasure map."

"Let me down!" cried the gargoyle. "A real treasure map! Oh boy!"

Hilary placed the gargoyle on the map and he hopped around it, examining it from every angle. "I don't know, Jasper," he said after a few moments. "It doesn't look like a treasure map to me."

"And why's that?"

"Well," said the gargoyle, "X marks the spot, right? On treasure maps, I mean?"

"That's right," said Jasper. "It's standard VNHLP policy."

The gargoyle wrinkled his stone brow. "But there's no X."

"Gold star for the gargoyle, too," said Jasper. "Therein lies our conundrum. This map was drawn before the days of the VNHLP—in fact, it was not even drawn by a pirate." He picked the gargoyle up and planted him by the bottom left corner, near the cannonball. "See anything unusual in front of you, my friend?"

The gargoyle studied the map for a moment. Then he began to hop so enthusiastically that the *Pigeon* shook beneath him. "It's her mark!" he cried. "The mark of the Enchantress! Do you see it, Hilary?" He poked his tail toward a small figure eight lying on its side in the bottom corner of the map.

"The symbol of the infinite," Miss Greyson murmured. "However did you recognize it, gargoyle?"

The gargoyle hopped up to her and raised his left wing. There, carved into the smooth stone of his back, was the same figure eight. "The Enchantress gave me her mark when she made me," the gargoyle said. "Does that mean she made this map, too?"

Jasper nodded. "I believe it does. The figure eight in the corner there is her signature, and this map will tell us the location of her treasure."

"You can't be serious," said Oliver. "Do you really think this Enchantress was foolish enough to take everyone's magic and leave it sitting on an island full of pirates? The whole thing sounds like a fairy story; it's preposterous."

The gargoyle bared his teeth. "I think *you're* preposterous."

(5) Unbelievegle

Miss Greyson clapped her hands together three times. "Calm down, everyone," she said. "I, for one, am quite interested in what Mr. Fletcher has to say."

"Thank you, Miss Greyson. Now, Oliver, I know the story of the Enchantress seems a bit fantastic, but I believe you'll find it's all a matter of historical fact. When the Enchantress discovered that certain people were using magic for rather nasty purposes, she collected as much magic as she could and hid it away somewhere safe. Luckily for us, she had enough presence of mind to draw this map before she so carelessly disappeared forever. And this map is no fairy story." Jasper looked straight at Hilary. "Whoever finds that treasure will control nearly all the magic in the kingdom. I can't think of a more valuable prize."

Oliver shrugged. "If all this is true—and I'm not saying it is—how come no one's dug up this treasure already?"

"Plenty of folks have gone looking for it, haven't they?" said Charlie. "My parents used to tell me stories about the Enchantress's treasure. Some pirates even died searching for it—or that's what my mam said, at least."

"She was right, I'm afraid," said Jasper. "Most of them tried to use their own magic bits to lead them to it, but it seems this treasure can't be found with a simple wish on a coin. I suspect the Enchantress magicked up a few protections to keep it well hidden."

"That sounds like something she would do," the gargoyle agreed.

"Anyway, there's not much use in searching for her treasure unless you've got a map, and no pirate has ever had one." Jasper tapped his finger on the papers. "Until now, of course."

"How'd you get your hands on it, then?" said Oliver. Hilary wondered if a good, thorough dunk in the sea would make him less contrary, but she rather doubted it.

Jasper, however, kept his temper. "Oh, the usual way," he said. "A bit of plunder here and there can be surprisingly effective."

Hilary knelt down next to the gargoyle to get a closer look at the map. "I don't understand how it's going to help us, though. The gargoyle's right; there's no X to mark the spot. We'll have to dig up all of Gunpowder Island if we want to find the treasure."

"Oh, we certainly won't be doing that," said Jasper. "The place is absolutely packed with pirates. They'd never allow us to shovel through their sitting rooms or mess about in their vegetable patches."

Hilary looked up at him. "Then what will we be doing?"

"That, Hilary, is the question I need you to answer."

"Me?"

"You remember our deal, don't you?"

Miss Greyson stiffened. "What deal? Hilary! You made a deal with a pirate?" She pressed her fingertips to her forehead. "For heaven's sake, did I teach you nothing?"

Hilary stared at her rope-burned hands and nodded. Find the treasure or return to Miss Pimm's with a blackened name: the terms of the deal were hardly forgettable.

"I'm leaving this map in your hands," said Jasper. "I've set our course for Gunpowder Island. By the time we arrive, I expect you'll have discovered where the treasure is buried, and we'll all dig it up and have a round of grog." He smiled down at Hilary. "Don't worry. I'm sure you'll figure it out; that's why I hired you."

Oliver snorted. "A useless map to an imaginary

treasure . . . and you're counting on a girl to find it for you. Perfect."

Hilary simply couldn't tolerate it. She stood up and moved toward Oliver, but before she could give him a really satisfying slap, the gargoyle nudged her boots with his snout. "Don't pay any attention to him. He doesn't know anything; he's not a real pirate like we are. Besides," he added, "I'll help you find the treasure."

"So will I," said Charlie quietly. "I'm no expert at treasure hunting, but I won't let the lot of us end up like"—he hesitated and shoved his hands into his pockets—"like the pirates in my mam's stories."

Jasper clapped Charlie on the back. "Good lad," he said. "I shall be no help at all, I'm afraid." He rolled up the map, secured it with a shabby red ribbon, and handed it to Hilary. "I'll be captaining the ship and consorting with my budgerigar if you need me."

"Thank you," said Hilary, hugging the map close. It *was* a real treasure map, no matter what Oliver said—and somewhere out there a real treasure was buried, and somehow she would find it. A true pirate could do no less.

Miss Greyson shook her head and turned back toward her cabin. "Consorting with budgerigars," she said with a sigh. "I've clearly wound up on a ship for the insane. Now, if you'll excuse me, I have to sharpen my knitting needles. I want to be able to defend myself when we reach Gunpowder Island."

JASPER FLETCHER, FREELANCE PIRATE
TERROR OF THE SOUTHLANDS
VNHLP CERTIFIED IN BATTLE,
TREASURE HUNTING, & PARROT MAINTENANCE

✠ ✠ ✠ ✠ ✠

Dear Claire,

Please don't be too alarmed—I had to swipe some stationery from Jasper's cabin, but it's really me, Hilary. Thank you for your letter. The postal courier sailed out to deliver it to our ship yesterday. He told me he had to ask for a Pirate Hilary at fifteen different pirate ships before he found me, so I think I may be the only one. You can address all further correspondence to me in care of the Pigeon. I think it's a ridiculous name for a pirate ship, and when I asked Jasper about it, all he would say was that he likes pigeons. If you want to know the truth, pirates can be even sillier than Miss Pimm's girls, although they are not nearly as cruel.

Thank you very much for the beard. It does fit, and I have to say it looks quite handsome in a bold sort of way—I borrowed Miss Greyson's mirror to admire myself. Did I tell you that my governess is on board? I have no idea how she tracked me down, and I am feeling very suspicious, but she does not approve of suspicion so I am forced to hide my feelings. I also suspect that Jasper is wildly in love with her. I think you would find him very dashing, but he is even older than Miss Greyson and a good deal less sensible.

I am quite concerned to hear that everyone is looking for me. Could you tell them to stop, please? Miss Greyson has written to Miss Pimm to explain that I won't be coming back to school, so maybe I will not need the beard after all. (Of course, I will still wear it if I ever need a disguise.) If my father sees my picture in the newspaper, he will most likely send all his warships to collect me, but he is not too fond of newspapers, so I hope I will be safe for now.

We are sailing to Gunpowder Island! I hope I have not upset you too much by writing its name here. Perhaps your parents have protected you from hearing of it: It is an island off the coast of Nordholm, in Gunpowder Bay, and it is absolutely famous for piracy. I think it was once a summer palace for the queen, or someone important like that, but pirates took it over by firing cannons at it, hence all the gunpowder. I believe the most fearsome scallywags on the High Seas often spend their summer holidays on the island, organizing their treasure chests and sending their enemies' ships up in flames. I'm afraid I can't reveal why the Pigeon has set her course for Gunpowder Island, but it is quite a thrilling mission, and I shall tell you all about it someday.

Oh dear, the gargoyle is calling me to come watch a performance of the Royal Augusta Water Ballet, for their (troupe) has floated in front of our ship. He says they are very talented, but I will let you know my own opinion when I write again.

⑦ Group of performers

ARR! (That is a pirate (valediction) of which I am sure the handwriting mistress would not approve.)

⑧ Expression

Hilary

KINGDOM OF AUGUSTA
OFFICE OF THE ROYAL RECORDS KEEPER

FORM 118M: INTENTION TO SET SAIL

INSTRUCTIONS: Please write legibly in ink. Forms completed in blood will be rejected upon receipt. All questions are mandatory.

NAME OF CAPTAIN:
James Westfield, Admiral

NAME OF VESSEL: *HMS Augusta Belle*

TYPE OF VESSEL: *Fastest clipper on the High Seas, and don't you forget it*

HOME PORT: *Queensport, The Southlands*

DESTINATION: *That's confidential.*

GENERAL PURPOSE OF VOYAGE
(please check one):
☒ BUSINESS ☐ PLEASURE ☐ PIRACY

If PIRACY is checked, the Kingdom of Augusta reserves the right to send the Royal Navy to attack your vessel if necessary. Do you accept these terms?
Happily. I presume I will be the one doing the attacking.

NUMBER OF CREW MEMBERS: 30

NAMES OF CREW MEMBERS (please list):
Do you think I have the time for this? I'm taking my best men. Surely you can figure out the details.

PRIMARY OBJECTIVE OF VOYAGE:
None of your business.

NUMBER OF FLOTATION DEVICES ON BOARD:
The Augusta Belle meets all naval regulations, and I'm offended that you would dare to imply otherwise.

NUMBER OF WEAPONS ON BOARD:
As many as I can fit.

If you PERISH AT SEA, would you like a MEMORIAL PLAQUE installed in your honor at the Royal Palace?
☒ YES ☐ NO
And make sure it's one of those extralarge plaques with my portrait on it.

Thank you for complying with the rules and regulations of the Kingdom of Augusta, and enjoy your voyage!

CHAPTER EIGHT

THE SUN HAD sunk below the sea, made a hasty journey around half the world, and poked a few tentative rays over the rim of the horizon again, but Hilary hadn't slept a wink. Her thin, lumpy mattress was a poor substitute for her feather bed in Westfield House: It smelled faintly of mildew, and her toes stuck out over the edge. The waves rocked the *Pigeon* to and fro in a vaguely alarming fashion; a square of hardtack and a mug of water were hardly sufficient for a good night's rest; and on top of all this, Miss Greyson was snoring, primly but unmistakably, in the next cot. Hilary hadn't thought governesses were capable of snoring.

She could have tolerated it all quite well, though, if it hadn't been for the treasure map squashed under her pillow. She'd spent half the night worrying about the blasted thing. Generations of pirates had failed to find the Enchantress's treasure; what made Jasper so sure that Hilary would succeed? What would happen to her if she couldn't find the treasure after all? Or—and this was a thought nearly too horrifying to contemplate—what if she led the pirates directly to the treasure, only to find herself betrayed? Surely Jasper would never lie to her; surely Charlie could be trusted. But they *were* pirates, and the treasure map they'd plundered looked suspiciously similar to the scroll those thieves had stolen from Westfield House. Whatever were they up to?

Daylight slithered in through the porthole, and a cold snout nudged Hilary's arm.

"Are you awake?" the gargoyle whispered. "I can't sleep."

"Neither can I. Do you need another blanket?" Hilary had made a cozy spot for the gargoyle on the floor next to her bed after he had refused to perch in the Gargoyle's Nest all night, arguing that he was an indoor gargoyle at heart.

"No, the blanket is fine." The gargoyle sighed. "But it's not like my doorway. It's not like home."

Hilary picked up the gargoyle and tucked him in under her thin sheet. "It's all bumpy and wavy," the gargoyle continued, "and my stomach feels strange. They don't mention that part in *Treasure Island*."

"Poor gargoyle. I'm sure you'll get your sea legs soon— if you'll pardon the expression." Hilary patted the place where his legs would have been if he'd had any. The gargoyle snuggled up to her, and she lay back on her pillow, which crunched ominously under her head. "As long as we're both awake, would you like to look at the map?"

The gargoyle nodded, and Hilary unrolled the treasure map as quietly as she could, so as not to wake Miss Greyson. Both of them stared at the thin black letters that curled across the page. Unfamiliar place names were scattered across the map, and coves and hills were sketched in with only the faintest nod to accuracy. Little illustrations of houses and trees indicated villages and forests, and in the center of Gunpowder Island stood a smiling, beautiful young woman who was doubtlessly intended to be the Enchantress herself, looking very similar to her portrait in the stained-glass window of Westfield House. Hilary was disappointed to see that the Enchantress had not sketched the likenesses of any pirates. Perhaps the island hadn't been overrun by scourges and scallywags in the Enchantress's day.

The Enchantress had, however, written a long and looping phrase across the southern portion of Gunpowder Bay. It was too long to be a label and too intentional for a mere decoration. The gargoyle hopped over to the line of text and poked at it with his tail. "What does this say?" he asked.

Hilary squinted. "It says, 'Fear no more the heat of the sun.'" She exchanged a glance with the gargoyle. "That's very strange. I wonder what it means."

"It means," said the gargoyle, "that you're not supposed to be afraid of the sun."

"Yes, I know that. But why would anyone write it on a treasure map?"

"Maybe she was feeling poetic," said the gargoyle. "It's a line from Shakespeare, you know. I would have chosen something from Keats myself." He tapped his tail in response to Hilary's stare, in much the same way that Miss Greyson tapped her foot. "You really don't pay attention to your lessons, do you?"

Hilary pulled the sheet over the gargoyle's head. "If I ever want another governess, I will let you know at once. For now, however, I am finding one governess to be more than enough." She traced her finger over the letters of the strange phrase. "If we're not supposed to fear the sun, that means we must have to move toward it."

"So we sail east," said the gargoyle. "Toward the sun."

"But the sun isn't *always* east, just in the mornings. Besides, Gunpowder Island is north of here." Hilary muttered a minor pirate curse she'd heard Jasper use when he discovered a small fish in his coffee. "Maybe we're thinking too hard. Maybe all she wants us to do is take the map out into the sunlight."

The gargoyle poked his head out from under the sheet. "What difference would that make?"

"Well, maybe we'll be able to see something that's hard

to make out when it's too dark. A secret message, maybe, or an *X* to mark the spot."

"What are we waiting for, then?" cried the gargoyle, hopping up and down on the bed. Miss Greyson rolled over and mumbled something about handkerchiefs. "Let's go!"

"All right," said Hilary. She swung her feet onto the cold wooden floor and swapped her nightdress for a shirt and trousers. Then she tucked the gargoyle under one arm and the map under the other. "We'll have to be quiet," she whispered, "so we don't wake anyone."

The gargoyle nodded. "My lips are sealed. Not really, of course; I need a way to let the spiders in. But you know what I mean."

HILARY TIPTOED TO her cabin door, turned the handle, silently cursed the squeaky hinges—and walked straight into Oliver.

She dropped the map, nearly dropped the gargoyle, and winced as the cabin door shut far too loudly behind her. "What are you *doing*?" she said when she had recovered herself. "Lurking outside my cabin? Plotting a way to string me upside down from the mast?"

Oliver's sneer settled comfortably on his face. "I'm on night watch," he said. "Or didn't you remember?"

Now that he mentioned it, Hilary did remember. Jasper had given them their watch assignments the previous evening. "Fine," she said. "In that case, you can just watch somewhere else. I assure you that Miss Greyson and I don't need protecting. Besides, it's morning now."

"My shift lasts another hour," said Oliver. "What are you up to, anyway? Sneaking out of bed is hardly ladylike."

"Well, I'm not a lady."

"Obviously. No lady would have that monster for a best friend."

"Why, you little *mold spore*," cried the gargoyle. "Hilary, let me at him!"

"You know," said Hilary, "I just might."

"And no lady," Oliver continued, "would be tiptoeing about with this." He bent down and picked up the map.

Hilary grabbed for it, but Oliver held it over her head. "You give that here," she said as calmly as she could. Under her arm, the gargoyle gnashed his teeth.

"No thanks," said Oliver. "I'd rather keep it. I could use a little light reading."

"Jasper entrusted it to me, not to you."

"Looks like you're not as trustworthy as he thought, then. Can't even hold on to it for a single day."

"What in the world would you want with it? You don't even believe the treasure exists."

"True," said Oliver, "but I enjoy watching you turn purple."

"I'll let the gargoyle bite you, I swear. In fact," said Hilary, "I'll bite you myself."

"I doubt your father would approve of that behavior."

"Stop talking about my father!" Hilary jumped up and snatched at the map, but Oliver held on tightly, and she didn't dare tear it. "If you care so much about what he thinks, why don't you jump in the sea and swim back to him?"

"Hey, now, what's going on here?" A door opened behind them, and Charlie stepped out of his cabin, brandishing his sword.

Oliver transformed his sneer into something that faintly resembled a smile. "Hilary dropped her map," he said, "and I was helping her retrieve it. Here you go, Hilary."

Hilary grabbed the map from Oliver's outstretched hand. "Oh, you were a tremendous help."

Charlie looked back and forth at the two of them, then slid his sword back into his belt loop. "Glad that's all sorted out," he said. "Any luck with that map, Hilary? Find the treasure yet?"

"Actually," she said, "the gargoyle and I have a theory. With any luck, we'll be heroes within the next five minutes."

BUT LUCK, IF any of it was to be had, chose to bypass the *Pigeon* that morning. Hilary unrolled the map on the deck, in the brightest patch of sunlight she could find, but no secret messages revealed themselves, and no X rushed in to mark any sort of spot. "So much for heroism," Hilary said as she rolled the map back up. "I believe I'm starting to loathe the Enchantress."

"It was a good idea," said the gargoyle. "Almost as good as one a gargoyle might have."

"And what idea might a gargoyle have?" Charlie asked.

The gargoyle ground his teeth together thoughtfully for a few moments, sending small bits of rock trickling across the deck. "I'm still working on it," he said at last. "You'd better make me a figurehead again, so I can watch for scurvy sea dogs."

Charlie and Hilary helped him hop into the Gargoyle's Nest, and Charlie watched as Hilary tied the knots that kept the gargoyle secure. "That's the finest bowline in the Southlands," he said when she'd finished. "Where'd you learn to do that?"

Hilary hesitated. "I've been good at knots since I was young." Admiral Westfield had refused to teach her a skill as unladylike as knot tying, of course, but Hilary had spent hours studying the hitches and bends he tied on his ships. Soon enough she'd worked out how to knot them herself, and she'd even replaced a few of the knots her father's apprentices had gotten wrong.

"Did you grow up on ships, then?" Charlie frowned, and his voice became sharp as a cutlass. "You don't come from a naval family, do you?"

"No!" said Hilary. "I mean, certainly not. My father is a sailor"—that much was true, at least—"but he wants nothing to do with the navy. He says they're a terrible nuisance."

"He's right about that. A nuisance was the nicest thing

my own pa ever called the navy."

"Your father was a sailor, too?"

"He was a pirate!" said Charlie. "Nat Dove, Scourge of the Northlands. He was even more fearsome than Jasper, though you'll never hear Jasper admit it. But he wasn't around long enough to teach me my knots."

"I'm sorry," said Hilary.

Charlie shrugged. "It's all right. When Jasper took me in, I told him I'd be a pirate just like my pa, and he got my bowlines and hitches in order. He even let me train with the VNHLP, although he thinks they're nearly as useless as the navy. If I'm ever Scourge of the Northlands myself, it'll be thanks to him." He pulled a piece of hardtack from his coat pocket and broke off a corner with a cracking noise that Hilary hoped came from the biscuit and not from his teeth.

"So," he said through a flurry of crumbs, "how's your sword fighting? We'll need a crackerjack swashbuckling team if we're headed to Gunpowder Island. Plenty of pirates who've sailed there have left a limb behind."

"Actually," Hilary admitted, "I haven't gotten much practice. I'm afraid they don't teach sword fighting at Miss Pimm's."

"They wouldn't." Charlie brushed the hardtack crumbs from his hands. "All right, then. If you grab your sword, I might be able to teach you a few things myself. I can't promise you'll be the new champion of the High Seas, but at least you'll be able to defend yourself from scoundrels."

Not to mention from Oliver. "Thank you, Charlie," she said. "That would be wonderful. I'll do my best not to slice your nose off."

HILARY RETURNED TO her cabin to find that Miss Greyson was no longer snoring. In fact, she was wide awake, wearing a pressed calico dress, and peeling an orange. Her bedclothes were neat as a pin, and the cabin floor looked suspiciously as though someone had swept it.

"Good morning, Miss Greyson!" Hilary buried the treasure map back under her pillow and accepted the segment of orange her governess held out to her. It tasted perfectly sharp and juicy, especially compared to hardtack. "I hope you slept well."

Miss Greyson chewed a slice of orange thoughtfully. "Yes, I suppose I did," she said. "I'm finding all of this piracy to be rather exhausting. But I must summon up my strength, and so must you, because it's nearly time for your lessons."

"My lessons?" Perhaps it was a joke—but Miss Greyson never joked. "Blast, Miss Greyson! Pirates don't have lessons!"

(5) Acquire or to get

Miss Greyson procured her most devastating gaze and aimed it directly at Hilary. "Do not say 'blast,'" she said. "Say 'pardon me,' if you must say anything at all. You are missing a good deal of school, and I can't abide ignorance, in pirates or anyone else."

"But I won't be ignorant. Charlie is about to give me a swashbuckling lesson, so I'm utterly swamped at the moment. Taking on any more lessons would . . . well, it would strain my constitution." (6) Mind and Body

"Now," said Miss Greyson, "you're just being silly."

"Perhaps I am. But you don't want me to be cut to bits on Gunpowder Island, do you? Aren't you always saying that young ladies of quality must be able to defend themselves?"

Miss Greyson frowned at her orange. "I do often say that. But I've never meant to suggest they should use swords." She put the orange aside and fiddled with the crochet hook tucked into her hair bun. "I can see I won't be able to prevent you from buckling swashes, or whatever it is you plan to do. But I'll expect you back here in two hours' time for history lessons. Are we in agreement?"

"I suppose so." Hilary was fairly sure she was the only pirate in the kingdom who had to do battle with a governess. "May I go now?"

"You may," said Miss Greyson, "once you've tidied up your things. Even the most fearsome of pirates must fold their blankets and retrieve their nightdresses from the floor."

IT TURNED OUT that Claire had been right: Sword fighting was very much like waltzing, though it was also a good deal more violent. Hilary had no trouble following the footwork patterns Charlie demonstrated for her, but she found it difficult to make her sword behave itself. When she wanted it to slice, it squiggled; when she wanted it to stab, it swooped out of her hand and into the air, nearly skewering Jasper's hat on one occasion. Jasper warned her at this point that if she did not improve quickly, she might find herself cutting and parrying at the bottom of the sea. "And we're on the High Seas now," he said, "so you'll find the bottom is a long way off."

Charlie was an excellent fencer, so skillful that the gargoyle declared that if a real sword fight ever broke out on the *Pigeon*, he would choose Charlie's legs to hide behind. "Did you learn all this from your pa?" Hilary asked.

Charlie shook his head. "From my mam, actually. Pa was away most of the time—well, you know how it is when your pa is a sailor." Hilary nodded. "And my mam always wanted to be a pirate. She would have made a fine one, too; she could beat Pa handily in a duel. But the League wouldn't tolerate it."

"Of course they wouldn't," said Hilary fiercely. The VNHLP didn't seem to tolerate much of anything, really. "Couldn't your pa let her on board his ship anyway?"

"He did, once," said Charlie. "He took her off on the *Cutlass* on a treasure hunt, and I never saw them again. The navy sank their ship with no apologies."

Hilary dropped her sword. "But that's horrible!"

"Yes," said Charlie, "but I'd expect no less from the navy. From what I hear, the naval officers fired the first shots, and the *Cutlass* had no hope of fighting back."

Admiral Westfield may not have cared for pirates, but Hilary couldn't believe he'd let any of his ship's captains behave so cruelly. "It doesn't make sense."

"No," said Charlie, "it doesn't. And that's not the strangest part. Mam and Pa had found treasure, but when the wreck was searched, there wasn't a magic coin in sight." Charlie picked Hilary's sword up from the deck and passed it back to her. "I still can't work out what happened, but I'd swear that stash of magic got my mam and pa sent to the bottom of the sea."

"And that's why you won't touch the stuff."

"That's right. I've got no use for magic, and I doubt it's got much use for me."

"It's very kind of you, then, to help us search for treasure," said Hilary. "Do you mind very much?"

"Mind?" Charlie looked surprised. "What pirate worth his salt minds treasure hunting? If I'm going to be Scourge of the Northlands like my pa, I've got to be the fiercest, boldest pirate on the High Seas. Finding the Enchantress's magic stash should be a good start, even if I don't plan to keep the loot." He sheathed his sword and tightened his belt around his waist. "Besides," he said, "I won't let my friends get sunk the way Mam and Pa did."

"I'm sure your parents would be impressed," Hilary said, "and it's quite a fine thing to impress one's parents." She slipped her own sword back into her belt. "At least, that's what I've heard."

In the Gargoyle's Nest, the gargoyle cleared his throat. "I'm sorry to interrupt," he called, "but what am I supposed to say if I see another ship?"

"'Shiver me timbers, there be buccaneers ahead,'" Hilary said.

"No, that won't work," said the gargoyle. "I don't think they're buccaneers, and they're not exactly ahead. They're more behind, and a little to the right."

"*Who's* not buccaneers?" said Jasper.

"That big ship heading right for us," said the gargoyle, pointing his snout toward starboard. "The one with all the blue and gold flags."

"Blue and gold?" Jasper ran to the side of the ship and retrieved his spyglass. "You're sure?"

"Of course I'm sure. Gargoyles have excellent eyesight."

Jasper peered through his spyglass in the direction the gargoyle pointed. "Blast!" he cried.

"If Miss Greyson were out here," Hilary murmured, "she'd want you to say 'pardon me.'"

But Jasper did not seem to care. "Blast, blast, and once again blast!" he said. "You'd better improve your swordsmanship in a hurry, Hilary. The Royal Navy's fastest ship is heading our way, and she's got battle colors flying."

A LETTER FROM ROYALTY!

HER ROYAL HIGHNESS

Queen Adelaide of Augusta

Urgent and Confidential
Admiral James Westfield
HMS Augusta Belle
The High Seas

Dear Admiral Westfield: ⑦ Little Hospital

My records keeper informs me that you have already set sail
on a private voyage, but I sincerely hope that when you receive
this letter, you will adjust the course of your journey as quickly as
possible in order to assist your queen and your country.

 I have just paid a visit to the royal treasurer, who currently
occupies a bed at the Queensport Infirmary. He is confined there
for the moment because, as you may be aware, he was bashed
over the head with a priceless porcelain vase whilst guarding the
Royal Treasury last week. We have gone to great lengths not to
distribute this information to the public, but I fear I must tell you
that a robbery of grave proportions followed the assault, and the
palace's entire inventory of magical coins has been simply wiped out.

This inventory was not large, as you know, but I am concerned that this crime is only the latest in a string of troubling incidents involving the remnants of our kingdom's magic. Without a magical reserve of my own, I shall find it quite difficult to combat whoever is responsible for this thievery.

I would not trouble you with any of these details, as I know you are ever so busy, but upon regaining consciousness, my royal treasurer was able to report that his attackers wore masks and smelled distinctly of seawater. Furthermore, their boots left damp markings on the floor of the treasury. I am convinced that this evidence—the masks, the seawater, the lust for treasure—points firmly and unquestionably to pirates. As your queen, I command you and your officers to stop any pirate ship you spy on the High Seas and question its captain thoroughly, searching belowdecks for treasure if you believe such a step is prudent and warranted.

I have just read in the <u>Gazette</u> of your daughter's disappearance, and my thoughts are with you at this difficult time. If you are searching for her, I hope your search ends happily and quickly so you will be free to pursue this crucial investigation.

Fondly,
The Queen

an extract from

Treasure Hunting for Beginners:

THE OFFICIAL VNHLP GUIDE

HOW TO USE YOUR TREASURE:

If you are lucky enough to dig up a treasure chest, you will need to know what to do with your newfound riches. Bits of magic sparkle pleasantly in the sunlight, to be sure, but pirates must not stand about like silly High Society girls admiring their treasure all day! No, dear pirate, you must *use* your treasure.

All pieces of magic—coins, goblets, toothbrushes, and so forth—operate in the same way. A pirate who wishes to perform an act of magic must first grip his coin (or goblet or toothbrush) firmly in one hand. Then, in a loud and fearsome voice, he must command the magic to do his bidding. For example, if the pirate wants to sharpen his hook, he must say, "Sharpen my hook!" When these words are spoken, the magic piece will draw power from the pirate himself. If this power has been properly channeled into an appropriate magical item, it will transform his wish into reality: in no time at all, the hook will be sharp enough to skewer a coconut. Be warned, however, that the use of magic can be draining. Most pirates are not powerful enough to perform more than a few magical acts without pausing for a nap and a spot of grog.

When you command the magic to do your bidding, it is important to keep your focus entirely on your wish. If your focus wavers, your magic will not work exactly as you intend it to, and you are likely to receive an unpleasant surprise: if you wish for a bit of soap but allow yourself to be distracted by a flock of geese in the middle of your wish, for example, you may find yourself scrubbing your clothes with a goose. This activity is likely to be extremely unpleasant.

⑧ Enough

While a single magic coin is sufficient for small chores such as hook sharpening, more ambitious tasks require additional magic. Pirates who uncover large treasure troves often attempt to use their newfound magic to sail through the air in flying pirate ships or defeat all their enemies in combat. We at the VNHLP must stress, however, that these activities are not recommended! Even the most powerful and skilled magic users frequently discover that using large amounts of magic can be exhausting, unpredictable, and dangerous. So please, dear pirate, take care with your treasure, and use it wisely.

CHAPTER NINE

JASPER RANG THE ship's bell so loudly it set Hilary's teeth vibrating, and the gargoyle pressed his ears against his head in an attempt to block out the noise. "All hands!" cried Jasper. "Oliver, Miss Greyson, we need you at once!"

Oliver came running from one direction with his sword outstretched, and Miss Greyson rushed in from the other direction, clutching her skirts. "Whatever is the matter?" she said.

Jasper let go of the bell and began to pace the deck. "What in the blazes is the navy doing here?"

"The navy?" Oliver nearly dropped his sword. "The *Royal* Navy?"

"Yes, of course it's the Royal Navy. What other navy

would it be?" Jasper kicked the side of the *Pigeon*, damaged his toes, and hopped about, scowling. "If they're after us, we're done for. Finished. Our goose is cooked."

The gargoyle started to suggest that goose might make a tasty change of pace for dinner, but Hilary hushed him. Pirates were unpredictable, after all, and an angry pirate might very well demote the gargoyle from figurehead to anchor.

"Now, see here, Mr. Fletcher." Miss Greyson pulled a chair from somewhere and set Jasper in it. "It's thoroughly unproductive to break one's toes before a battle. You'd better let me take a look."

Charlie peered at the ship on the horizon, and his hands tightened around the spyglass. "It's a navy ship, without a doubt," he said. "They're probably blasting pirates for sport."

"Oh, they wouldn't!" Hilary grabbed the spyglass and scanned the waves for the navy ship. "Surely they're not that horrid."

"You give the navy a great deal of credit," said Jasper. "Ouch! Please take care with that sock, Miss Greyson. It's quite usual for navy ships to be out and about, but that's the admiral, and he's flying battle colors. He's in a foul mood for some reason, and I don't like it."

"I don't like it either," Hilary murmured to the gargoyle. She had never been allowed to set foot on the *Augusta Belle*, Admiral Westfield's prize ship, but she recognized its billowing sails in the spyglass lens immediately. Her father had discovered the truth of her disappearance, no doubt, and he'd commanded his fastest ship to drag her back to Miss Pimm's. Truthfully, it would have been flattering if it weren't so immensely inconvenient.

And inconvenience was hardly the worst of it. Admiral Westfield was not known for being lenient with pirates. If he caught Jasper and Charlie, the best they could hope for was that they'd never set foot on the *Pigeon* again, and the worst—well, Hilary couldn't bring herself to imagine what the punishment for enrolling the admiral's daughter in a life of piracy might be. She had wanted her father to see what a fine pirate she was, but she certainly hadn't intended to send the *Pigeon* and its crew to the bottom of the High Seas. A wave of seasickness rose in Hilary's stomach; she set down the spyglass and clutched the gargoyle. "This is all my fault," she whispered. "I've cooked our goose for sure." I really messed things up.

The gargoyle buried his head under Hilary's chin. "When the navy gets here, will they make me walk the plank?" He sniffed. "I'm very likely to sink, you know."

Miss Greyson wrapped a piece of cloth around Jasper's foot and used her golden crochet hook to tuck its ends in place. "I wish your injuries would heal promptly," she said as she replaced his sock. "While we wait for them to do so, however, I believe we should develop some sort of strategy. Shall we stand and fight, or shall we surrender?"

Jasper wiggled his toes and drew his breath through his teeth. "Miss Greyson," he said, "we shall do neither. We shall run and hide."

Hilary looked up from scratching the gargoyle's ears. "Do you mean you don't want to blast that ship out of the water?"

"I would enjoy nothing more," said Jasper, "but I'd like to be certain that I'm blasting it for a good reason. Perhaps the navy isn't after us at all, and if we stay ashore for a day or two we'll be safely out of their way. Or perhaps we're all scheduled to be blown to bits in a few hours' time. Either way, I'd like to make some inquiries about the admiral's intentions, and we happen to be near a place where I can do exactly that."

"Ah," said Charlie. "The Scallywags Den?"

"Exactly."

"Hold on a moment," said Hilary. "What's the Scallywags Den?"

Jasper looked at her as though she'd grown a second head. "It's a den. For scallywags."

Miss Greyson handed Jasper his boot. "It doesn't sound particularly savory."

"No," Jasper agreed, "it's not. And that, my dear Miss Greyson, is precisely the point. Charlie, set us a course for Middleby. If I use my magic piece to speed us along, we should be there by afternoon, assuming the navy doesn't board us before then. Why they're always attacking innocent pirates, I just don't know."

Hilary hugged the gargoyle tightly and wished very much that she didn't know, either.

The trip up the coast to Middleby was brief, but it lasted entirely too long for Hilary. Charlie attempted to pick up their ⟨swashbuckling⟩ tutorial where they'd left off, but both of them kept glancing over their shoulders at the ship on the horizon. It looked no larger than a child's toy boat, but a few hours before, it had only been the size of Hilary's thumbnail. Admiral Westfield enjoyed bragging to anyone who would listen about the *Augusta Belle*'s speed, and it was clear that his boasts hadn't been exaggerated.

It was late afternoon when the *Pigeon* pulled into Middleby Harbor. "Land ho!" cried the gargoyle, a bit belatedly, as Jasper lowered the anchor and Charlie prepared the dinghy that would take them to land. Jasper had insisted that as the ship's resident scallywag, he should be the only person to make the trip to the Scallywag's Den. But Charlie said that it would be too dangerous for Jasper to go alone, and Hilary said she couldn't possibly miss an opportunity to see a real pirates' den, and Miss Greyson would certainly not let Hilary go into a pirates' den unaccompanied, and the gargoyle announced to everyone that if they were all going ashore, they had better not leave him behind.

In the end, it was decided that Oliver would remain on board the *Pigeon* to guard it from suspicious ⟨personages,⟩

① person

and everyone else climbed into the dinghy. "Like a tin of anchovies," Miss Greyson remarked. Sandwiched between Charlie and the side of the boat, with the gargoyle on her lap in her canvas bag and Fitzwilliam perched too close to her shoulder for comfort, Hilary wasn't sure whether Miss Greyson was referring to the squash of bodies in the dinghy or to the harbor's distinctly fishy smell. Despite the smell, however, the harbor was cheerful and pretty. Small sailboats in a rainbow of colors were tied up along the docks, and planters of tulips bloomed in the midsummer light. Wooden stalls along the waterfront offered clams dipped in butter and potatoes crisped in oil, and Jasper swore on his fourth-best hat that he could smell blackberry pie.

They tied up the dinghy under a sign marked PIRATES ONLY and followed Jasper like a trail of ducklings as he strode along the dock and down the cobblestone length of Middleby's main street. The Scallywag's Den was hard to miss: It stood only a block from the water, a low wooden building with shuttered windows and a flapping skull-and-crossbones flag over its doorway. Outside the door stood a burly pirate in a red bandanna and blue striped shirt who was looking about in a bored sort of way, cleaning his fingernails with his cutlass.

Jasper tipped his hat to the burly pirate as he passed through the door. "Ahoy," said the burly pirate. "Very welcome ye be to the Scallywag's Den. 'Tis a fine parrot you have there."

"He's a budgerigar," said Jasper.

But as Hilary tried to follow Jasper through the doorway, the burly pirate stuck out his (burly) arm in front of her. "Go away, little girl," he said. "Pirates only."

Hilary tried to walk through the pirate's arm, but it wouldn't budge. "Excuse me, sir, but I *am* a pirate."

The burly pirate looked at Jasper, and Jasper nodded. "She is. She's a member of my crew."

"Sorry," said the pirate. "Even if that's the case, she be a pint-size pirate, and we don't allow children in this here establishment." He tapped his cutlass against the sign beside him, where the words NO CHILDREN were clearly written in chalk. "Same goes for the middling-size pirate behind her."

"But I'm first mate!" said Charlie. "My father was Scourge of the Northlands!"

"Don't matter," said the burly pirate. "Full-grown pirates only, and those be the rules." He glanced up at Miss Greyson and, without a word, pointed his cutlass a few inches lower on the sign, where it said NO GOVERNESSES.

"Hmph!" said Miss Greyson.

"What about gargoyles?" Before Hilary could stop him, the gargoyle poked his head out of the bag and examined the sign. "It doesn't say no gargoyles, does it?"

The burly pirate heaved a sigh, reached in his pocket for a piece of chalk, and wrote, in large letters at the bottom of the sign, ABSOLUTELY NO GARGOYLES.

"What a shame," said Jasper far too cheerfully. "I'll meet you all back at the ship in three hours' time." He poured a few coins out of a leather pouch and pressed them in Miss Greyson's hand. "You can hire a rowboat to take you back to the *Pigeon*."

Then the burly pirate closed the door between them, and Jasper was gone.

"You heard him," said the burly pirate. "Off with the lot of ye." He stared hard at Hilary and Charlie, who stared just as hard back at him. "Stubborn little pirates, aren't ye?"

"Yes," said Hilary, "we are."

"Walkin' about with a great lump o' magic?" The burly pirate eyed the gargoyle. "That's awfully bold."

The gargoyle bared his teeth. "Did you hear that, Hilary? He called me a *lump*!"

Hilary drew her sword. "If you even touch him," she said, "I'll call for the Terror of the Southlands, and he'll squash you under his boots."

"Assuming we don't squash you first," Charlie added helpfully.

The burly pirate shrugged. "In that case," he said, "ye'd better clear out." He pulled a handful of golden coins from his pocket and cleared his throat. "Send the small pirates away!" he said firmly to no one in particular.

A wall of air hit Hilary hard in the stomach and sent her staggering back into the street. She landed on the cobblestones a good ten feet from the Scallywag's Den, and Charlie crashed to the ground beside her.

"Of all the nasty tricks!" cried the gargoyle. "If you've bruised my tail, you'll never hear the end of it!"

"'Small pirates,' he called us," Charlie muttered. "I've got a few names I'd like to call him myself."

Hilary waved her sword in the general direction of the burly pirate, who merely crossed his arms and looked away. "You may have magic," she said, "but you've got no right to knock other people about with it. It's a shame you haven't met Philomena; I think the two of you would get along swimmingly." *Getting along well*

Miss Greyson gave the burly pirate an unmistakable look of fury, as though she very much wished that she could send him to his room without supper. Then she grabbed Hilary by one hand and Charlie by the other. "Come along, both of you," she said, "before he's tempted to run us all through."

"But he shouldn't be allowed to act that way," Hilary protested as Miss Greyson dragged her down the street. "It can't possibly be legal."

"Oh, it's not," said Charlie, "but who'd stop it?"

The gargoyle hung his head. "I could have stopped it," he said quietly. "If you'd grabbed hold of me, Hilary, and if you'd said, 'Gargoyle, please protect me,' I could have helped."

"Nonsense," said Hilary. "I promised I'd never let anyone use you. I know how much you hate it, and I won't let your heart go all fluttery. Besides, a pirate should be able to defend herself." She waved her sword in the air. "The next time a scallywag threatens either of us, I'll simply run him through."

"It's the only proper thing to do," Charlie agreed.

"It most certainly is not!" said Miss Greyson. "And Hilary, put that sword away before you slice somebody's nose off. Now, let us stroll the streets like respectable citizens, and please speak up if you see a market. I discovered this morning that I'm nearly out of oranges."

BEHAVING LIKE A respectable citizen was rather tedious work. Hilary looked up and down Middleby's main street for the town market, but it wasn't nestled in the rows of spiky pine trees that lined the avenue, nor was it hiding behind the whitewashed cottages. Her shoulder strained under the gargoyle's weight, and her stomach ached from the burly pirate's magic. Still, hadn't she just been in her first pirate battle? The thought cheered her considerably. Then they turned a corner, and Hilary saw the sign.

It was nailed to a nearby tree, and sketched upon it— rather unflatteringly, she thought—was a drawing of her face. Underneath the image, a great many bold and blackened words marched along the page:

"Oh, curses!" Hilary cried. She ripped the poster down
with both hands and shoved it in her bag, ignoring the gargoyle's protests. Then she looked down the street: Whoever
had hung the posters had been thorough. Her face was

nailed to trees and signposts in both directions. There was nothing to do but tear the signs down as quickly as possible.

"What are you doing?" Charlie called. "Hey, what's that?"

Hilary raced toward the next sign, but Charlie got there first. "Hilary Westfield," he read. He gave a low whistle. "So that's it—you're Admiral Westfield's daughter. No wonder you know all those knots."

Hilary ripped the sign from the tree, but Charlie pulled it away from her. "Hold on," he said. "I haven't finished reading yet." His voice was calm, but it sliced through the air just as it did whenever he mentioned the navy. "Did your father send you here, then? To spy on Jasper and me?"

Hilary looked at Charlie and quickly decided she'd prefer to look anywhere else instead. "I'm so sorry," she said to her boots. "All I want is to be a pirate, but I thought you'd never let me join the crew if you knew who my father was."

Charlie snorted. "You're right about that."

"I swear I'm not a spy, though, and even if I were, I doubt my father would be interested in my reports. He'd probably pat my head and tell me to stop playing silly games. That's what he did when I told him I wanted to be a pirate."

"He sounds like an absolute treasure."

"He's not so bad, truly, but—"

"Not so bad? After what the navy's done to pirates? Surely you can't believe that!"

Hilary felt certain that walking the plank of the *Pigeon* would be a good deal less painful than facing Charlie's stare. "You've got every right to loathe him," she said at last. "And I suppose you'll loathe me, too, now that the navy's chasing us. I'm sure they've been sent to bring me home." She paused, but Charlie didn't reply. "I really am sorry," she said once more. "Please, you've got to believe me."

Charlie's knuckles tightened around the sign in his hand. He didn't say a word, and he didn't stop staring at Hilary.

Miss Greyson, who did not approve of running, finally arrived behind them. "What's going on?" she said. "Hilary, you look like a damp dishrag. Is everything all right?"

"Not at all," said Hilary. She handed one of the signs in her bag to Miss Greyson. "Read this."

A cloud gathered over Miss Greyson's face as she read. "A rogue governess indeed!" she said. "What nerve!"

The gargoyle squirmed out from under the sign Hilary had stuffed on his head. "I," he said proudly, "am a fearsome beast."

Charlie crunched his sign into a little ball. "Does Jasper know who you are?" he said at last.

"No," said Hilary, "and please, you can't tell him. He'll kick me off the ship."

"Probably. He can't stand old Westfield." Charlie

thought for a moment. "Do you swear," he said, "that you're telling the truth? That you've got nothing to do with your pa?"

"I swear it," said Hilary. "Pirate's honor."

Charlie relaxed his grip on the sign, but he didn't look much happier than he had before. "I'm not sure I believe you," he said, "but if you help us against that navy ship, I won't say anything to Jasper—not yet, at least. If you betray us, though, I'll run you through."

Hilary had no doubt he was telling the truth. She nodded. "I'm sorry I lied to you—about my father, I mean."

Charlie shrugged and turned away from her. "When you spend your time with pirates, you get used to lies."

Before Hilary could say another word, Miss Greyson cleared her throat. "I'm not fond of rushing about," she said, "but I'm afraid we must collect the rest of these signs as quickly as possible, before some well-meaning citizen comes along and arrests us all. I have no desire to develop a reputation as a rogue governess."

"Too bad." The gargoyle nestled down inside Hilary's bag. "I was starting to enjoy being a fearsome beast."

THEY PULLED DOWN all the MISSING signs along the waterfront and on half a dozen side streets, too. Charlie helped a bit, but he hardly said a word. He didn't even smile when the gargoyle tried to offer him a spider. Worst of all, he wouldn't look at Hilary, and she felt certain she'd never be able to patch up the hole between them. Claire would have known just what to do, she thought, but Claire was leagues away at Miss Pimm's.

Hilary's feet were sore from walking, and she could feel blisters forming in her boots, but pirates never complained about those sorts of things, so she didn't. The gargoyle, on the other hand, complained constantly: He couldn't see out of the bag, and he didn't enjoy swinging back and forth so frequently, and the growing number of signs on top of his head was starting to weigh heavily upon his ears. "You'd better find a place to get rid of these things," he said, "because they're not going into the Gargoyle's Nest, and that's final."

Although Middleby was still a few leagues away from the Northlands, it was much farther north than Hilary had ever traveled before. The summer sun stayed up later here; even though dinnertime must have come and gone, the sky was still nearly as light as it had been hours earlier. Hilary wondered how the people who lived in the North-lands ever got any sleep at night if the sun didn't bother to go to sleep itself, but Miss Greyson took her question as an opportunity to launch into a sneaky lesson about longitude and latitude, and it was a great relief when their wanderings through Middleby's side streets brought them at last to the market.

Middleby's town square was smaller and less grand than Pemberton's, and the market vendors were just packing up for the evening. Miss Greyson made a beeline for the woman selling oranges, leaving Hilary and Charlie to watch a group of men lighting a bonfire in the middle of the square. Although the sun was still up, the air was chilly this far north, and Hilary was grateful for the bonfire's warmth.

Charlie took his hands out of his pockets and looked sideways at Hilary. "I've got an idea," he said quietly. Then he took a handful of signs out of Hilary's bag and tossed them into the flames. They crackled in a satisfying sort of way as their edges caught fire; the signs closer to the center of the bonfire crumbled to ashes almost immediately, while the ones along the edges turned a toasty brown before they disintegrated.

Hilary grinned. "Thank you," she said. Charlie didn't return her smile, but after a while, he nodded.

They stood there without talking, tossing signs onto the fire, until the whole bundle was alight. It was rather disconcerting, Hilary thought, to watch one's own face go up in smoke. Sometimes the heat made little patterns along the paper, like charred water stains or unexplored coastlines.

"Very clever," said Miss Greyson, handing them each an orange and warming her hands over the flames. "When you're finished, I think it's time we returned to the *Pigeon*. It wouldn't be polite to keep Jasper waiting."

As they left the town square, they discovered that

people were lighting smaller bonfires on every street corner. The flames grew brighter and the air grew colder as the sun began to set at last, and Hilary hurried from fire to fire, stopping to warm herself up at each one. The heat felt delightfully cozy against her cheeks, as long as she didn't lean in too close. "Fear no more the heat of the sun," she murmured to herself. That strange phrase from the Enchantress's treasure map seemed particularly appropriate as she rubbed her hands together and hoped Charlie and Miss Greyson would hurry up. Really, she thought, it should be "Fear no more the heat of the fire." Fire was much more fearsome, after all, and it was quite a good source of heat when the sun simply wasn't as warming as it should be. In fact—

"Charlie! Miss Greyson!" She ran back to them and took their hands, though neither Charlie nor Miss Greyson looked terribly pleased about being pulled along behind her. "We have to get back to the *Pigeon* at once!"

Miss Greyson frowned. "Really, Hilary, you must learn to be more patient. I know I said we shouldn't keep Jasper waiting, but—"

"Oh, blast Jasper!" cried Hilary. "I think I've figured out how to read the treasure map."

MISS GREYSON HIRED the fastest rowboat in all of Augusta—or so the oarsman claimed—to deliver them back to the *Pigeon*, and they clambered onto the deck without even bidding the oarsman goodnight. Although Miss Greyson did not approve of running, she proved to be a superb sprinter, and she was first to reach the door of the cabin she shared with Hilary.

Oliver was just coming out of it.

Miss Greyson skidded to a halt. "Young man, whatever were you doing in my private quarters?"

Oliver shrugged. "Sorry, ma'am. Wrong cabin."

"Very wrong indeed." Miss Greyson clicked her tongue and brushed past him through the door. "You may atone for your mistake by fetching us some matches. I believe I have a candle in here somewhere."

Oliver smirked, and Hilary resisted the urge to trip him as he skulked by. "I do *not* like him," the gargoyle muttered once Oliver was out of earshot.

"That makes at least two of us," said Hilary. She joined Charlie and Miss Greyson in the cabin and rummaged about under her pillow until she found the treasure map. Miss Greyson produced a candle from the depths of her carpetbag. It was a new-looking candle, squat and sturdy, and unfortunately, it was purple. A white candle, or even a yellow one, would have been more piratical, but this was no time to be picky. Oliver reappeared with a half-empty box of matches, and Hilary lit the candle's wick.

Immediately, a strong scent of lilacs filled the cabin. Charlie coughed, and Miss Greyson looked embarrassed. Hilary didn't care, though; she unrolled the treasure map and held it carefully over the flame.

"What do you think you're doing?" said Oliver. "You'll burn it up!"

"No, I won't," said Hilary. At first, however, very little seemed to happen. The map turned warm all over, and its underside began to scorch where it hovered over the candle.

"Oliver may be right," said Miss Greyson reluctantly. "But I see what you're getting at, Hilary. Perhaps there's another solution." She reached under her bed and pulled out her iron and ironing board.

"Please, Miss Greyson," said Hilary, "tidiness isn't important at a time like this!"

Miss Greyson simply smiled and removed the map from the flame. Then she held the iron over the candle until its flat bottom was warm to the touch. "Perfect," she said. "Place the map on the ironing board please, Hilary. I'd hate to scorch the floor."

Hilary did as Miss Greyson asked, and Miss Greyson placed the iron gently on top of the map. She moved the iron slowly back and forth over the paper. As the iron traveled from one end to the other and back again, markings emerged in its wake, faint at first, but turning browner and browner with heat.

"It's working," said Charlie. "I can't believe it."

"I want to see!" said the gargoyle. Hilary pulled him out of her bag and held him up for a better look. "Now, *that*," he said as he examined the markings, "is a treasure map."

It was true. Most of the map was unchanged, but now, in the middle of Gunpowder Island, a dotted brown line began directly above the sketch of the Enchantress and traveled due north before bending like an elbow and hopping along to the west. Next to the first part of the line was a label reading "ninety paces from the statue" in the Enchantress's curled handwriting, and a label that said "fifty paces toward the ash tree" appeared along the second part of the line. At the very end of the line stood a bold and unmistakable *X*.

"An *X* to mark the spot," the gargoyle said happily. "Just like in books."

The only other new addition to the map was a couplet scrawled in the wide blankness of Gunpowder Bay. "Perhaps the Enchantress was a poetess as well," said Hilary. She read the couplet aloud.

> *May my treasure rest with me,*
> *Hidden for eternity.*

"Not great literature," said Miss Greyson, "but it gets the message across."

Hilary wasn't so sure. If the Enchantress had really wanted her treasure to be hidden for eternity, why had she bothered to draw a map to its location? She had certainly done her best to make things complicated for future treasure seekers. Maybe Admiral Westfield had been right after all when he'd called the Enchantress a Meddling Old Biddy.

"She probably planned to retrieve the treasure herself someday," Charlie said, "but she never got the chance."

"And now," said the gargoyle, "it's our turn. Arr!"

Hilary let loose a hearty round of pirate cries as well, and even Miss Greyson uttered a prim and proper "ahoy."

"Perhaps I'll be Scourge of the Northlands after all," said Charlie. He looked up from the treasure map, and Hilary thought she saw him smile.

"I hate to interrupt your celebration," said Oliver from the doorway, "but you might be interested to know that Jasper's back."

Oliver was right: Out on the deck, footsteps approached, and someone demanded to know why the *Pigeon* smelled distinctly of lilacs.

Hilary blew out the candle and ran out to meet him. "Jasper," she called, "we did it! We've figured out the treasure map!"

Jasper beamed in the moonlight and gave Hilary a hug. His expedition to the Scallywag's Den had left him smelling of wood smoke and parrot, which was rather a friendly combination. "Well done," he said. "I knew you'd do it. And just in time, too."

"What do you mean?"

Jasper sighed and took his hat in his hands. "It appears," he said, "we're not the only ones looking for this treasure."

JAMES WESTFIELD, ADMIRAL
AUGUSTA ROYAL NAVY

FIVE-TIME RECIPIENT OF THE SOARING OSTRICH
MEDAL OF (PERSEVERANCE)

To Her Highness: ① Keep going no matter wh

I am very disturbed by your report of the magical
thefts from your palace. There is no doubt in my
mind that pirates are to blame: everyone knows
they are treasure-grubbing, power-hungry thugs.
I fear these pirates plan to challenge your claim
to the throne. But do not fear: I shall personally
search the High Seas for the scallywags and
force them to return your stolen magic. I can
guarantee this mission will be successful—in the
twenty-seven years of my illustrious naval career,
I have never once failed, and I do not plan to
start now.

As I have been whacked over the head with
vases myself in the past, I can advise the royal
treasurer to put some ice on that bruise.

Thank you for your concern regarding
my daughter. I had not been aware of her
disappearance—I've been terribly busy, and I'd
believed she was safely at finishing school.
The education system these days is a disgrace.

J.W.

Visit Sunny *Middleby!*

Where
Every Day
is a Delight*

*excluding
Wednesdays

Ahoy, Miss Pimm,

I've spotted that girl yer lookin' for. I thought she were a pint-size pirate when I saw her, but I didn't know ye wanted her then. Just saw yer sign on my afternoon juice break. If ye be travelin' to Middleby in search of her, yer always welcome for a free pint of grog at the Scallywag's Den.

Best regards,

BURLY BRUCE McCORKLE

P.S. About that reward: Do I get paid in magic coin, or in gold? I prefer magic if ye got any.

CHAPTER TEN

ALTHOUGH JASPER HAD called an emergency meeting in his private quarters, Jasper himself was the last to arrive. The others huddled around a large oak table that took up a good portion of the room. No one spoke; the only sound was the grumble of stone as the gargoyle ground his teeth.

Jasper appeared at last, carrying a box packed to the brim with tins of beets. Without a word, he deposited the box on the cabin floor and disappeared again, returning a few minutes later with an even larger box of beet tins. He hurried back and forth for some time, until it was nearly impossible to move through the cabin without bumping into a beet.

"That's the last of it," said Jasper as he dumped a dozen more tins on the floor. "Everyone still here? Fantastic." He slid into the slightly bedraggled chair at the head of the table. "I'm pleased to report that my visit to the Scally-wag's Den was most instructive. The scallywags proved to be tremendously helpful."

Oliver glanced around the cabin. "They must have instructed you to invest in beets," he said.

"They did not," said Jasper icily. He popped open a tin with his sword and helped himself to a beet slice. "They did, however, have plenty of gossip to share about that navy ship, the *Augusta Belle*."

Hilary shifted in her chair. She rather wished she could dive under the table, but such behavior wouldn't be the least bit piratical. Miss Greyson gave her hand an encouraging squeeze, but it didn't cheer her one bit.

"The *Augusta Belle* left Queensport unexpectedly a few days ago. Admiral Westfield himself is the captain, and he took care not to advertise the purpose of his journey. Some of the pirates believe it's routine naval business, nothing more. But a few of them," said Jasper, "disagree."

Charlie slumped down in his seat. "So he's after us."

"Not quite." Jasper raised an eyebrow. "Admiral West-field is after the Enchantress's treasure."

"But that's impossible!" Hilary suddenly found herself standing up; her face burned as she slipped back into her chair. "I only mean," she said more quietly, "that I've heard the admiral doesn't approve of treasure hunting."

"Perhaps he doesn't, when the treasure hunters are pirates," said Jasper, "but he's been collecting quite a bit of treasure himself these days. I have it on good authority that he's stolen a number of magical objects from High Society households."

Hilary could have sworn the *Pigeon* was rocking back and forth more violently than usual. Maybe the waves were to blame for her queasiness. Maybe it was the close quarters, or the strong smell of beets.

Miss Greyson frowned. "Are you referring to the string of magic thefts in Queensport? Surely Admiral Westfield has nothing to do with that."

"My good Miss Greyson, he has everything to do with it. It seems a few High Society scoundrels are gathering as much magic as they can lay their manicured hands on— mostly through theft. And I believe James Westfield is the ringleader. A number of—well, let's call them 'reliable sources'—in the Scallywag's Den confirmed my suspicions."

The rocking sensation had gotten worse; Hilary was almost sure of it. If only the room weren't so warm; if only Miss Greyson weren't sitting so close; if only the cabin walls would stop leaping about and settle down properly. But no one else seemed to mind the rocking or the warmth; no one else even seemed to notice it. Hilary supposed that real pirates never fell victim to queasiness. "I'm sorry," she said, "but I've got to get some fresh air. Please don't stand up, Miss Greyson; I'll be perfectly fine in a moment."

THE OVERTURNED DINGHY was still damp and cold after its journey to Middleby, but Hilary hardly noticed the chill as she leaned against it. The gargoyle had hopped after her when she'd left Jasper's cabin; now he rested his stone cheek against her leg and wound his tail around her ankle in a comforting sort of way. Bits of starlight dotted the ocean, and in the distance the *Augusta Belle*'s lanterns flickered across the waves. Being pursued by a villain on the High Seas was all part of being a pirate, Hilary knew, but she had never expected that the villain would be her father. It rather dampened the thrill of the whole adventure.

"It's not fair," said the gargoyle. "None of the pirates in *Treasure Island* have villainous fathers."

"Perhaps Jasper's made a mistake," said Hilary, but she knew Jasper had done no such thing. On the day she'd left for Miss Pimm's, Admiral Westfield had been too busy to say good-bye to her, too busy even to bestow his usual dis- ①
tracted kiss on her forehead. Had he been busy stealing Give
magic? Hilary buried her face in her hands. It was lucky she was a pirate now, because pirates didn't let anything bother them. They sailed forth and dug up priceless treasures, and when they returned home in a haze of victory, their parents were undoubtedly proud.

Footsteps hurried toward the dinghy, and Hilary peered through her fingers at the lantern that bobbed above her in the darkness. "I told you I'd be fine, Miss Greyson," she said. "There's no need to come after me."

Charlie slid down next to her. "That's the first time I've been mistaken for a governess," he said. "You really didn't know old Westfield was rotten, did you?"

Hilary shook her head. "He's a thief," she said. "He's a rat. And I didn't know a thing."

"I'm sorry I thought you were in league with your pa," Charlie said after a while. "You look so awful right now that I know you're not."

Hilary nearly laughed in spite of herself. "That's kind of you to say." She held out her hand. "Shall we be friends again?"

"Friends," Charlie agreed, and they shook on it.

"I'm awfully glad for a friend right now," said Hilary. "When Father's ship began following us, I thought he wanted to send me back to finishing school—to keep me safe. But I suppose he only cares about the safety of his treasure."

"That's not quite all he cares about," said Charlie.

"What do you mean?"

Charlie hesitated. "It might upset you . . ."

"It's all right," said Hilary. "I'm fairly sure I can't feel much worse, so you'd better tell me, whatever it is."

"All right, then." Charlie took a deep breath. "Admiral

Westfield wants to rule Augusta. Or that's what Jasper's saying, at least. That's why your pa's been stealing magic—he wants to use it to get rid of the queen."

The rocking sensation had started again. "He does love ordering people about," Hilary said quietly.

"Well, if he gets his hands on the Enchantress's treasure, he'll be ordering us all about. He and his High Society mates will have most of the magic in the kingdom, and no one will be able to stop him from doing whatever he wants." ②Crime against own country

It was treasonous talk, but it all made a horrid sort of sense. "No wonder he hates pirates so much. The more treasure we dig up, the less there is for him." Hilary peered at Charlie in the lantern light. "How long have you known what he's been up to?"

"I just found out this evening, same as you. But I think Jasper's suspected for a while. The scallywags say your pa's been looking for the Enchantress's treasure map for years, and he finally got his hands on it a few months ago, but Jasper found out somehow. We did some pilfering at Westfield House a while back—Jasper wouldn't tell me what we were pinching, but it turned out to be that map." ③ Stealing

"You made an awful scene with that hole in the wall. Father practically turned purple."

Charlie laughed. "You saw that? It was Jasper's idea, I swear. He loves a good spectacle."

"I've noticed that," said Hilary. "I want to know what

he's got planned with all those beets."

The gargoyle shuddered. "I don't."

"Let's go back and find out, then," said Charlie, "unless you're still feeling rough. If you are, I don't blame you. Finding out your pa's a villain is enough to make anyone seasick." *Antagonist*

Hilary pulled herself to her feet and picked up the gargoyle. Seasick or not, she couldn't allow her father to seize that treasure for himself. He was likely to rule Augusta as imperiously as he ruled the halls of Westfield House, and Hilary could hardly imagine the unpleasant things he might do with a stash of magic. He might lock her up in finishing school or enchant her away from the High Seas for good; the thought was too horrid to bear. "Thank you," she said to Charlie, "but we'd better hurry back. I've got to find that treasure before Father does."

"I'M AFRAID I don't understand," Miss Greyson was saying as Hilary and Charlie slipped back into Jasper's quarters. Hilary could tell by the way Miss Greyson was tapping her fingers on the tabletop that Jasper was in for a scolding. "If you're trying to keep Admiral Westfield from finding the treasure, why not steal the map and leave it at that? It seems to me, Mr. Fletcher, that if you claim the Enchantress's treasure for yourself, you'll be no less dangerous than the admiral."

Jasper leaned back in his chair and placed a

melodramatic palm against his forehead. "She thinks so little of me!" he cried. "She has so little faith! Actually, Miss Greyson," he said, sitting up, "I must admit that I'm not quite as much of a Terror as I used to be."

Charlie snickered. In response, Fitzwilliam flapped down from Jasper's shoulder and pecked at Charlie's earlobe until the snickering stopped.

"Now, I won't have you spreading the news of my virtue outside this room," Jasper continued, "but I don't want to keep that treasure for myself. If Westfield doesn't find it, someone else might, and that person might be twice as villainous as the admiral. As I figure it, the only way to protect ourselves—pirates and commoners—from tyrants like Westfield is to find that stash of magic and hand it out to the people of Augusta. Fairly and equally, of course. Give them a chance to fight back. That's what I plan to do," he said, "and I hope you all will help me."

Miss Greyson flushed. "Well," she said. "In that case. If everything you say is true, it's very noble of you."

"What he won't tell your governess," Charlie said to Hilary, "is that after he's shared that magic all over the kingdom, he won't hesitate to pinch a bit and bury it on a nice deserted island somewhere."

"And what's wrong with a little treasure plundering of an afternoon?" Jasper replied. "I meant what I said about fairness and all that, but surely you don't expect me to stop being a pirate." He rapped his knuckles on the table.

"What we have to do now is beat Westfield and his crew to the treasure. Unfortunately, the *Augusta Belle* is the fastest ship on the seas. My magic coin can speed us along a bit, but I'm sure Westfield's brought along a magic piece or two of his own, so ours isn't likely to be much help. However, we have one thing the admiral doesn't." He pointed to Hilary. "The map, which Hilary has so helpfully deciphered for us. Westfield may beat us to Gunpowder Island, but he won't find the treasure without that map."

"Does he know we're hunting for the treasure, too?" asked Charlie.

"According to the scallywags, he's suspicious. He'll be wanting the map back, of course, so our job now is to avoid him if we can. And that," said Jasper, holding up a tin of beets, "is where these come in."

"No!" cried the gargoyle. "Don't make me eat them!"

Jasper laughed. "Perk your ears back up, my friend. These aren't our supper—they're our disguise."

"THIS," THE GARGOYLE announced, "is completely undignified." He spit out a strand of curly yellow hair that had detached itself from his wig. "I'd rather eat beets."

"I, for one, think you look radiant." Hilary smoothed the shiny green fabric around the gargoyle's torso and adjusted the seashells on his top. "You're the most beautiful mermaid I've ever seen."

The gargoyle snorted. "If anyone sees me looking like this, my name is mud back in the quarry." proud ⑤

"But you're disguising yourself for a (noble) cause." Hilary patted his yellow curls. "And you're not the only one who looks ridiculous." The beard that Claire had crocheted for her was starting to itch, and she scratched her chin in much the same way that Admiral Westfield often scratched his own—a villainous way, she supposed. But a true pirate wouldn't let herself be distracted by such thoughts.

"You're right," said the gargoyle as he examined Hilary's beard. "Purple really isn't your color."

Jasper had explained that while Admiral Westfield would certainly be suspicious of a pirate ship like the *Pigeon* sailing toward Gunpowder Island, he'd hardly be likely to pay attention to a less exciting sort of ship, like the ship of a minor beet merchant. They had worked all night and into the morning, stacking the decks high with beet tins and dressing in the costumes that Jasper had conjured up with his magic piece. Jasper himself, clad in a pink feather boa, had painted over the *Pigeon*'s name on the stern and (rechristened) it the *Friendly Vegetable*. Miss Greyson had lowered the skull and crossbones and replaced it with a flag she'd sewn herself, upon which a vivid beet hovered over two crossed carrots. Even the gargoyle had grudgingly allowed himself to be transformed into a more traditional figurehead. Having a mermaid on the prow of the ship

⑥ Renamed *183*
(For a ship)

was supposed to make the *Pigeon* less noticeable, but Hilary couldn't help admiring the gargoyle's iridescent green tail as it sparkled in the sun.

"Well done, crew," said Jasper as he examined the *Pigeon*'s transformation. "Well done indeed." One end of his boa dripped with seawater, the other end dripped with paint, and he had refused to relinquish his pirate hat. Still, Hilary had to admit he looked nothing at all like the Terror of the Southlands. "Anchors aweigh!" he cried. "We're off to Gunpowder Island—though why a group of simple beet merchants would want to travel there, I've no idea."

"To deliver beets, of course," said Miss Greyson. "Even pirates must eat their vegetables." She was dressed in overalls and a wide-brimmed straw hat, as was Charlie. Their costumes were effective, but a little dull, and Hilary much preferred Oliver's outfit: he was dressed as a beet.

"Every good beet merchant needs a mascot," Jasper had said when he'd handed Oliver the round purple tunic and leafy green hat. At this moment, Oliver was attempting to raise the anchor, but the chain kept getting caught up in his roots.

Once the *Pigeon* had gotten some wind in its sails, Miss Greyson picked up the spyglass and squinted through it across the High Seas. "Oh, dear," she said. Even without a spyglass, Hilary could tell that the *Augusta Belle* was gaining ground: She could practically make out the crew members climbing its ropes.

"We've got nothing to worry about," said Jasper. "With any luck, they'll sail straight past us, and we'll slip into Gunpowder Bay right under the tips of their mustaches."

"Or they'll sink us with a single cannonball," said Charlie.

Miss Greyson put a hand on Charlie's shoulder. "You mustn't think that way. It isn't good for one's nerves. I'm sure the navy won't give us any trouble at all."

Still, Miss Greyson allowed Hilary to skip that day's lessons in order to work on her sword fighting with Charlie. By the end of the afternoon, Hilary had thrown her sword in the air only twice, knocked Charlie's sword out of his hand once, and successfully skewered six tins of beets. The *Pigeon* was bathed in the blood of massacred vegetables, and Jasper ordered both of them to swab the deck. Murderd

Night fell at last, only to be replaced by another thinly stretched day and another brief wrinkle of night. The *Pigeon* sailed straight through all of it. So did the *Augusta Belle*. Trees along the coastline shrank and grew stubby, the chilly wind carried the scent of sod and pine, and finally, early one morning on Hilary's watch, the *Pigeon* sailed past a salt-stained wooden sign. It read, in faded letters:

YOU ARE NOW ENTERING
THE NORTHLANDS
DANGER: TREACHEROUS WATERS AHEAD
IF YOU SURVIVE, ENJOY YOUR STAY!

The choppy gray sea churned ahead of the ship, all studded with islands and rocky outcroppings, but in Hilary's opinion, it didn't look half as treacherous as what lay behind them: The *Augusta Belle* had caught up at last, and her deck was loaded high with cannonballs.

"Yikes," said the gargoyle. Under his wig, he turned even more gray than usual. "We'd better get the others out here."

"They'll probably pass us by," Hilary whispered, "like Jasper said." Still, her handmade beard suddenly felt very thin, and she was sure Admiral Westfield would be able to see right through it. She couldn't make him out at the *Augusta Belle*'s helm, which was a slight relief—she couldn't think of anyone she'd be less thrilled to see. Even Philomena would have been something of an improvement. Hilary rang the ship's bell, and the crew straggled out of their cabins to join her on the deck.

Jasper squinted up at the *Augusta Belle*. "All right, everyone," he said, "it's time. Now, let us all act like beet merchants."

This order resulted in significant confusion as everyone realized at once that they had no idea how beet merchants acted. Hilary settled for waving tins of beets in the air and calling, "Beets! Get your tinned beets here! Best in Augusta!" while Charlie juggled three tins at once, and Miss Greyson stacked the rest into elaborate pyramids that fell down whenever the *Pigeon* bumped into a wave. Oliver had gone back to his cabin, and Hilary didn't entirely blame him—it would be quite embarrassing for one's former employer to see one dressed up as a root vegetable.

A shadow fell over the *Pigeon* as the *Augusta Belle* passed between the ship and the sun. Hilary had seen her father's fastest ship hundreds of times before, but it had never looked quite so ominous or smelled quite so strongly of gunpowder. She resisted the urge to hide behind the nearest stack of beet tins.

"Ahoy!" called a naval officer from the deck of the *Augusta Belle*. "Greetings to the *Friendly Vegetable* on this fine morning!"

Jasper gave the officer a cheerful wave. "Ahoy, sir! We are simple beet merchants, and definitely not pirates!"

"That's fortunate, Captain," said the officer. Hilary didn't know his name, but she'd seen him roaming the halls of Westfield House over the past few months. He had a distinctive orange mustache in which he took great pride, probably because it was the only thing standing between him and baldness. "If you were pirates, we'd be obliged to do battle with you, and it would be terribly messy. I don't care for mess." The officer peered at them through his spyglass. "As a matter of fact, we've been looking for a pirate ship on these waters—a boat called the *Pigeon*. Have you seen it?"

Hilary groaned, and Charlie dropped a tin of beets onto the deck, where it splattered. "The *Pigeon*, eh?" said Jasper. "Foolish name for a pirate ship. Captained by Jasper Fletcher, isn't it? I hear he's the Terror of the Southlands."

"I wouldn't know," said Orange Mustache. Jasper raised his eyebrows, and Miss Greyson kicked him in the shin.

"Anyway, officer, I'm sorry, but we haven't seen so much as an eye patch or a peg leg for days now. We did pass a pirate ship anchored in Middleby, though—perhaps that's the boat you're looking for?"

"Perhaps." Orange Mustache shrugged. "Thank you for your help, and for the important . . . er, the important vegetable services you provide to the people of Augusta." He turned away. "All is well, Admiral Westfield," they heard him call. "They're simple beet merchants, and definitely not pirates. They say they might have seen the *Pigeon* in Middleby."

"But that's leagues away. It's impossible." Admiral Westfield sounded nearly as irritated as he had when Hilary had eaten the last piece of cake at his birthday gala. He had been quite furious with her after the cake incident, but if he spotted her on the deck of the *Pigeon*, she'd receive a lecture a thousand times worse, assuming her father was feeling generous. And Admiral Westfield hardly ever felt generous.

Hilary pulled her beard more tightly around her chin

and readied her sword. At the prow of the boat, the gargoyle shivered.

"Give me that spyglass," said Admiral Westfield. "Let me talk to them." Orange Mustache handed the spyglass over, and the admiral's bulky silhouette appeared over the *Augusta Belle*'s railing. He looked them over, first from right to left, then from left to right. On the third sweep of the spyglass, Admiral Westfield paused.

"What a surprise," he said slowly. "I'd know that face anywhere."

Hilary braced herself for the worst.

"If it isn't Jasper Fletcher," said the admiral. "Thought I wouldn't recognize you in that feathery thing, eh? Well, if you're a beet merchant, I'm the queen of Augusta."

"Oh, blast!" said Miss Greyson. She slapped her hand over her mouth.

Jasper tossed his boa aside and drew his sword. Charlie and Hilary drew theirs as well, rather shakily in Hilary's case, and the gargoyle did his best to hide under his wig. "I'm glad someone on your ship has heard of me," said Jasper. "Care for a beet, Admiral?"

Admiral Westfield laughed and pulled out a sword of his own. "Ready the ropes, men!" he cried. "Those rascals are pirates, and we're going aboard!"

Miss Pimm's Finishing School for Delicate Ladies

Where Virtue Blossoms
OFFICE OF THE HEADMISTRESS

TO: All students

FROM: Miss Pimm

Please report to the Great Hall promptly at one o'clock in the afternoon for an important announcement. Second-year girls and above, be sure to bring your golden crochet hooks. Girls with sailing or boating experience should gather in Miss Pimm's office directly after the assembly. All classes are canceled for the remainder of the day.

Miss Pimm's Finishing School for Delicate Ladies

Where Virtue Blossoms

Dear Hilary, (1) Unusual personality

You will never believe it, but I am sure Miss
Pimm has misplaced her wits. Violet says she has
always been eccentric, but really, no one here
knows what to make of today's peculiar events, and
I must tell you about them at once to entertain
you in case life on the High Seas is at all tedious.

I will get straight to the heart of things, which
is this: Miss Pimm called a special assembly and
announced that the whole school will be going on
an ocean voyage! Even though it's the middle of
term and we'll end up missing all of our classes
for weeks, Miss Pimm has decided to give us what
she calls an "alternative educational experience."
I think this means that she will try to stuff our
ocean voyage positively full of lessons. I can't
imagine trying to waltz on the deck of a moving

ship, can you? Or perhaps you have already tried it. Miss Pimm did not tell us exactly where our ocean voyage would take us, but she did mention new cultural experiences, so I suspect that we may be visiting the Northlands. Perhaps our ships will cross paths and we will get a chance to see each other! Isn't it funny that you ran away to sea, but if you had stayed here, you would have gone to sea all along? Of course, you wouldn't have gotten to be a pirate, but still, that is one of those sorts of things that the literature mistress would call coincidental. I call it just plain strange.

Our ship is to be called the Dancing Sheep (what else?), and horrid Philomena has been appointed first mate. I don't entirely know what that means, but I suspect that Philomena will be yelling at all of us even more than usual for the next few weeks. She certainly has the lungs for the position. I have been assigned to help in the galley, peeling potatoes and convincing the cook not to make anything absolutely revolting like rat's-tail stew. Is there such a thing as rat's-tail stew? It seems like something one might eat on a ship, but I hope I am making it up.

We leave in the morning, and I must admit

that I am slightly terrified. Miss Pimm says we
may meet all sorts of rapscallions and scoundrels
on our voyage, but we must remember our manners
at all times and behave as High Society ladies
would in every situation. But who ever heard of
High Society ladies going to sea? It is all faintly
ridiculous, and that is why I fear Miss Pimm has
gone round the bend entirely.   going crazy

   I hope that if we do meet a rapscallion or a
scoundrel, it turns out to be you. Please be careful on
Gunpowder Island, and do not get kidnapped or
blown to bits or anything unpleasant like that. I
would not get a chance to hear your stories about the
High Seas, and I would miss you terribly.

   Your unexpectedly seafaring friend,
   Claire

CHAPTER ELEVEN

OUTSIDE OF THE grand balls at Westfield House, Hilary had never seen so many uniformed naval officers in one place. In some ways, in fact, the battle taking place on the deck of the *Pigeon* was very much like a ball: the floor swarmed with flushed and grumpy-looking gentlemen, the metallic clashing of swords sounded a bit like badly played music, and the duelers leaped from port to starboard with the trademark grace of High Society dancers. However, Hilary had never attended a ball at which gentlemen routinely plunged into the sea. Nor had she ever attended a ball at which she had stayed for more than five minutes, pressed up against a wall and passing out strained curtsies to her parents' friends before retreating to the safety of her bedroom.

Here, however, retreat was not an option, and curtsies were highly impractical. Hilary kissed the gargoyle on the nose and charged into the fray, holding on to her beard with one hand and scanning the deck for Admiral Westfield. She couldn't make him out, and she couldn't see Jasper, either, but she did catch sight of Miss Greyson clutching her golden crochet hook in one hand and giving a naval officer a swift kick in the pants. "I'm afraid he was shockingly rude," Miss Greyson explained as the officer sailed across the deck and splashed into the sea. "Now, who shall be next?" The officers closest to Miss Greyson dropped their swords and backed away in a hurry.

But Hilary did not get to find out whom Miss Greyson selected as her next victim, for a young naval officer chose this moment to approach her with sword in hand. "I suppose we'd better fight, then, eh?" he said, sounding a bit irritated at the prospect. "You're awfully small for a pirate, if you don't mind my saying so."

Hilary gritted her teeth. Didn't the officer think she was fearsome? Taking care not to let her sword shake in her hand, she pointed it at his stomach. "I don't care to listen to your insults," she said, "and I'll have you know that I've never lost a duel." She dearly hoped the officer couldn't tell that this duel was, strictly speaking, her first.

"My goodness," said the officer, holding up his own blade. "That *is* impressive. Are you one of those famous scallywags I've heard so much about, then?"

Hilary hesitated. "Not yet," she admitted, "but I assure you I will be."

The young officer was not much better at dueling than Hilary was, but several of his wild blows came dangerously close to her head. After ducking his blade for a fifth time, Hilary decided she had had quite enough of this tiresome gentleman and his rusty swordplay. When the officer's sword whizzed past her ear again, she clutched her hands to her chest, gave a dramatic gasp, and sank into a simple swoon that Miss Pimm herself would have admired.

The young officer wrinkled his brow. He coughed a few times and wrung his hands. Then he put down his sword, walked up to Hilary, and prodded her with his boot. "Pirate?" he said doubtfully. "Are you quite all right?"

Hilary grinned. Before the officer had a chance to retrieve his sword, she leaped up and pointed her own blade at his throat. "I'm perfectly well, sir," she said, "but thank you for your concern."

"Oh dear," said the officer. He looked down at his sword and shook his head. "I'd better hop in the sea, then, hadn't I?"

"Yes, I think you'd better," said Hilary, and she waved good-bye as the officer swam back to the *Augusta Belle*. In fact, though she'd never admit it to Jasper, she was relieved the officer had suggested this course of action; she had felt awfully uncomfortable holding her sword against his throat. Surely one could be a successful pirate without separating people's heads from their necks.

To her left, Charlie was fighting two officers at once and hardly breaking a sweat; to her right, Miss Greyson was sending a first lieutenant or a cabin boy soaring overhead once or twice a minute. The gargoyle waved his shiny green tail back and forth like a pennant and cheered the pirates on from the prow, although Hilary noticed that he squeezed his eyes shut whenever the battle threatened to become bloody. All in all, however, there was not much blood, because the naval officers were proving to be surprisingly useless at dueling. A few of them put up a decent fight against Hilary, but even they didn't seem to be trying very hard. By the time Hilary had encouraged four officers in a row to swim back to the *Augusta Belle*, she was feeling rather suspicious.

Charlie and Miss Greyson were holding their own against the dwindling band of sailors, and even the gargoyle took occasional breaks from cheering to bite those naval officers who were unlucky enough to wander past his perch. Jasper, however, was still nowhere to be seen. Perhaps the Terror of the Southlands had decided to run and hide in the captain's quarters—or perhaps he was actually in trouble. Hilary made her way around the edge of the deck, tripping a few naval officers along the way, until she reached the door to Jasper's cabin. The door was open, and inside, two people were arguing. One of them was Jasper. The other was Admiral Westfield.

"Halt!" said a voice behind Hilary. She whirled around to find Orange Mustache pointing a very shiny, very sharp sword in her direction. "Back away, pirate fiend," said Orange Mustache. Hilary was pretty sure he was trying to look threatening, with his eyes narrowed and his lips curled into a snarl, but his mustache spoiled the whole effect. "I've got orders to protect the admiral from the likes of you."

"Surely," said Hilary, "the admiral can protect himself."

In response, Orange Mustache sliced her beard neatly from her ears. Her left cheek stung where the officer's sword had grazed it. Hilary winced and pressed a hand to her face. At least Orange Mustache didn't seem to recognize her; he had been in the habit of gazing several feet above her head whenever they'd passed each other at Westfield House. ② Fusion

"Thank you, officer," she said. "I hear being clean-shaven is all the rage this season. Perhaps I'll return the favor." She held her sword to his nose and trimmed a few unruly hairs from the ends of his mustache.

③ Oct of controll

"How dare you!" Orange Mustache cried, and the duel was on. Unlike his fellow officers, Orange Mustache was very handy with a sword—much handier, even, than Charlie. As Hilary dodged Orange Mustache's blade and attempted to whack him with her own, she performed several waltz steps, a twirl, and a handful of improvisational moves that would have sent Miss Pimm's dance mistress into hysterics. She was more nimble than Orange Mustache, and equally fierce, but he showed no signs of wanting to jump into the sea as they dueled up and down the deck of the *Pigeon*. Even worse, he showed no signs of running out of breath. It turned out that sword fighting was far more exhausting than treading water for thirty-seven minutes, and Hilary could feel her strength leaking out of her and sloshing onto the deck. At last, she fell back against the ship's rails, breathing hard. Behind her was the open sea, and to either side tall stacks of beet tins barred her way. Orange Mustache stood in front of her, with his sword at her throat: he had her cornered.

"Drop your sword, pirate scum," said Orange Mustache. Hilary dropped it, and Orange Mustache kicked it away, out of her reach.

"Very good." His mustache twitched in the breeze like a small and curious rodent. "You're a fearsome little fighter, and it would be a shame to kill you. Perhaps I'll take you hostage. I'd be the toast of Queensport with a pirate hostage of my very own. Or perhaps I'll adopt you and civilize you! Wouldn't you like to be civilized?"

"I'd prefer not to be, if you don't mind," Hilary said. "They've already tried to civilize me at finishing school, but I'm afraid it hasn't stuck."

Orange Mustache took a step back. "Finishing school? But you're a pirate! Whatever do you—?"

Before he was able to complete this line of questioning, however, Hilary struck him in the head with a well-aimed tin of beets. The tin popped open, and purple juice trickled down his forehead as he slumped to the deck. Hilary tossed a second tin at him just to make sure he'd stay unconscious; the splattered beets made a pleasant pattern on his bald head. She felt a little guilty—Orange Mustache didn't care for mess, and now he was lying in a thick pool of beet juice—but he had wanted to civilize her, *and* he had destroyed her beard in the process. That sort of behavior simply couldn't be tolerated.

She stepped over Orange Mustache, taking care not to slip in the beet juice, and retrieved her sword from the deck. The argument in the captain's quarters was louder than before, and Hilary wasn't quite sure whether to barge in to defend Jasper's honor or run as far away from Admiral Westfield as possible. Running did seem to be the more practical option, but pirates didn't run from villains or parents, did they? Perhaps pirates stood awkwardly outside open doorways, trying to gather up their courage.

"I swear to you," Jasper was saying, "I don't have your blasted map!" This was true enough, Hilary realized; the map was still tucked safely under her pillow. "And I don't appreciate having power-mad government officials abuse my crew for sport."

Hilary ducked behind a crate of beet tins as Admiral Westfield pushed his chair back from the long oak table. "You expect me to believe," he said, "that you're not after my treasure?"

"You have my word," said Jasper.

"And what is a pirate's word worth to me? You're nothing but scamps and liars, the lot of you." The admiral scratched his chin. "But you swear the map's not on board."

"I do."

"In that case," said Admiral Westfield, "there's nothing to prevent me from blasting this ship to smithereens."

Jasper spun his magic coin on the tabletop. "Just like you blasted the *Cutlass*?" he said.

Behind the beet crate, Hilary clutched her sword. Hadn't Charlie's parents been aboard the *Cutlass* when they'd been sunk by the navy? Surely her father couldn't be villainous enough to send an entire pirate crew to the ocean floor.

"I'm not here to discuss the *Cutlass*," said the admiral. "The whole event was regrettable. But they refused to give up their treasure, and I had no choice but to sink them. Now, if you'll excuse me, I'll have my men prepare the cannons at once."

"Hold up!" said Jasper. "You don't want to sink this ship."

"I don't?" Admiral Westfield paused. "Whyever not?"

"Because," said Jasper, "I've got your daughter on board."

Hilary gasped, feeling rather like she'd been hit with an exploding beet tin herself. Had he known all along? Had he seen the signs in Middleby? Regardless, Jasper was discussing her now as if she were some sort of hostage, and Hilary did not care for it one bit. If Admiral Westfield sliced him to ribbons right then and there, she wasn't entirely sure she'd mind.

But Admiral Westfield refrained from slicing anyone to ribbons. Instead, he merely sighed. "So that's where she's run off to. Foolish child."

"It would be rather unseemly to sink one's own daughter," said Jasper. His coin clinked to rest on the tabletop, and he set it spinning again. "I doubt they go in for that sort of thing in High Society."

"They certainly don't." Admiral Westfield put both hands on the table and leaned toward Jasper. "Look here, Fletcher, I don't have time to deal with my daughter's little pranks. You'll have to return her to Miss Pimm's at once. With all of her limbs intact, if you can manage it."

"We make no bargains," said Jasper, "until you remove yourself from the *Pigeon*. And take your band of (sycophants) with you, please." (8) Poor behaving people .

"Very well." The admiral plucked Jasper's spinning

coin from the tabletop. "But I'll be taking this with me. Can't leave my enemy with a magic piece, you understand. And if I catch you near my treasure——"

"Believe me, Westfield," said Jasper, "you won't catch me anywhere."

Hilary stayed hidden behind the beet crate as Admiral Westfield marched out of Jasper's quarters, but she soon realized that she needn't have bothered to hide: her father did not seem at all interested in searching for her. Instead, he caught sight of Orange Mustache lying in a pool of beet juice and nudged the officer with his boot. Soon enough, all the naval officers had departed the *Pigeon*, and the *Augusta Belle* sped away in a flurry of blue and gold. It should have been a relief, but the sight of Admiral Westfield's ship disappearing in the distance was sharper than a dozen of Orange Mustache's swords at Hilary's throat.

She watched the *Augusta Belle* until it was hardly more than a smudge on the horizon. Then she knocked on the door to Jasper's quarters and entered without waiting for a response.

Jasper looked up at her and smiled as if nothing at all terrible had just occurred. "Hello, Hilary. That went rather well, don't you think?"

Hilary straightened her shoulders and drew herself up to her full height, which was not nearly as high as she had hoped. Still, Jasper was sitting down, so at least she was able to look him in the eye. "How did you know?" she asked.

"How did I know the battle went well? We've still got our map, and we're all still alive—or at least I assume we are. I'm sure the screaming would have been quite a bit louder if anyone had gotten themselves run through."

"No," said Hilary, "that's not what I meant." Did he think she was a foolish child, too? "How did you know Admiral Westfield is my father?"

Jasper crossed his arms and kicked his boots up onto the table in front of him. "Ah," he said. "Frankly, the clues were obvious: your distinct High Society accent, your familiarity with naval protocol, and of course your stubbornness, which you could have only developed as a result of living with a tyrant like Westfield."

Hilary gaped at him. *Nefarious Person*

"Oh, all right. If you must know, I caught sight of you at Westfield House when I was preparing to pinch the treasure map. And I recognized you at once when we met on the train. I must admit I had no idea you'd come work for me, though I could hardly turn you away when you did. Employing the enemy's daughter—now *that*'s a trick worthy of the Terror of the Southlands." Jasper gave a little bow from his chair, as though he expected Hilary to applaud.

"A trick?" Despite her excellent posture, Hilary felt

even smaller than before. "You mean you only hired me to get at my father?"

"Oh dear," said Jasper. "When you put it that way, it sounds quite heartless. But I hoped you might have certain information about Westfield's plans. I thought, for instance, that he might have taught you how to read that blasted map of his."

"And you thought it would be handy to have me as a hostage if he tried to sink your ship."

Jasper looked awkwardly down at Fitzwilliam, who was resting in his lap. He shrugged and said nothing. Hilary rather wished Fitzwilliam would bite him on the nose.

"So you didn't really think I was brave, or bold, or an excellent knot tier, or any of those things?" If she shrank any smaller, she'd slip through the slats in the floorboards and end up in the bilge; it was too upsetting to contemplate. "You didn't think I was a pirate?"

"Now, wait a moment," said Jasper.

But Hilary had no interest in waiting. "If you don't believe I'm a pirate," she said icily, "then I won't stay on the *Pigeon* a moment longer. Good day, Mr. Fletcher." Then she marched out of Jasper's quarters, stopping only to kick a stray beet tin, which burst in a magnificent purple explosion all over the deck.

Hilary didn't stop marching until she reached the Gargoyle's Nest, where she set about freeing the gargoyle from his ropes. "What a battle!" the gargoyle cried. He was still dressed as a mermaid, although he'd lost his wig in all the excitement. "Did you see me bite those officers? They tasted awfully salty." He looked up at Hilary, and his ears drooped. "Are you crying?"

Hilary blinked hard. "Of course not. A pirate never cries." She helped the gargoyle out of his costume and tucked him under her arm. "Let's go."

"Where are we going? Why can't I stay in my Nest?"

"We're going on a pirate ship—our *own* pirate ship. The Terror of the Southlands doesn't think I'm a true pirate, and I plan to show him otherwise. The first thing I'll do is steal his dinghy."

"We're going to sail the High Seas? By ourselves? In that tiny boat? With waves and everything?" The gargoyle gulped. "Are you sure this is a good idea?"

Hilary nodded. "We're pirates, aren't we?"

"Of course we are," said the gargoyle.

"Then we've got to leave at once. A true pirate wouldn't tolerate one more moment on board this ship."

"But what about Charlie? And Miss Greyson? Won't they miss us?" The gargoyle squirmed under Hilary's arm. "Will there be spiders?"

"I'm sure Charlie and Miss Greyson will manage perfectly well without us," said Hilary. A rather unpleasant lump was forming in her throat; no matter how hard she swallowed, it remained stubbornly in place. "And as for the spiders—"

She stopped so suddenly that she nearly lost hold of the gargoyle. There, where the dinghy should have been, was nothing but a tangle of ropes. Two of the ropes hung overboard, but their ends dangled loose above the waves, and the dinghy was nowhere in sight.

"Oh, blast," Hilary whispered. Had the navy taken the dinghy with them when they left the *Pigeon*? No, most of the naval officers had plunged into the sea. But who else could have set it loose from its ropes? Jasper was still in his quarters, and Hilary could see Miss Greyson and Charlie chatting on the other side of the ship—but she couldn't see Oliver anywhere.

"Oh, double blast!" she cried. She hurried to Oliver's cabin and flung open the door without knocking, but the cabin was empty. Then she cursed Oliver's name heartily, ran into her own cabin, and pulled her pillow from her bed.

The treasure map was gone.

JASPER FLETCHER, FREELANCE PIRATE
TERROR OF THE SOUTHLANDS
VNHLP CERTIFIED IN BATTLE,
TREASURE HUNTING, & PARROT MAINTENANCE

✠ ✠ ✠ ✠ ✠

Dear Captain Blacktooth:

It has come to my attention that the Augusta Royal Navy is sailing to Gunpowder Island. Under the direction of Admiral James Westfield, the navy has already attacked my pirate ship, injured my crew, plundered valuable items, and (our resident governess informs me) behaved very rudely in general. I believe that Admiral Westfield poses a direct and immediate threat to all pirates on the High Seas, and I hope that the staff at VNHLP Headquarters on Gunpowder Island will act accordingly. Please send your best pirates, fastest ships, and most ominous cannons to attack the Augusta Belle at once, before she gets anywhere near Gunpowder Bay. There is no time to waste.

I would also appreciate it if you would refrain from attacking my ship, the Pigeon, when it arrives in Gunpowder Bay. As you read this message, you may be remembering the recent VNHLP banquet at which I described you as "more useless than a bucket of sea cucumbers," but I am sincerely sorry that you overheard me, and I will make every attempt not to be overheard in the future.

I am sending this message via my budgerigar, Fitzwilliam. Please enclose your response in his beak and send him back to me; he will know where to find me.

Grudgingly,

Jasper Fletcher

Mr. Fletcher:

We are disturbed to hear of Admiral Westfield's attack on your ship and crew. Unfortunately, however, we cannot attack the Augusta Belle as you have requested. You may be aware that the VNHLP's relationship with the Royal Navy is unsteady at best. You may also be aware that Admiral Westfield himself is in possession of quite a lot of cannons. We are pirates, and we do not normally avoid a hearty battle, but considering the admiral's extreme distaste for piracy, we would prefer not to provoke him unless it is absolutely necessary. And frankly, Mr. Fletcher, defending your honor is not our greatest concern at this time.

Please be assured that if the Augusta Belle does engage us in battle as we are minding our own business, we will do our best to send the ship to the bottom of the bay. It would be convenient for us to have a new shipwreck in this location to serve as a spine-chilling warning to passersby. Our existing shipwrecks have become homes for interesting varieties of fish and are more of a delightful tourist attraction than a spine-chilling warning.

We are concerned by your report that you are employing a governess. Mr. Fletcher, pirates do not have governesses. This fact should be obvious to even the most hopeless amateur. Furthermore, a little bird tells us that one of the members of your crew is a young girl. We sincerely hope that the little bird is mistaken, since as you are no doubt aware, young girls are not permitted to be pirates. Any pirate who violates this rule may find himself on the uncomfortably sharp side of the VNHLP's sword of justice. If you are indeed employing a governess and a young girl, please dispose of them immediately. Tossing them over the side of your ship should suffice. Satisfactory 11

And no, we have not forgotten about the sea cucumbers.

Arr!
Captain Rupert Blacktooth
President, VNHLP

JASPER FLETCHER, FREELANCE PIRATE
TERROR OF THE SOUTHLANDS
VNHLP CERTIFIED IN BATTLE,
TREASURE HUNTING, & PARROT MAINTENANCE

✠ ✠ ✠ ✠ ✠

Captain Blacktooth:

Thank you for your response. I am disappointed to learn that you will not be able to put every effort into stopping Admiral Westfield, but I understand that keeping up the appearance of piracy is more important than actually thwarting one's enemies.

Thank you also for the advice about disposing of my crew members. I shall cheerfully ignore it.

Eagerly anticipating a blow from the sword of justice,

Jasper Fletcher!

CHAPTER TWELVE

ALTHOUGH JASPER AND Charlie searched the ship from keel to crow's nest, and Hilary and Miss Greyson scoured it from starboard to port, no one could find any trace of the treasure map. "Do you really think Oliver took off with it?" Charlie asked. "He can't be planning to row that dinghy all the way to Gunpowder Island; it would take months to get there."

Hilary groaned and flopped onto her bed. "But he won't be rowing," she said. "He'll be sailing there on the *Augusta Belle.*"

Charlie stared at her. "Why would a pirate climb aboard a navy ship?"

"He's not a pirate." Hilary wanted to kick herself. Of

course; Admiral Westfield had never dismissed Oliver at all. "Don't you see? He's a spy. He must have been working for Father all along." She shut her eyes. "He used to be Father's apprentice." *Learn the profesion*

"Did he?" said Jasper. "Oh, blast it all, Hilary; why didn't you tell us?"

"I couldn't! He said he'd tell you that I was the admiral's daughter." Hilary hesitated. "Of course, you knew that all along. But I thought he'd had a fight with Father; he said he wanted to help you in your battles against the navy. . . . Oh dear," Hilary said. "I've mucked things up terribly." *(messed things up)*

"Nonsense," said Miss Greyson. "You are certainly not responsible for that boy's treachery. I should have said something myself."

"And I should have let you drop that cannonball on his foot," said Charlie.

"Well, I was foolish enough to hire the lad in the first place," said Jasper, "so there's no use assigning blame." He set down his hat and mopped his forehead with a bandanna. The gargoyle hopped eagerly toward the hat, but Jasper frowned at him. "Don't even think of it, gargoyle. A pirate must have his hat in times of crisis."

"So must a gargoyle!" the gargoyle protested, but it did no good at all.

"If Oliver's been working for the navy," said Charlie, "and Westfield knew all along that Oliver would be able to get him the map, does that mean the whole battle——"

"Was nothing more than a distraction? Yes, I'm almost sure of it." Jasper squashed his hat back down onto his head, where it settled like a fat black raincloud. "I have to give Westfield some credit—it was a tidy little plan. Sneak a man onto my ship, cause a ruckus, scurry off with the loot while we're all looking the other way. And he stole my magic piece for good measure! I hate to say it, but it's textbook piracy."

This observation only served to make Hilary feel worse. Judging by the way everyone else was staring at the floor and scowling, she wasn't alone in her misery.

"If it's any consolation," she said at last, "Oliver is still dressed as a beet."

Charlie snickered. "I hope someone stews him."

"I should have bitten him when I had the chance," the gargoyle said. "Could have had a nice big chomp on his leg."

"Now, really," said Miss Greyson, "this is hardly the time for vengeance."

"Miss Greyson, if you please," said Jasper, "we are pirates. It is *always* time for vengeance."

Miss Greyson rolled her eyes toward the heavens. "Mr. Fletcher, I'm afraid that's a highly impractical approach to life. If you are good, you may have your vengeance later, but first we must plot a course of action. If I'm not mistaken, Admiral Westfield not only has our treasure map and our magic coin; he also has the fastest ship on the High Seas. If we don't act at once, we'll have no hope of beating him to the treasure."

"Yes, of course. Right you are." Jasper bowed to Miss Greyson and tipped his hat.

Hilary had always assumed that Miss Greyson was incapable of blushing, but to her astonishment, Miss Greyson blushed right then and there on the deck of the *Pigeon*. Before Hilary could ask her if she was feeling quite well, Jasper clapped his hands together.

"All right, crew," he said. "Barring a storm or some other piece of luck, we've got no chance of catching up to Westfield, and no magic to speed us along. I've sent a request for help to the VNHLP"—Jasper squinched his lips together as though he'd tasted something sour—"but their response makes it clear that those overstuffed fools will be no help at all. So it's entirely up to us. I want each of you to think hard about ways to make this ship fairly leap through the waves like a young gazelle.

Miss Greyson busied herself by explaining the concept of a gazelle to the gargoyle, and Charlie set off in search of extra sails and oars, but Jasper pulled Hilary aside before she could leave. "If you don't mind," he said, "I'd like to have a word with you."

They walked together out onto the deck, where the summer sky showed no hint of a storm or any other force that might stop Admiral Westfield in his tracks. Hilary crossed her arms in front of her chest and stared up at Jasper. Fitzwilliam, who was perched on Jasper's shoulder, ruffled his feathers. Jasper smiled down at her, but she didn't smile back.

"You've got every right to curse my name," Jasper said at last, "and I don't blame you for storming out of my quarters, but I hope you'll hear me out. You were perfectly right about me: I didn't think you were a pirate, not at the start. But tell me, how many naval officers did you defeat in combat today?"

Hilary thought for a moment. "Five. But I don't think four of them were trying very hard."

"Still, a win's a win in my book. Besides, you lied to me about your identity—a very piratical thing to do. And you deciphered that treasure map, didn't you?"

Hilary nodded. "You were wrong, by the way," she said. "My father never told me a thing about it."

"After today's events, I have no trouble believing that." Jasper placed both of his hands on her shoulders. "Now, I am about to be perfectly honest with you. Engaging in perfect honesty is something I do quite rarely, so I hope you'll pay attention."

The smile had disappeared from Jasper's face. Even Fitzwilliam stopped preening and stared at him.

"Hilary Westfield," said Jasper, "you are a true pirate, and I am honored to have you on my crew. I hope you'll forgive me for ever thinking otherwise. ★ *Paternal*

If Hilary had been a Miss Pimm's girl, she would have curtsied. If she had been a High Society daughter, she would have blushed. But she was a pirate. A warm feeling swept from her forehead down to her boots—it was rather like the sensation that came from drinking grog, only nicer.

"And you won't take me back to finishing school?" she asked.

"Certainly not," said Jasper. "I need you to help me find the treasure, and you can't do that while you're waltzing about in a bathing cap, or whatever it is those girls do at Miss Pimm's."

The warm feeling drained away. "But we've lost the map. Father will reach the treasure first, and you'll have to blacken my name, and—" (3) *Kept*

"As far as I'm concerned, you've upheld your end of our bargain. I have no intention of blackening your name." Jasper paused. "However, if your father gets his hands on that treasure, my good opinion will hardly matter. The queen tolerates us, but what do you think life will be like for pirates under the rule of James Westfield?"

"'The kingdom,'" said Hilary slowly, "'would be far better off without all those pirates sailing through it.' That's what Father always says." She could practically picture him leaning back in his chair with his boots up on his desk, dusting off his hands after ridding the High Seas of pirates. "He'll toss us all in jail, along with the other things he can't abide—like books and newspapers and square-shaped windows." She swallowed. "Or he'll sink us, like he did the *Cutlass*."

"Yes, I think you're right. Jail if we're lucky, the ocean floor if we're not. I'm sorry to say it, but if we can't find our way to the treasure before he does, you'll never be a pirate again—and neither will anyone else."

NINETY PACES FROM the statue, fifty paces toward the ash tree. Or was it fifty paces from the statue and ninety toward the ash tree? No, Hilary was almost certain she'd been right the first time. She refused to let Oliver—Oliver, of all people!—get the best of her. He might have stolen her map, but that didn't mean she couldn't remember the Enchantress's instructions. Ninety paces from the statue, fifty paces toward the ash tree. She could beat Oliver in a footrace, if it came to that; she'd had no trouble running away from him hundreds of times at Westfield House. Beating Oliver, Admiral Westfield, and thirty additional naval officers in a race across Gunpowder Island might prove to be slightly more difficult, but Hilary preferred not to think about that if she could help it.

"Ninety paces from the statue," she said to the gargoyle.

"Yes, yes, and fifty paces toward the ash tree. Why is Gunpowder Island so far away?" The gargoyle hopped around his Nest. "I haven't gotten to say 'Land ho!' in days."

That was hardly the worst of their troubles. Without his magic coin to toss from one hand to the other, and with no hint of a breeze in the air, Jasper had wrapped himself in a foul temper, and Hilary was growing worried. If even Jasper had lost hope, their chances of being first to arrive at the treasure must be very grim indeed.

Miss Greyson appeared to be worried as well, for she had canceled all of Hilary's lessons, and she spent a good deal of time walking up and down the deck, clutching her golden crochet hook. "I do wish we'd catch a favorable wind," she said quietly as she walked past Hilary.

At the helm of the *Pigeon*, Jasper sniffed the air. "The wind's picked up, my friends," he said. "There may be some hope for us yet. Charlie, Hilary, tend to the sails."

But Hilary didn't move: She kept her eyes locked on her governess. A breeze had sprung up at the very moment Miss Greyson had wished for one. It was odd, now that she thought about it: Miss Greyson kept that crochet hook with her at all times, but Hilary had never actually seen her use it. She sewed, of course, and knitted thick and itchy woolen sweaters in the winter, but the crochet hook served only to help keep Miss Greyson's hair tidily in place. She often clutched it when she was nervous or worried; Hilary believed she'd even been holding it on the night she'd arrived at Jasper's bungalow. Perhaps it was simply a small reminder of civilization in the midst of piracy—after all,

Miss Greyson did very much enjoy civilization. Or perhaps it was not so simple after all.

"Miss Greyson," she said, "I hope you'll forgive me for being impolite. But I'm almost certain you have magic."

Miss Greyson stopped pacing. The color drained from her face, and she sucked in her cheeks. "What a preposterous suggestion!" she said at last. "I'm sure I don't know what you mean." (4) Outrageous

"But you just used your crochet hook to summon a wind." Hilary had gotten Jasper and Charlie's attention by now. "Didn't you?"

Miss Greyson let the crochet hook clatter to the deck. "I did no such thing."

Because Miss Greyson was not a pirate, she was not a very good liar. "And you've used it before," said Hilary. "To find me on the train to Miss Pimm's, and to find me again when I ran away. You must be terribly good at magic if you tracked me all the way to Little Herring Cove."

Miss Greyson started to say something about governesses having their ways, but Jasper retrieved the crochet hook from the deck and weighed it thoughtfully in his palm. "Fetch me a drink!" he said to the hook.

A silver serving tray appeared on the deck. In the center of the tray, a pink china teacup perched on a lace doily, accompanied by a small pink bowl of sugar and a small pink pitcher of milk. The cup was filled nearly to the brim with steaming black tea.

Jasper picked up the teacup, sipped, and made a face. "I was hoping for grog," he said, "but I should have known a governess's magic piece would deliver a tea service. I do wish it had thought to send along some biscuits."

Two biscuits popped onto the tray.

"That's quite enough!" said Miss Greyson. "I believe you've made your point."

"I always wondered why my ears tingled during lessons!" the gargoyle said. "I thought that was just what learning felt like."

Jasper held the crochet hook up to the sunlight. "It's a fine piece of work," he said. "Wherever did you get it?"

"I really can't recall," Miss Greyson said quietly.

Hilary stared at her. "But you got it from Miss Pimm! You said so yourself, just last week."

Miss Greyson looked around from one end of the ship to the other, as though she expected Miss Pimm to walk across the deck at any moment. "I did, didn't I? Oh dear, now I've really put a finger in the porridge." She lowered her voice. "You mustn't tell a soul, any of you. Miss Pimm would have my head on a pike if she knew how careless I'd been. The hooks are only to be used in emergencies, and I felt that our current situation qualified."

Charlie helped himself to a biscuit. "It's typical High Society nonsense," he said. "Why would anyone want to hand out magic to a bunch of finishing-school girls? Aren't those girls terrifying enough as it is?"

"I'm not aware of Miss Pimm's reasons," Miss Greyson said tightly, "but I'm sure they are practical ones. There is quite a bit of magic floating around High Society—or there was until your father got his hands on it, Hilary—and perhaps Miss Pimm feels that her girls should be familiar with it. Don't look so horrified, Mr. Fletcher; Miss Pimm herself gives deportment classes to instruct her charges in the use of magic." ⑥ Behaviors

⑦ Pic.

"Do you mean to tell me," said Jasper, "that a posse of magical young ladies is currently dashing about Pemberton?"

"Certainly not!" said Miss Greyson. "They are hardly a posse. And Miss Pimm's girls never dash." She plucked her crochet hook out of Jasper's hand. "Now, if you'll excuse me, I believe I need to lie down. I feel quite exhausted, and being interrogated is hardly improving matters."

"Hold on a moment." Jasper caught Miss Greyson by the elbow. "You do look pale. Just how much magic have you been using?" ⑧ Asked questions

"I felt it was very important"—Miss Greyson took a long breath—"to help the *Pigeon* move along as rapidly as possible." She breathed again. "I suppose I may have over-exerted myself."

Hilary caught Miss Greyson's other elbow to prevent

her from tipping over. "Will she be all right?" she asked Jasper.

He nodded. "Magic can be quite draining, but it's nothing a bit of sleep and a good chunk of hardtack won't cure. You must rest, Eloise. We'll take over from here."

"Take over?" Miss Greyson went rigid. "Whatever are you proposing?"

"Simply that Hilary and I take turns using the crochet hook while you rest. We'll drive the *Pigeon* forward without exhausting ourselves too terribly. What do you say?"

Jasper put out his hand to accept the crochet hook, but Miss Greyson merely scowled at him. "Absolutely not."

"Miss Greyson, please!" Hilary had never discovered quite how to win an argument with a governess, but she would put in her best effort nonetheless. "Let us help you. I've read a bit about using magic, and I'm sure I'll be able to work it out. Besides, Jasper will oversee everything."

To Hilary's surprise, Charlie agreed with her. "I can't say I like the plan, but I don't see that we've got much of a choice. That crochet hook is the only piece of magic we've got—apart from the gargoyle, of course, but we can't use him to speed up the ship."

"I should think not!" The gargoyle shuddered.

"And if we don't reach that treasure before Westfield does," Charlie continued, "he'll sink us all sooner or later. I don't know about the rest of you, but I'd rather put up a fight while we still can."

"Oh, very well." Miss Greyson placed the crochet hook in Hilary's palm. "I suppose I do need some help. But I'll fetch a chair and supervise the whole ordeal to make sure those two don't transform themselves into tea cakes. And I dearly hope," she said as she walked toward her cabin, "that Miss Pimm never finds out about this."

HILARY HAD ALWAYS imagined that magic would be exciting, but watching Jasper hold a crochet hook and say things like, "Hurry up, ship!" was an awfully dull way to spend the morning. To Hilary's disappointment, Jasper did not change anyone into a tea cake, although he did conjure up a gust of wind that sent Fitzwilliam soaring all the way up to the crow's nest. Up in the rigging, Charlie stretched bedsheets and blankets into makeshift sails to catch the breeze, and the *Pigeon* soon looked more like a laundry line than a pirate ship. But it sailed onward faster than ever, and Miss Greyson relaxed enough to fall asleep in her chair.

Finally, Jasper pressed the crochet hook into Hilary's hand. "I don't think I can manage another round," he said. "You'd better give it a try."

The crochet hook was smooth and cool against her fingers, like the gargoyle's ears when she scratched behind them. It was such a small thing, more delicate than she'd thought; it certainly didn't feel powerful.

"Just hold on tight," said Jasper, "and tell it what you'd like it to do."

Hilary nodded. "Hello, magic," she said. A thrill unfurled in her chest and began to travel down her arm, toward the crochet hook. "I'd like you to help our ship sail faster, if you please."

"You don't have to have a conversation with it," Jasper said. "This isn't High Society—my goodness!" The crochet hook apparently enjoyed being greeted in such a civilized manner, for it had summoned up a wind that knocked Jasper's hat right off his head.

"It is from Miss Pimm's, after all," Hilary reminded him. "It probably thrives on good manners."

The wind continued to blow, and the thrill continued to thrum in Hilary's chest. It was a lovely feeling—she rather thought she could take on the entire Royal Navy at the moment, and Philomena besides. Perhaps she could even get into the Scallywag's Den without allowing the burly pirate to knock her onto the cobblestones. When the breeze died down, she asked the crochet hook politely for another push, and it obliged.

Hilary wondered for an instant if the rush of wind had been tugged out of her lungs. "It's harder the second time," she said between breaths, "and not nearly as nice."

She would have liked to hold on to the crochet hook a bit longer, but Jasper took it away and tucked it in his pocket. "That's quite enough for now," he said. "You'll be able to use the magic longer with practice."

All the thrill had left Hilary's chest by now. "It was exciting," she admitted, "when the wind picked up." She considered for a moment. "But it wasn't nearly as exciting as piracy."

"Of course it wasn't," said Jasper. He walked back to the ship's wheel and gave it a good spin as Fitzwilliam settled down on his shoulder. "Then again, what is?"

At the prow of the *Pigeon*, the gargoyle nearly hopped out of his knots. "Trees!" he cried. "Trees!"

Jasper frowned. "I hardly think trees are more thrilling than piracy."

"No," said the gargoyle, "I see trees out there! And grass, and sand—lots of it." He puffed out his chest and cleared his throat. "Land ho, everyone! Land ho!"

Jasper Fletcher, Freelance Pirate
Terror of the Southlands

VNHLP Certified in Battle,
Treasure Hunting, & Parrot Maintenance

Dear Claire,

Please forgive me for taking so long to reply to your letter. It seems that doing battle on the High Seas does not leave one with much free time, and I have only just caught a spare moment in which to steal a page of Jasper's stationery.

I cannot believe that the entire staff and student body of Miss Pimm's has taken to sea! You are right—this is entirely strange. I do not know all that much about High Society, but I am fairly sure that Mother never swabbed any decks when she was in finishing school. (As she positively refuses to come within ten feet of a mop at home, I cannot imagine that she would behave any differently on board a ship.)

10
Moped
cleaned

I have discovered something else quite surprising about Miss Pimm's, and I must admit that I don't know what to make of it. I've been sworn to secrecy on this matter, but I can't bear to keep it a secret from you, so you must simply swear to secrecy as well.

Have you sworn? Good. Now that you are prepared, here is the shocking truth: the golden crochet hooks that Miss Pimm distributes to her students are made of magic, and Miss Pimm herself instructs her students in their use.

I shall give you a few moments to recover.

If you are anything like me, you are probably shaking your head and muttering to yourself, "But that's impossible!" I suggest that you stop shaking your head: You will only succeed in making yourself seasick, and I promise you that I am telling the truth. In fact, I am quite sure that Philomena used her very own golden crochet hook to enchant your fish sticks, though I still can't believe Miss Pimm would have approved of her behavior.

As you can probably guess, I am simply swamped with questions, and here is a sampling of them: Why is Miss Pimm instructing her students in magic? How does she know anything at all about the subject? Where in the world does she find all of those crochet hooks, and why has she given one to someone as horrid as Philomena?

Oh, Claire, things are getting rather tangled out here on the High Seas, and I wish you were here on our pirate ship instead of on the Dancing Sheep. As long as you are there rather than here, however, you might try to observe the older girls as they use their golden crochet hooks. Do be careful, though, and stay as far away from Philomena as you possibly can. I'd be simply devastated if she turned you into a toad.

ARR!, which is the pirate way of saying that I miss you very much,

Hilary

CHAPTER THIRTEEN

ILARY, JASPER, AND Charlie all raced for the spyglass, but Hilary claimed it first. Through its lens, she could make out a flat coastline trimmed with crenellated towers and sharp, proud steeples. She caught glimpses of gardens, apple orchards, and what appeared to be rows upon rows of cannons. There was no question about it: They'd reached Gunpowder Island at last.

Hilary hurried to wake Miss Greyson, and Charlie took the spyglass. "I don't want to dampen the mood," he said after a while, "but there are naval flags flying in Gunpowder Bay."

"Curses," said Jasper. "They've gotten here first."

Hilary peered through the spyglass again, just as a

cannonball from the island smacked into the water off the starboard side of the *Augusta Belle*. "Yes," she said, "but it looks like they're distracted at the moment."

"Old Westfield never could resist provoking the VNHLP," said Jasper, borrowing the spyglass from her. "I must remember to send Captain Blacktooth a token of my appreciation. A pie, perhaps, or a nice bouquet." He nodded and put the spyglass down. "But we must be careful. If the navy notices we've arrived, they're not likely to arrange a welcoming tea in our honor."

"I'd wager," said Charlie, "that the navy won't pay us any notice at all. They'll be far too busy noticing *that*." He pointed behind them, and Hilary turned to look. There, in the not-so-far distance, was a vast wooden ship. It hurried toward Gunpowder Island, kicking up wave foam on all sides, and its green and silver sails puffed confidently in the wind. From the mainmast flew a silver flag adorned with what looked like a large green blob. When Hilary grabbed the spyglass for a closer look, however, the blob transformed into a carefully embroidered dancing sheep.

"Oh, bother it all!" She cleaned the spyglass lens with her shirt, but when she looked through the glass again, nothing had changed: the embroidered sheep was undoubtedly dancing the hornpipe. "What in the world is Miss Pimm doing here?"

"Miss Pimm?" Miss Greyson wrinkled her brow and made her own examination through the spyglass. "Surely not, Hilary. A woman of her stature would never—dear me, that *does* look awfully like a dancing sheep."

"Hold on a moment," said Jasper. "Is this the same Miss Pimm who has a fondness for crocheting?"

"The very same," said Hilary. "And she thinks you all are nefarious scoundrels."

"Ah. I like her already." Jasper turned back to the helm. "I wish I could impress her with my nefarious deeds in person, but we hardly have the time right now. I hope she won't be offended if we avoid making a social call."

Along the edge of Gunpowder Island, where the wide gape of the bay bumped impolitely into the coast, dozens of standing stones rose up from the waves. Their surfaces had been polished by centuries of water rushing past, and they reminded Hilary of the unsmiling guards who stood at the palace gates in Queensport. Jasper maneuvered the *Pigeon* in and out between the stones, taking care to shield the ship from the battle taking place in the middle of the bay. Every so often, the boom of a cannon set all the deck's planks shaking, and Hilary wondered how long the VNHLP could possibly hold off the Royal Navy. When she was very young, she would curl up on her mother's lap and ask how long it would be until Admiral Westfield came home again. Her mother always gave the same answer: "He'll be gone until he's gotten the job done, and not a moment sooner. Your father can be stubborn as an ox." And Hilary always laughed, imagining an ox dressed to the nines in full naval uniform, pacing the deck of a grand ship. Now, however, Hilary desperately wished that her mother had compared Admiral Westfield to something a good deal less fierce— an otter, perhaps, or a rabbit. She felt almost certain that she could face a rabbit.

The *Pigeon* pulled up behind the standing stone closest to the coast. "Drop anchor," said Jasper, "and lower the sails. We'll have to abandon the ship, I'm afraid. Westfield's already got us outnumbered, and we can't afford to leave anyone behind to look after the *Pigeon*. Normally, of course, we'd take the dinghy to shore, but since we've been careless enough to lose it . . ." He looked them all up and down. "Miss Greyson, in that monstrous handbag of yours, did you happen to bring along a bathing costume?"

SWIMMING TO SHORE turned out to be a particularly unpleasant task. The cold waters of Gunpowder Bay turned Hilary's arms and legs an unfashionable shade of blue, and to make matters worse, she had to lie on her back and propel herself by kicking as she held the gargoyle up above her head. The gargoyle couldn't stop trembling, and he squirmed whenever his tail dipped into the ocean or a drop of sea spray landed on his snout.

"Just stay calm," Hilary said as clearly as she could, "and please don't wiggle." It was difficult to talk when half the High Seas poured into your mouth each time you opened it. "We're almost there, I promise."

"I had no idea piracy would be so terrifying," said the gargoyle from between his clenched teeth. "You hear all about the swords and cannons, but no one ever mentions a thing about swimming."

Finally the ocean floor was close enough to touch, and Hilary hauled the gargoyle out of the water and onto the rocky beach. She set him down safely on the shore, where he began to introduce himself to all the resident pebbles and boulders.

Charlie, who had been the first to float ashore, was sharpening his sword on a nearby rock, but Miss Greyson and Jasper were still bobbing about in the waves, holding large metal spades in the air above them. Atop Jasper's head sat his very best pirate hat, and atop the hat sat Fitzwilliam. Jasper, Fitzwilliam, and the hat all looked terribly bedraggled, and bits of seaweed clung to them for dear life.

Miss Greyson brushed off her long woolen sleeves and marched out of the sea as though she were a particularly brusque and responsible ocean goddess. "There's nothing like a cold bath to bring color to one's cheeks, don't you think?" she said. Hilary wondered if blue was the color to which Miss Greyson referred.

In front of them, a stone wall laced with vines and roses stood twice as high as Jasper. Hilary looked down the beach in both directions, but the wall didn't seem to end, nor did it shrink: if anything, it grew taller. "I've been here once before," said Charlie, "for VNHLP training. If I'm remembering it right, this wall goes all around the island. We can get in at the west gate, though, and it's not too far from here."

Miss Greyson picked up her spade and started walking. "Well, then, that's where we must go."

"You intend to march up to the west gate and announce yourself to the pirates on duty?" Jasper shook his head, and seaweed flew from his hat. "I wouldn't recommend it. They have cannons, you know, and they don't take kindly to governesses."

Hilary suspected that Miss Greyson could have made short work of the pirates on duty, but they all agreed that it would be practical to avoid unnecessary skirmishes. "Which means," said Jasper, "that we must go up."

"Up?" The gargoyle looked doubtfully at the sky.

"Up," said Jasper, "and over." He began stacking rocks against the side of the wall like stairsteps. "If you hop this way, gargoyle, I'll give you a boost."

Scrambling up to the top of the ancient wall was quite easy—Hilary found toeholds in the vines and in the places where stone had crumbled away over the years—but getting back down to the ground on the other side proved to be more of a challenge. From her wall-top perch, Hilary took a good look at Gunpowder Island, scanning the landscape for any sign of a buried treasure. The helpful X on the Enchantress's map was not likely to appear on the ground itself, and all Hilary could see were miles of winding, old-fashioned cobblestone streets lined with shops and houses, bustling with pirates, and punctuated by the occasional tree or well-tended flower bed. Gunpowder Island may have been home to the most fearsome scourges on the High Seas, but it appeared that the VNHLP liked to keep things tidy.

Jasper handed the gargoyle up to Hilary. Slowly, balancing him under one arm, she lowered herself to the cobblestone street below. She had to let go of the wall a good five feet above the ground, and she landed rather painfully on the seat of her pirate breeches. Miss Greyson's head popped over the top of the wall, and soon enough, all of Miss Greyson crash-landed next to Hilary.

"I hope you won't think I'm being rude," said Hilary, "but I never thought I'd see you fly through the air like that."

"Governesses," said Miss Greyson, "are full of surprises." She adjusted the skirt of her bathing costume. "I certainly wasn't about to let you visit a pirate stronghold without a chaperone."

"Miss Greyson, I don't think you're being perfectly honest with me."

Miss Greyson flushed and smiled at Hilary. "If you must know," she whispered, "I am enjoying myself immensely. But you mustn't tell a soul!"

"Pirate's honor," said Hilary.

Charlie chose this moment to clamber over the wall,

with Jasper following close behind him. "All right, treasure seekers," said Jasper, "where do we go from here?"

"Well," said Hilary, "the first clue on the Enchantress's map is 'ninety paces from the statue.' Is there a statue anywhere on Gunpowder Island?"

Charlie nodded. "There are loads. The town square is full of them—memorials to notorious pirates and that sort of thing. It's too bad the Enchantress didn't say which statue she was thinking of, though. It'll take hours to mark out ninety paces from each of them."

"We've got nowhere else to start," said Hilary, "so we might as well start there. Which way to the town square?"

At Charlie's direction, they picked up their spades and turned left down the cobblestone street. "Remember," Jasper whispered over his shoulder, "don't make eye contact, and look as ferocious as you possibly can. You might even mutter a curse or two, if you're up for it. It will help us blend in with the crowd."

JASPER HAD BEEN right about Gunpowder Island's beauty: Roses bloomed in every color imaginable, as well as a few colors that Hilary had never thought to imagine. The narrow streets marked the routes along which generations of pirates had strolled. Intricate faces of animals and monsters were carved into some of the rooftops and stone walls; the gargoyle greeted them politely, but they appeared to be decorative rather than magical. Small wooden signs offered up smartly painted street names like Mutineer's Way and Scurvy Lane, and timber-fronted shops advertised everything from sword-sharpening services to sail repair, from mapmaking to (millinery.) The gargoyle gazed longingly at the elegant display of pirate hats in the milliner's window, and Hilary would have loved to stop in each and every shop, but what good would a new hat be if they didn't reach the treasure before the Royal Navy did?

On the outskirts of town, they had been the only people on the street, but as they drew closer to the center of the island, they found themselves caught up in coarse and salty crowds of pirates going about their daily errands. Quite a few pirates were discussing the battle taking place in the bay, but it did not sound as though battles were an unusual or unexpected part of life on Gunpowder Island, and most of the pirates' discussions soon turned to which groggery they would visit to celebrate their inevitable victory later that day.

"Your pa and I used to rest our weary breeches at the Sword and Seahorse," Jasper said to Charlie. He pointed to a groggery across the street with a cheerful red door and window boxes full of tulips. "We'd plot our next adventures and discuss how to make ourselves more fearsome." He patted Charlie's shoulder. "Perhaps when the treasure is ours, we can all stop by for a celebration."

Charlie nodded, but he didn't say a word—not even a pirate curse—until they'd reached the next street corner.

On one side of the street was a dusty old shop where pirates could exchange their magic coins for other magical items, though its windows were boarded up and cobwebs hung from its signs. On the other side of the street was an ice cream parlor, and small knots of pirates sat outside chatting under pink-striped umbrellas. "I think," said Charlie, "that the town square is just around the next— oh, curses!" He stopped short, and Hilary nearly crashed into him. "We've got to hide. Quick."

They hurried behind the nearest pink-striped umbrella, and Hilary peered past Charlie to get a better look at what had alarmed him. There, a few yards down the street, stood a man and boy in plain black clothes. They both looked damp and drippy, as though they'd recently gone for a swim, and their pants were torn and scuffed at the knees, as though they'd recently climbed over a city wall. Unlike the pirates around them, they were not chatting or challenging each other to duels; they were huddled close together, studying a seawater-stained square of parchment. The man glanced about uncomfortably, and the boy sneered.

Admiral Westfield (for it was he) pointed to the trea-sure map and mumbled to Oliver. Oliver looked over his shoulder at something around the corner and nodded. Then Admiral Westfield rolled the map up and patted Oli-ver's shoulder. "Well done, lad," he said loud enough for Hilary to hear. "I'm proud of you. Shall we proceed?"

"Oh, they wouldn't dare!" said Hilary. In her arms, the gargoyle growled. She lunged toward Admiral Westfield, but she hadn't taken three steps before Jasper's hands clamped down on her shoulders, and Miss Greyson's hands pressed over her mouth. "Let me *go*," she said, although the muffling effects of Miss Greyson's palm made it difficult to give orders. "We've got to go after them!"

"You're only half right," said Jasper. "Someone must go after them, it's true. But I intend to be that someone."

Admiral Westfield and Oliver hadn't paid any attention to the scuffle taking place behind them—there were at least two additional pirate scuffles on the street at that moment, so a third one must not have seemed worth noticing—and they had almost rounded the corner, out of Hilary's view. "They're getting away!" said the gargoyle, whipping his tail frantically to and fro.

"Yes, yes, I know." Jasper wiped the sweat from his brow. "Which of us is the Terror of the Southlands?" He let go of Hilary's shoulders and handed her his spade. "Now, listen carefully. I will deal with the admiral and Oliver. While I am doing that, *you* must find the treasure."

"But—"

"I'll hear no *but*s or *however*s," said Jasper, sounding discomfortingly like Miss Greyson. This, Hilary supposed, was what came of letting governesses sail about on pirate ships. "It's perfectly simple: One of us has to distract them while the others dig up the treasure. You know the map better than I do, and besides, I think you'd be wise to keep your distance from your father. With Miss Greyson's crochet hook and Charlie's sword, you should all be perfectly safe."

Hilary had never used a spade before—her mother's gardeners highly discouraged unauthorized digging on the grounds of Westfield House—and this one felt heavy and awkward in her hands. "But you can't fight them off singlehandedly, Jasper," she said. "Oliver never fights fairly, and you know Father. He's stubborn as an ox." An ox with a ship full of cannons at its disposal, Hilary thought.

"This whole plan is highly impractical," Miss Greyson agreed, "and there's only one solution I can see. Mr. Fletcher, I will help you distract the evildoers." She tugged her crochet hook from her bun, sending a shower of hairpins clattering down on the cobblestones. Even in her bathing costume, with her loose curls flowing over her shoulders, Hilary thought she looked terribly fearsome. "I'm useless at digging," she said, "and I believe Mr. Fletcher would benefit from having a bit of magic on his side."

Hilary stared at her. "You mean you won't come with me?"

In response, Miss Greyson behaved very oddly indeed: She bent down and kissed Hilary on the cheek. "I am confident," she said, "that you will do wonderfully well without a governess. Now, for goodness' sake, hurry along and find that treasure!"

Dear Hilary,

I must know at once: Is your ship still bound for Gunpowder Island?

If it is, you must tug on its reins and turn it around as fast as you can!

You will want to know why, of course, but a decent explanation would take far too long, and I'm afraid you would hardly believe it, so you will have to trust me when I tell you that something peculiar is going on, and Gunpowder Island seems to be at the center of it all. Oh dear, now Philomena is looking daggers at me, and I must get this message to the postal courier without her noticing. Do be careful, Hilary, and please stay away from Gunpowder Island!

Yours in haste,

Claire

POSTAL COURIER
COULD NOT DELIVER.
REASON: MISS WESTFIELD IS BELIEVED
TO BE ASHORE ON GUNPOWDER ISLAND.
IF SENDER THINKS POSTAL COURIER IS
SETTING FOOT ON THAT GODFORSAKEN ROCK,
SENDER MUST KINDLY THINK AGAIN.

CHAPTER FOURTEEN

ONE MOMENT, THE town square on Gunpowder Island (2)
was a pleasant, quiet open space. An elaborate marble Details
fountain burbled in the center of the square; skull-and-
crossbones flags hung cheerfully from open windows;
pirates strolled past, singing sea chanteys; and statues of
legendary sea captains watched over the whole scene. Near
the fountain, a man and a boy studied a map. To a casual
observer, they might have looked like travelers on a grand
tour of famous pirate hideaways. To Hilary, however, they
looked like danger. She would have been a bit less nervous
if Oliver had still been dressed as a beet.

The next moment, all was madness. Jasper ran toward
Admiral Westfield with his sword in hand, shouting all

sorts of words that were impolite even to think about in High Society. Miss Greyson was hot on his heels, clutching her crochet hook in one fist and swinging a spade wildly with the other. Admiral Westfield and Oliver looked up from their map. They looked at each other. They looked back at Jasper and Miss Greyson. Then they unsheathed their swords and began to shout unsavory sentiments of their own.

"Fletcher, you fiend!" cried Admiral Westfield. "And— my goodness, aren't you that horrid governess?"

"This man," Jasper called to the pirates who'd already gathered to watch the confrontation, "is the admiral of the Royal Navy, and an enemy to pirates everywhere!"

At once, several of the pirates in the square drew their own swords and leaped into the fray. Some of them fought alongside Jasper and Miss Greyson, but many of them didn't seem to care whose side they were on, and they brandished their weapons at anyone who happened to be within reach. Word traveled fast on Gunpowder Island, and within minutes the square was positively full of sword-waving pirates.

Hilary, Charlie, and the gargoyle watched the battle from behind a statue of a pirate who was portly enough to conceal all three of them. Hilary reminded herself that pirates were never squeamish, but there was something distinctly uncomfortable about watching Jasper and Miss Greyson go into battle against her father. She didn't want them to lose, of course . . . but what would happen to Admiral Westfield if they won? She shook her head in an attempt to clear that particular thought from her mind. Miss Greyson and Jasper had charged her with finding the treasure, and she did not intend to disappoint them.

The gargoyle poked Hilary with his tail. "What do we do now?"

Hilary closed her eyes and pictured the treasure map. "We've got to count out ninety paces from the statue," she said, "heading north."

"That sounds easy enough," said Charlie. "But which statue?" Dozens of statues filled the town square, and none of them looked like a particularly suitable starting point for a treasure hunt.

"Maybe the Enchantress chose the statue she liked best. Like that one." Hilary pointed to a polished stone sea captain a few yards away. "He looks quite trustworthy."

Charlie coughed. "Trust me," he said. "It's not that statue; I'm certain of it."

"But you haven't even looked at it!" Hilary tucked her spade under one arm and the gargoyle under the other. Then she hurried through the crowd of battling pirates to the sea-captain statue and knelt down to examine the words carved into its base.

"'Nat Dove,'" Hilary read aloud. "'Scourge of the Northlands.'"

The gargoyle's ears drooped.

"The Enchantress wouldn't have known about this statue," Charlie said behind them. "Pa only died ten years ago, and her treasure was hidden long before that."

"Oh, Charlie, I'm sorry. He must have been a very great pirate." Hilary looked up at the statue of Charlie's pa. His stone arms crossed his chest, and his stone mouth was pressed into a stubborn line, but she decided his eyes looked friendly. "He looks a bit like you."

"Not really," said Charlie. "Everyone said I looked more like my mam. She should have a statue of her own, but the VNHLP wouldn't allow it."

"When you're Scourge of the Northlands someday, I'm sure they'll change their minds," said Hilary.

"They'd better," said Charlie. "But if I'm going to be Scourge of the Northlands, we've got to find that treasure. I don't want to embarrass myself with my pa looking on."

"I understand completely." The pirate battle had grown fiercer than ever around them, and a small part of Hilary wished she could abandon her hiding place and dash across the square with her sword glinting in the sun, like a hero out of a pirate yarn. *That* would have given her father and Oliver something to think about.

The gargoyle had apparently been thinking about something, too. "If the Enchantress hid her treasure a long time ago," he said slowly, "shouldn't we look for a really old statue? That one over there is even more crumbly than

I am." He jabbed his tail toward a worn and weathered statue standing to one side of the town square.

"Good thinking, gargoyle," said Hilary. The gargoyle bowed and looked terribly pleased with himself.

Jasper and Miss Greyson had managed to lead the battle down a side street, so no pirates gave Hilary or Charlie any trouble as they crossed the square to the ancient-looking statue. When they'd drawn close enough to make out its features, the gargoyle gasped. Then, quite without warning, he began to flap his wings and wriggle about.

"Whatever is the matter?" said Hilary.

"Don't you see?" The gargoyle wriggled so fiercely that he nearly tore a hole in Hilary's sleeve. "It's the Enchantress!"

Time and weather had worn away the statue's features, and generations of pirates had scraped their swords against its surface, but unlike the other statues in the square, this one wasn't wearing a billowing coat or breeches, and it certainly didn't have a three-cornered hat atop its head. In fact, it seemed to be wearing a gown. On its polished face, Hilary could just make out the trace of a thin-lipped smile. The smile was familiar, and why shouldn't it be? She'd passed that smile—or a stained-glass version of it, at least—nearly every day of her life in the halls of Westfield House. At the base of the statue, Hilary could just make out the faint imprint of a figure eight.

Charlie began to laugh. "Of course," he said. "I'm beginning to think the Enchantress was awfully interested in herself."

Hilary thought back to the treasure map and groaned. "Oh dear. She actually drew a picture of herself on the map, you know, right at the place where the path to the treasure began. It must have been a clue." She rapped the statue's left foot hard with her knuckles; missing a clue on a treasure map was hardly piratical behavior. "This is the starting place; I'm sure of it."

Aside from a few pirates watching the battle through their spyglasses, the path due north from the statue was clear enough. Hilary handed her spade to Charlie, who rested it on his shoulder. "Now," she said, "we've got to pace."

A GOOD PIRATE always knows which way is north, and Hilary and Charlie paced in that direction, counting each step together under their breaths. The gargoyle tried to count, too, but he got confused somewhere around forty-six. "I've never been much good at counting," he complained. "It's because I don't have hands."

Counting out ninety northward paces didn't seem terribly difficult at first, but Hilary soon realized that she had no idea how large an Enchantress-sized pace might be. The Enchantress had probably been taller than Hilary—most people seemed to be—but what if she'd had uncommonly short legs? The gargoyle said that the Enchantress had been taller than *him*, but that was not much help either. Eventually, Hilary decided to match Charlie's paces, which were a bit longer than her own.

By the sixty-seventh pace, however, she began to worry that she'd miscalculated badly. A high, sand-colored brick wall bordered the town square, leaving gaps only for the streets that radiated out from the square like spokes in a wheel. No street lay in front of the treasure hunters, however, and the wall was fast approaching. They'd never be able to take twenty-three more steps without smashing their noses against the bricks, and that was sure to cause a scene among the handful of onlooking pirates. Hilary could practically feel the weight of their spyglasses on her already.

The seventy-ninth step brought them up to the wall. "It must not have been around in the Enchantress's day," Charlie said.

Hilary looked back at the statue of the Enchantress. "I'm sure we're going in the right direction. We'll just have to climb over the wall and start counting again on the other side." But the wall was very high, and the bricks were smooth, with hardly any helpful juts or crags to assist hopeful climbers. Charlie tried to lift Hilary over the wall, and then Hilary tried to lift Charlie, and then the gargoyle insisted on trying to lift them both with his snout. No matter how high they stretched, however, they couldn't come close to reaching the top.

"Oh dear," said the gargoyle after Hilary and Charlie had crashed down on the ground beside him for the third time in a row. "I think I've bruised my snout."

"Don't worry," said Hilary. She scooped up the gargoyle and gave his snout a little pat. "All self-respecting pirates are simply covered in battle scars."

Charlie kicked at the wall with the toe of his boot. Then he tried to chip away at the bricks with his sword, but he only succeeded in creating a good deal of dust. "I blame the Enchantress," he said, "and her blasted magic. If she magicked this wall, we haven't got a hope of getting over it."

The gargoyle hopped closer to the wall and wiggled his ears experimentally. "It doesn't *feel* like magic," he said at last. "And I'm sure the Enchantress wouldn't have wanted to make things harder for us. She was a very thoughtful person."

Hilary ran her fingers over the bricks in the wall, searching for any small crack or bump that might make a decent foothold for climbing. At last her hand bumped into a square-shaped brick that stuck out a few inches more than the others. It didn't look like it could possibly hold her weight, but she pressed her hands against the wall and placed her foot carefully on the edge of the brick.

The brick spun wildly under Hilary's boot, and she tumbled to the ground. "That foothold's no good, then," said Charlie. "Curse that Enchantress!"

"Wait a moment," said Hilary. "There's something very strange about this brick." She brushed it with her palm, and it spun under her hand like a loose doorknob.

The only natural thing to do with a doorknob was to turn it, so Hilary did just that. It made a soft crunching noise as she spun it clockwise, and the whole wall creaked as she pressed her shoulder against the bricks. Slowly, letting loose the scent of moss and earth, a small door opened inward.

"A secret passage!" said the gargoyle. "Oh boy! Let me at it!" Without a moment's hesitation, he hopped through the doorway.

Charlie seemed to have cheered considerably. "We'd better go after the gargoyle," he said, "before he digs up the treasure for himself."

The doorway was large enough for a pirate to squeeze through, though not much larger, and Charlie had to remove his hat as he crawled into the passage. When they had both reached the other side of the wall, Hilary pulled the door shut to discourage curious pirates or angry Royal Navy admirals from following them to the treasure.

When she stood up again and brushed the brick dust from her breeches, she found she was standing in a garden. An overgrown lawn stretched before her, and delicate yellow and blue flowers sprang up from the grass, determined to claim every spare inch of soil as their own. More

Gunpowder Island roses bloomed here, too, scrambling up the garden walls. A wooden swing hung from a tree with leaf-covered limbs reaching in every direction, and the air hummed with the summer buzz of bees. At the far end of the garden, a jumble of stones cast mossy shadows over the ground. Perhaps a great mansion had stood here once, long ago, before the days of pirates.

"Where are we?" Hilary whispered, for it seemed right to whisper in this place. It was nothing like the manicured lawns of Westfield House, where her mother's gardeners constantly reminded Hilary that swordplay in the flower-beds was strictly forbidden. It had been a long time, Hilary guessed, since a gardener had bothered to scold anyone here.

"It's pretty enough," said the gargoyle, "if you like flowers and that sort of thing. But I don't know—it still doesn't feel like magic. Are you sure the treasure's nearby?"

"Yes, it's got to be." Hilary stood with her back against the wall and counted off the last of the ninety northward paces. "All right. Now it's fifty paces toward the ash tree." She looked around the garden at the trees that lined its borders—green and brown and golden-leaved, wide and bushy, thin and creaky. "What does an ash tree look like?" she said at last. "I don't believe Miss Greyson ever tried to teach me about nature."

"It's that huge old tree, the one with the swing," said

Charlie. "They grew all around our house in the North-lands."

Hilary turned to face the ash tree. "Fifty paces, then." She tried as hard as she could to keep from wobbling as she paced, but her legs were growing shakier by the second. How many pirates had tried to find the Enchantress's lost treasure? However many had tried, they'd all gone home empty-handed. But now that very treasure was only fifty, forty-nine, forty-eight paces away. As they walked, Charlie told treasure-hunting stories he'd heard from his mam and pa, and the gargoyle wondered aloud if they would get their pictures in the *Queensport Gazette*, or if the VNHLP might commission a statue for Gunpowder Island in recognition of the kingdom's most heroic gargoyle. There were thirty paces left to walk, and then there were only twenty. The ground under Hilary's feet felt soft and earthy—easy to dig. Ten paces left. Hilary began to count out loud, slowly and precisely, and Charlie and the gargoyle soon joined in. At last, in the shadow of the ash tree, they stopped pacing.

Hilary looked down at the gargoyle. "Is this the spot?" she asked. "Does it feel like magic to you?"

The gargoyle wrinkled his snout. "I don't feel anything yet," he said. "It must be covered by a whole lot of dirt."

"In that case," said Charlie, sinking the spade into the ground, "there's nothing to do but uncover it."

Hilary and Charlie passed the spade back and forth

between them, and the gargoyle assisted by scooping up bits of earth with his tail. "Which do you think sounds better," he said, "National Gargoyle Day? Or National Day of the Gargoyle?" He flipped another tailful of dirt over his shoulder. "I want to be prepared when the queen creates a holiday in honor of me."

"I think," said Hilary, "that National *Pirate* Day would be more suitable."

The gargoyle harrumphed. "And watch where you're throwing that dirt," he said. "You nearly got some in my mouth, and it doesn't taste as good as you'd think."

They dug in silence for a while. The pit in the garden grew deeper and wider, until Hilary feared they'd reach the fiery core of the globe before they reached the treasure. "My arms are so sore," said Charlie, "that they might fall off at any moment. And then where will I be?" He passed the spade to Hilary and rubbed at his shoulder. "There are plenty of pirates missing a leg, but who's ever heard of a pirate with no arms?"

"It's not so bad," said the gargoyle, "once you get used to it."

Charlie and the gargoyle were still discussing the ideal number of arms for a pirate to possess when Hilary's spade struck something hard. "Hush for a moment, both of you!" she said. "I think I've hit something."

"Probably just another rock." The gargoyle rolled his eyes toward the large pile of rocks they'd already collected.

"No, this one feels different." Hilary tapped her spade against the thing in the earth, and it clanged distinctly. "It sounds different, too; I think it's metal." She scrambled farther into the pit and brushed away the dirt from the top of the object. Silver bands gleamed in the sunlight—silver bands wrapped around a wooden frame that looked for all the world like a treasure chest.

"We've done it!" the gargoyle cried. "The treasure is ours! Huzzah!" He hopped closer to Hilary and planted a chilly granite kiss on her nose. "We're the greatest pirates in the land!"

"And the finest on the High Seas," Charlie added.

"Yes, we are," said Hilary. "I'm afraid it can't be denied."

Then they all stared down at the treasure chest.

"No more finishing school," said Hilary.

"No more bathing caps," said the gargoyle.

"No more worrying about the blasted navy," said Charlie. "They'll put statues of us in the town square for sure." He cleared his throat. "But we'd better get this chest back to Jasper's house before old Westfield figures out what's happened."

THEY HAD JUST cleared the last of the dirt away from the treasure chest when, with a great deal of banging and panting, Jasper and Miss Greyson burst into the garden. The crochet hook in Miss Greyson's outstretched hand appeared to be tugging them along toward Hilary. "There you are!" said Miss Greyson. "Thank goodness."

Hilary waved at them. "Come quickly! We've found the treasure!"

Jasper ran to her, picked her up, and swung her about. "Well done!" he cried. Then he swung Charlie, Miss Greyson, and the gargoyle about, too. "And we've left Westfield and Oliver facedown in a (pig trough) halfway across the island. They're hopping mad, of course, but it should take them a while to recover their breath." ③ pig food dish pic.

"And," said Miss Greyson, "we borrowed this." From the sleeve of her bathing costume, she retrieved the treasure map and handed it to Jasper. "I suppose we won't be needing it now, but it should make it much more difficult for the navy to find us while we're hauling up this treasure."

With the help of Jasper and Miss Greyson, it took only a few moments to pick up the treasure chest and slide it out of the pit. "It's an awfully small box to hold most of the magic in the kingdom," said the gargoyle. He tapped it with his tail. "Can we open it now?"

Jasper said he didn't see why not, and Miss Greyson agreed that it would be (prudent) to examine the treasure before setting off for home, just to make sure everything was in order. "As long as the magic is out of Westfield's hands," said Jasper, "I don't care if it's shaped like ten thousand golden elephants." With his sword, he sliced off the chest's padlock. "Then I shall sail to every town in Augusta

④ Just, right or nobel

to give all the folks their fair share of magic, and perhaps they'll name a holiday after me. How does Jasper Fletcher Day sound to you all?"

"Ridiculous," said Charlie.

"Conceited," said Miss Greyson.

"Definitely not as good as National Day of the Gargoyle," said the gargoyle.

"Just open the treasure chest!" said Hilary.

And Jasper did.

A CLOUD OF dust escaped from the chest, and a large, irritated-looking moth followed close on the dust's heels. Jasper swatted the moth away, and they all leaned forward around the chest.

"But it's empty!" said the gargoyle. "Treasure chests aren't supposed to be empty, are they?"

Hilary squeezed her eyes shut in the hopes that when she opened them again, the Enchantress's treasure would magically appear. But the dusty wooden slats at the base of the treasure chest refused to disappear under a pile of coins and loot. "No," she said. "They are *not* supposed to be empty."

Charlie sat back on his heels and stared at the empty chest. "I don't know what's going on," he said, "but whatever it is, it's completely rotten."

"You're certainly right about that." A tall, white-haired woman strode through the garden toward them.

Her braid circled her head like a crown, and on the collar of her purple silk jacket she wore a pin in the shape of a dancing sheep. There could be no doubt: Miss Pimm had arrived on Gunpowder Island.

Behind her stood Oliver and Admiral Westfield. Oliver wasn't smirking anymore, and both of them looked bruised, bedraggled, and slightly embarrassed to be surrounded by a gaggle of Miss Pimm's girls, who stood stern and fearsome in their matching woolen dresses and green cardigans. Hilary searched the crowd for Claire but couldn't make her out. (5) Gaggle of geese

Miss Pimm herself reached the pirates first. She looked them up and down. Her gaze settled for a moment on Hilary, and a thin, familiar, stained-glass smile flickered across her lips. "I'm afraid," she said at last, "that you have all behaved rather poorly." She crossed her arms and shook her head. "It simply cannot be tolerated."

Collective nown
Special for geese
Rubbits:
Birds: Flalk
Lions: Pride
elephant: herde
kittens: kindle
Wolves: Pack
Dancers: Tropp
etc.

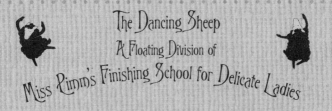

The Dancing Sheep
A Floating Division of
Miss Pimm's Finishing School for Delicate Ladies

Dear Queen Adelaide,

You may be quite surprised to hear from me, for we have never met. In fact, you may be under the impression that I no longer exist. I assure you, however, that this impression is false: I am alive and well, though I trust you will not advertise the fact to anyone beyond your closest royal advisers.

Since my retirement, I have not paid much attention to magical misdeeds in the kingdom. Such matters were, I believed, best left in the care of the royal inspectors. The recent string of magical thefts caught my interest, however, and I soon learned that your inspectors were making quite a hash of the investigation, so I decided to take matters into my own hands. I would have preferred to stay out of the mess entirely, but it seemed to be rather serious. Besides, one can't always do exactly as one likes, even when one is as old as I am.

I created a little trap to lure in the villains, and I must admit that I took the opportunity to amuse myself. (After all, one rarely has the chance to use invisible ink in the course of running a finishing school!) I am pleased to inform you that the trap has been a great success, and I have caught the scoundrels responsible for the magical thefts. You will not be surprised to hear that they are pirates, and they are quite a nasty lot—both thieves and kidnappers! They are led by one Jasper Fletcher, who is known to be the Terror of the Southlands. I trust the Royal Dungeons have sufficient security to keep him locked up for quite some time.

I have not yet recovered the stolen magical items, but Admiral Westfield has kindly offered to help me in this endeavor. We sail for Pemberton immediately.

@Activity

Your humble servant,

Eugenia Pimm
Enchantress of the Northlands (Retired)

an extract *From*
Treasure Hunting for Beginners:
THE OFFICIAL VNHLP GUIDE

WHAT TO DO IF YOU ARE **CAPTURED**:

Are you really so careless that you have been captured in the act of obtaining treasure? Are you entirely sure that you are cut out for piracy? We at the VNHLP are gravely concerned. Don't expect us to risk our necks rescuing you. You will have to get yourself out of this one on your own. *Stupidity, Lack of ability or ignorance* ⑦

Of course, since you have proven your (incompetence) in piracy by getting captured, it is highly unlikely that you will be able to escape. If you inform the VNHLP of your new address in the Royal Dungeons, we will send you greeting cards on your birthday and major holidays. Membership in the VNHLP is, of course, (revoked) upon your capture. If you are proven innocent, you may reapply for membership, but it is best to face the facts: you are a pirate, and pirates are never innocent. ⑧ *cancled*

CHAPTER FIFTEEN

dubling

"WHO," SAID JASPER, "is this terrifying woman?"

"It's Miss Pimm," said Hilary, at the same moment as the gargoyle said, "It's the Enchantress!"

Miss Pimm smiled and extended her hand to Jasper. "Both of your companions are correct," she said, "although their manners leave a good deal to be desired."

Hilary stared at her. "You're the Enchantress of the Northlands?"

"You mustn't let your mouth hang open like that, my dear," Miss Pimm replied, "unless you care to swallow a fly. I *was* the Enchantress. I am now retired." She paused. "My goodness, is that the gargoyle I carved for Simon Westfield? I haven't seen you in centuries. You must be the fearsome beast I've heard so much about."

Hilary picked up the gargoyle, who was beaming at Miss Pimm. "You used to look a lot younger," he said.

"So I did," said Miss Pimm with a sniff. "And I believe you had a full set of limbs when I saw you last."

"Simon Westfield?" said Hilary to the gargoyle. "The same Simon Westfield we've got in our stained-glass window at home? The aeronaut?" Claire had mentioned once that Miss Pimm had fallen in love with an aeronaut, but Hilary hadn't imagined he might have been one of her long-ago ancestors. And Simon Westfield had died over two hundred years ago! "You never told me you knew Simon Westfield."

The gargoyle shrugged. "There's not much to tell. He hardly ever came to visit me on my wall. And he wasn't very chatty."

Jasper had turned to Miss Pimm. "Forgive me for asking such an indelicate question," he said, "but how is it possible that you are the Enchantress of the Northlands? You'd have to be, er—"

"Two hundred and thirty-eight years old," Miss Pimm interrupted. "All I can say is that my work keeps me young." She nodded to the girls behind her. "Well, that and the magic, of course."

Charlie had ducked behind Hilary at the sight of an approaching army of finishing-school girls, but now he stepped forward. "If you really are the Enchantress," he

① Ridiculous

said, "why don't you tell us where your treasure is? It's obviously not here." He kicked the empty treasure chest.

But Miss Pimm simply laughed. "I've kept that information under lock and key for the past two hundred years," she said, "and it would be (absurd) to share it now, especially with a pirate." She peered down her nose at Charlie. "Aren't you a bit young to be a pirate, my boy? Shouldn't you be in school?"

Charlie tried to protest, but Miss Pimm had no intention of pausing. "And Miss Westfield," she said, turning to Hilary, "I can't tell you what a relief it is to find you safe and sound! I can only imagine how harrowing your kidnapping must have been. Abducted by common thieves! It's lucky you had the gargoyle to protect you. But never fear—we'll have you back at finishing school in three shakes of a lamb's tail. Your father must be just as relieved as I am. Why don't you go say hello to him, dear?"

happen quickly

Behind Miss Pimm, Admiral Westfield tugged at his collar and frowned. When Miss Pimm turned to look at him, however, he summoned up a feeble smile and opened his arms. "Ever so good to see you, Hilary," he said. "Been terribly worried, of course."

Hilary held on tightly to Miss Greyson's hand. "I'm afraid there's been a mistake," she said. "I wasn't kidnapped. I ran away, and it certainly wasn't Jasper's fault, or Charlie's or Miss Greyson's, either. Besides, they're not thieves." Hilary glanced at the stolen treasure map in Jasper's hand.

"Not usually, at least. They're pirates—and so am I."

Miss Pimm stepped forward and pried Hilary's hand out of Miss Greyson's grasp. "Oh, my dear," she said. "A sweet young girl like yourself a pirate? I know you've had a terribly confusing time, but you mustn't let these criminals addle your brain any more." Hilary tried to wriggle free, but Miss Pimm was surprisingly strong. She pushed Hilary forward into the waiting arms of Admiral Westfield, who smelled of tobacco and pig trough.

At this, Jasper drew his sword. "Let her go, you miserable—" he began, but at a gesture from Miss Pimm, the girls behind her raised their golden crochet hooks and murmured a muddle of polite-sounding requests. Jasper dropped his sword as though it had burned him. Charlie reached for his own sword in response, but his arm froze in midair, and Miss Greyson muttered a pirate curse as her hand came to a halt halfway to her crochet hook. None of them seemed to be able to lift their feet from the ground.

Hilary wished she could run to them, but Admiral Westfield held her tightly. How could Miss Pimm approve of such shocking behavior? Her girls were acting even more abominably than the burly pirate in Middleby had; no decent pirate would engage in such an unfair fight. "Please, Miss Pimm," she said, "you've got to let them go."

"I'm afraid," said Miss Pimm, "that the only place these scallywags will be going is the Royal Dungeons."

"The Dungeons?" Jasper sputtered. "And what, pray

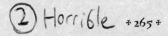
(2) Horrible ⁕265⁕

tell, have we done to deserve such treatment?"

Miss Pimm walked calmly in a circle around Jasper. "I should think it's perfectly obvious. You've been stealing magical objects from Augusta's most noble citizens for months. I've heard reports that a man and a boy have been involved in these thefts, and it's clear that you"—she gestured to Jasper and Charlie—"are the villains in question. I must admit that I don't know what you're planning to do with the magic you've stolen, but as you're the Terror of the Southlands, Mr. Fletcher, I assume it can't be anything good."

"But, Enchantress," said the gargoyle, "they haven't—"

"Don't bother defending the pirates, my dear gargoyle; it's no use. The very fact that they are here is evidence enough of their guilt. When I set out to catch these villains, I asked myself what a thief of magic would most desire. The largest stash of magic in Augusta seemed to be rather a safe bet, so I set loose a rumor that my treasure had surfaced at last. Then I drew up a map—the very map you hold in your hand, Mr. Fletcher—and sent it to a small museum in Queensport, where the guards simply sat back and waited for it to be stolen. I should congratulate you, Mr. Fletcher, for conducting the theft in very short order. I hoped my little game would lure the thieves to this spot so I could catch them in the act of stealing magic—and my hopes have been rewarded, for here you stand."

"A brilliant trap. Well done, Miss Pimm," said Admiral Westfield. "Well done indeed!"

Hilary spun around to face him. "Don't be ridiculous! You know perfectly well that *you're* the one who stole the map in the first place; you're the one who's been stealing the kingdom's magic. If anyone should be sent to the Royal Dungeons, it's you and Oliver!"

Admiral Westfield stepped back as though Hilary had struck him. "Don't you dare speak that way," he said quietly. "I am your father, and I will not have you spreading wicked tales about me." He looked at Miss Pimm and shrugged. "I apologize for the girl's behavior," he said. "This is what comes of spending time with pirates."

"I certainly understand," said Miss Pimm. "Actually, James, I must admit that I had my own suspicions about you at first. I had heard you were planning a treasure-hunting expedition to Gunpowder Island, and—well, you can imagine my reaction." Miss Pimm looked modestly down at her dancing-sheep pin. "Now, of course, I see that you were simply trying to track Mr. Fletcher down yourself. I would expect no less from a Westfield, and I commend you for doing your best to stop these pirates."

Admiral Westfield gave a little bow. "I'm proud to serve my queen and country."

"Oh," said Hilary, "this is all utter nonsense!" She reached down to draw her own sword, but the scabbard was empty: her father had removed the sword and tucked it into his own belt.

"Such a weapon is far too dangerous for a young lady," he said. "I'm sure you'll learn that when you're settled back at Miss Pimm's." He reached out to pat Hilary on the head, but just as his palm touched her hair, he yelped and drew back his arm. "What the devil?" he cried. "Your blasted pet rock sank his fangs into me!"

"Really? How dreadful." Hilary held the gargoyle well out of Admiral Westfield's reach. "His teeth must have slipped."

Miss Pimm frowned. "This is becoming a most uncivilized gathering. Girls, please collect the villains." Philomena and another tall, silky-haired girl in a cardigan tied thick ropes around Jasper's wrists and then Charlie's, using clumsy knots entirely unsuited to the task. "You'll want to secure Eloise Greyson as well," said Miss Pimm. "It pains me, Eloise, to see a Miss Pimm's girl come to this. No matter how dashing Mr. Fletcher might be, there is simply no excuse for being seduced into a life of villainy."

Miss Greyson looked very small inside the vast sleeves and pleats of her bathing costume, and she seemed to shrink even more when Philomena plucked the golden crochet hook from Miss Greyson's hair. "I suppose you won't believe a word I say," Miss Greyson said, "but I promise you, no good will come of this."

Miss Pimm clapped her hands together. "Well done,

girls. And well done, Admiral Westfield. The kingdom is safe once more. I'll have Mr. Fletcher and Miss Greyson shipped directly to the Royal Dungeons, and as for the lad"—she pointed at Charlie—"he is quite young, and he may still be cured of his villainy. I shall have to keep an eye on him until I can secure a place for him at the Queensport Academy for Difficult Boys."

"You wouldn't!" cried Charlie. "It's worse than the Dungeons!"

"Nonsense," said Miss Pimm. "You'll be polished up and fit for High Society in no time at all. Now, we mustn't linger on Gunpowder Island—there's no telling what nasty habits one might pick up here. Let us depart at once."

As Miss Pimm marched her captives through the winding streets of Gunpowder Island, pirates stood in gutters and poked their heads out of windows to see what all the fuss was about. They did not, however, charge into battle against Miss Pimm. In fact, some of them seemed to be snickering.

Hilary worked herself free from Miss Pimm's arm and ran over to Jasper. "How are you?" she whispered.

Jasper winced. "Pained."

Hilary wondered whether his pain was caused by the rope at his wrists, by the indignity of capture, or by standing too close to Philomena. "Why aren't the other pirates helping us? Shouldn't they be dashing to our rescue?"

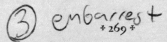

③ embarrest

"Pirates are only loyal," said Jasper, "when it's convenient. Consorting with captured pirates wouldn't do much for these fellows' image, would it? Besides, they're most likely all drooling at the thought of being the new Terror of the Southlands."

"Oh, don't say such things! You won't really be thrown into the Royal Dungeons, will you? You haven't done anything wrong; the queen must realize that."

"Ah, but I'm a pirate," said Jasper. "And Miss Pimm seems like the sort of woman who often gets her way."

"I'll talk to her; surely when she hears the truth——"

"Hilary." Jasper's voice was quiet but fierce. "You mustn't worry about me. I will be fine, and so will Eloise. But Westfield's still on the loose, and I'd bet my breeches that he'll be trying to get his hands on the Enchantress's treasure—the real one, that is. He's got to be stopped. I'd love to do the honors myself, of course, but as I happen to be a bit tied up at the moment, *you* must stop him."

Hilary nearly tripped over a cobblestone. How could she possibly stop her father on her own, when she was barely capable of convincing him to join the rest of the family for tea?

"A good pirate fights back," said Jasper, "and a good pirate finds treasure. Now you must be a good pirate— no, an *excellent* pirate—and find that treasure before your father does."

"I will," said Hilary. "I promise. And I'll clear your name, and free you and Miss Greyson, and get Charlie out of that horrid school—"

"That's all very kind, but finding the treasure will suffice for the moment. You must be the Terror of the Southlands in my place."

Hilary hesitated. "You do mean temporarily, don't you?"

"Of course," said Jasper, "though if you do find that dratted treasure, you'll be more worthy of the title than I am. But there is one more favor I have to ask of you. Will you look after Fitzwilliam? He doesn't do well in dark, dank places, and I fear the Royal Dungeons are both dark and dank."

The gargoyle groaned in Hilary's arms. "As if things weren't bad enough, we're stuck with that featherbrain? Are you kidding me?"

Hilary told the gargoyle to hush. "It's the least I can do," she said. "Fitzwilliam will be safe with me." She held out her arm, and Fitzwilliam hopped onto her shoulder, digging his claws in tight. Hilary supposed he was enjoying this new arrangement about as much as the gargoyle was.

They had reached the harbor, and Admiral Westfield cursed at the sight of the *Augusta Belle*. The VNHLP had peppered it with cannonballs, and the navy's fastest ship was sinking stern-first into Gunpowder Bay. "How inconvenient," said Miss Pimm. "But never mind, Admiral. You and your apprentice may travel with me, and I suppose we'll have to bring the captives on board as well. I do hope they won't tread mud on the carpets."

A fleet of delicate green rowboats waited to ferry them to the *Dancing Sheep*. "This way, pirate," said Philomena, dragging Jasper away with one hand and flipping her hair with the other. She looked over her shoulder at Hilary and wrinkled her nose. "I'll see you on board, Miss Westfield."

"Not if I can help it," said Hilary. Then Miss Pimm descended upon her once more, and she was swept up in a great deal of rose-scented purple fabric, which made it quite impossible to catch a glimpse of her friends as the little green boats floated out to sea.

THE *DANCING SHEEP* was nothing like the *Pigeon*. Silver curlicues decorated the railings all around the ship, and both the port and starboard sides were lined with benches cushioned in thick green velvet. On the lower deck, a vast dining room was set with crystal goblets and china plates that jangled against one another whenever the boat rocked to and fro. And on the upper deck was a sunny dormitory stacked high with bunk beds, each one dressed in crisp white linen.

Hilary couldn't stand it. Neither could the gargoyle. "There's no Gargoyle's Nest!" he said, burying his head under the down pillow on Hilary's bunk. "This is no place for pirates! Arr!" He sniffled. "My *arrs* don't even sound right here."

Hilary patted the gargoyle's back, but she didn't know what she could possibly say to console him. He was right to be miserable: Jasper and Miss Greyson were trapped belowdecks, and Charlie was locked in a tiny cabin guarded by girls with golden crochet hooks. Fitzwilliam had settled himself on the bunk above Hilary's, where he squawked and pecked at anyone who came near him. Gunpowder Island was little more than a blur on the horizon, and thanks to the vast supply of crochet hooks on board, the *Dancing Sheep* sped cheerfully toward Pemberton, Miss Pimm's, and a life piled high with doilies and doldrums. "Move aside, gargoyle," she said at last. "I'm joining you under that pillow."

Before she could do so, however, the dormitory door flew open, and someone collided quite enthusiastically with Hilary's rib cage.

"Oh, Hilary, is that you? It is, isn't it! Thank goodness you're all right!" Claire removed her arms from Hilary's middle. "I've been desperately worried. I haven't slept for *days*, or eaten much; the ship's food is terribly salty, and you can probably imagine all of the fish jokes I've been enduring out here on the High Seas. But never mind that; it's wonderful to see you! I'm ever so glad you're not a criminal."

Claire looked so earnest that Hilary laughed and hugged her back. "It's a good thing you're here. The gargoyle and I are rather in the depths of despair at the moment."

"It's all disastrous," the gargoyle agreed. "Scratch my head, please, Claire. I missed you."

As Claire scratched the gargoyle thoroughly behind the ears, Hilary gave a full account of her adventures, beginning with her interview with Jasper and ending with the horrible capture on Gunpowder Island. Claire was thoughtful enough to react dramatically at all the right moments, gasping when she learned of Admiral Westfield's villainy and cheering when Hilary knocked Orange Mustache unconscious with a tin of beets. But when Hilary described how Miss Pimm had accused Jasper and Miss Greyson of stealing magic, Claire punched a pillow so ferociously that it exploded into feathers.

"It's not fair!" she cried. "Putting those virtuous pirates in jail, and letting the rotten admiral get away with—oh, I'm so sorry, Hilary; I didn't mean—"

"It's quite all right," said Hilary. "He *is* rotten; this whole mess is rotten."

"I wish I'd been there—on Gunpowder Island, I mean." Claire brushed a few feathers from her cardigan. "I would have given them all a piece of my mind. It was terribly thrilling when Miss Pimm told us all that we were on a mission to protect the kingdom, but then she said the villains were pirates heading for Gunpowder Island, and I knew at once that it must be *you*, and I got into quite a row with Philomena over it, and she made me stay in the kitchen washing oatmeal pots instead of coming to save you, and you *know* how difficult it is to scrub dried oatmeal off things when they haven't even been soaked first!" She collapsed backward onto the bed. "But I don't have my golden crochet hook yet, and at this rate I never shall, so I suppose there's not much I could have done anyway. At least we'll be roommates again at Miss Pimm's; there's the bright spot in all of this."

"I suppose so," said Hilary, but it seemed like a very dim bright spot indeed. Miss Pimm's was no place for a pirate, and neither were the Royal Dungeons. If only she had her sword, or a golden crochet hook of her own, or any inkling at all of where the Enchantress's treasure might be . . .

The door banged open again. Philomena leaned against the door frame, looking bored. "Message for you, Miss Westfield," she said. "Your father wants to see you in his cabin at once."

Claire gave Hilary's hand a sympathetic squeeze. "I'll look after the gargoyle for you," she said. "After all, there's no need for both of you to go through torture."

PIRATES RESPONSIBLE FOR MAGIC THEFTS CAPTURED AT LAST

GUNPOWDER ISLAND, AUGUSTA—Noble families throughout Queensport breathed a sigh of relief recently when Queen Adelaide announced that the villains responsible for a series of thefts in the area had been brought to justice. In a thoroughly unsurprising development, the Gazette has learned that these villains are pirates. The ringleader of the vicious gang is said to be Jasper Fletcher, a minor freelance ruffian. Accompanied by a rogue governess and a few other individuals of no importance whatsoever, Mr. Fletcher entered the great noble households of Queensport and absconded with magical objects of incalculable value. The Royal Treasury itself was a target of Mr. Fletcher's highly improper operation to steal Augusta's magic.

"I, for one, am thrilled that these pirates will be

behind bars," said victim Admiral James Westfield, a fixture in High Society and a five-time recipient of the Soaring Ostrich Medal of Perseverance. "That's the proper place for pirates, if you ask me."

Captain Rupert Blacktooth, the president of the Very Nearly Honorable League of Pirates, denies any knowledge of Fletcher's scandalous actions. "Jasper Fletcher, eh?" said Blacktooth when asked to comment on the matter. "I hear he used to be the Terror of the Southlands, but that was a long time ago, and he must have lost his touch. No, I've never associated with him. I'm an honorable pirate! Or very nearly honorable, at any rate. Regardless, I assure you that the VNHLP had nothing to do with these shocking events."

Rumors that Fletcher and his gang were also responsible for the kidnapping of a sweet and innocent High Society girl have not been confirmed.

The Augusta Scuttlebutt

WHERE HIGH SOCIETY TURNS FOR SCANDAL

Everyone in Augusta knows that the Enchantress of the Northlands vanished two hundred years ago, but reports from a certain groggery on Gunpowder Island suggest that the Enchantress has returned to the kingdom! Our source claims he was enjoying his daily pint at the Sword and Seahorse when he caught sight of the Enchantress herself walking through the streets of Gunpowder Island, surrounded by pirates, naval officers, and schoolgirls.

We at the Scuttlebutt do not embarrass easily, but we find that we are blushing so warmly that we cannot continue to write this article. It is clearly nothing more than gossip of the lowest quality.

We apologize for wasting your time.

WE ASKED, YOU ANSWERED:
Do you think the Enchantress of the Northlands has returned?

"I hope so! Maybe if we had a real Enchantress again, she'd make sure everyone in the kingdom had a fair share of magic."—L. REDFERN, PEMBERTON

"She won't try to keep me from treasure huntin', will she? If ye muck about in the affairs of pirates, yer sure to find yerself walkin' the plank. That goes for Enchantresses, same as the rest."—B. McCorkle, Middleby

"If the Enchantress really has returned, I hope she's planning to give back all the magic she took from us. All my family's got left is a magic cheese knife, and it doesn't even cut cheese very well."—T. Garcia, Summerstead

"I don't care to have an Enchantress interfering with my private life and stopping me from doing as I please. I dearly hope the Enchantress has not returned—and if she has, she had better stay away from my antique magic shoehorn."
—G. Tilbury, Nordholm

"How did you get on this ship? Remove yourself at once!"—E. Pimm, Pemberton

CHAPTER SIXTEEN

HILARY FOUND ADMIRAL Westfield waiting for her in the cabin Miss Pimm had lent him, which had formerly been occupied by the embroidery mistress. He sat stiffly among heart-shaped cushions on a small pink sofa adorned with ruffles, and when Hilary entered the cabin, he did not stand up. The hearts and ruffles surrounding him did very little to soften the expression on his face.

For a moment, Hilary wanted nothing more than to turn around and dash back through the cabin door, but such behavior hardly suited the temporary Terror of the Southlands. She would have to do her best to behave as Jasper would—without most of the cursing and grog swilling, of course. She settled herself on a round pink tuffet across from Admiral Westfield. "You wanted to speak with me, Father?" Large pillow

Admiral Westfield picked up a ruffled bolster pillow and leaned forward. "Running away," he said, tapping the bolster pillow against his open palm for emphasis. "Con- Importance sorting with villains. Attempting to claim my treasure for yourself. And worst of all, going directly against my wishes. Hilary Westfield, I am deeply embarrassed. An admiral whose own daughter disobeys him—if this gets out, I'll never hear the end of it in High Society! And just think of your poor mother, who will surely faint when she hears of your impudence. I assure you, this is not how a young lady behaves herself."

Hilary steadied herself on the tuffet. "I know that, Father. It's how a pirate behaves herself."

"A pirate! Haven't you tired of that nonsense yet?" Admiral Westfield tossed the bolster pillow to the deck. "My dear, you must stop being foolish. You may have stowed away with those scoundrels—and how you managed that, I'll never know—but you are certainly not a pirate."

"I did quite a bit more than stow away! Why, I defeated your senior officer in a duel! And besides that—"

"I'll hear no more of it," said Admiral Westfield. "You're to return to finishing school and stay there until you've learned to behave like a young lady. I am fully aware that such a task may take decades, but I can't allow you to keep running about with the scum of the High Seas. Although I suppose I won't have to worry about that once I've abolished piracy."

Hilary sprang up from the tuffet, which went skittering across the deck behind her. "You couldn't!"

"Ah, but I could! And what's more, I will. Of course, I've still got to find that old biddy's treasure"—here Admiral Westfield frowned—"but once that's taken care of, I'll have enough magic to send the queen and her advisers somewhere damp and distant, and then piracy shall go down the drain at last." He propped his boots up on a heart-shaped cushion. "Pirates are the very height of impropriety, you know, always ignoring one's orders and trying to steal one's magic. I shall be the ruler who locks up those scallywags once and for all, and Augusta will be well rid of them."

Had her father thought Augusta was well rid of Charlie's mam and pa, then, when he'd sunk their ship and helped himself to their treasure? The thought lodged like a rough bit of hardtack in her throat. "I can't imagine," she said, "that the queen will be fond of being replaced."

Admiral Westfield shrugged. "I suppose not. But it is my duty, as a High Society gentleman, to do what is best for Augusta. Scoundrels mustn't be permitted to sail about freely with no regard for my authority, and magic can't be allowed to fall into untrustworthy hands. If the queen is unable to keep the kingdom shipshape and orderly, I must take charge of it myself. All for the good of Augusta, of course." The admiral leaned forward and dared to offer up a smile. "I imagine you understand that better than anyone, my dear. Haven't I always done what is best for you?"

It was fortunate, really, that Admiral Westfield had taken Hilary's sword away. Challenging one's own father to a duel would have been horribly improper, even by the standards of piracy. "You do realize," she said, "that I could leave this room right now and tell Miss Pimm exactly what you're up to."

"Of course you could, my dear," said Admiral Westfield, "but even the old biddy isn't foolish enough to listen to a child's fanciful stories."

This, Hilary realized, was most likely true. Even the Terror of the Southlands would need more than a good tale to convict the admiral of the Royal Navy of thievery. "Then I'll have Miss Pimm search Westfield House, and she'll find the magical objects you stole."

"Oh, come now. Do you think I'm foolish enough to store my treasure in my own home? Besides, if young Oliver does his job properly, several of those objects will soon decorate the shelves and tabletops of a certain bungalow. Twenty-Five Little Herring Cove is the address, is it not?"

He knew perfectly well that it was. "You intend to frame Jasper?"

"My dear, I do not *intend* to frame him. I *am* framing him."

"But that's horrible!"

"Perhaps," said Admiral Westfield, "but it is undeniably convenient. You know, I should pop down belowdecks and thank Fletcher for being the first to stumble into the old biddy's trap. I shudder to think how unpleasant it would have been if she'd caught me instead."

Hilary nearly pointed out that *she* had been the first to stumble into the Enchantress's trap, and Jasper had merely been following her lead, but this piece of information was hardly likely to impress Admiral Westfield. In fact, he seemed more impressed by the lace ruffles on the pink sofa than by Hilary. "I'm sorry, Father," she said, "but you must excuse me. I can't endure this conversation for another moment. As I will make every effort to avoid you for the rest of the voyage, I hope you have a pleasant journey." She strode to the door, letting the heels of her boots slap against the deck.

"All right," said Admiral Westfield. "Run along, then, and be a good little girl."

Hilary paused in the doorway. Surely Admiral Westfield would never tell the real Terror of the Southlands to be a good little girl. "If I'm going to be good," she said, "I'd prefer to be a good pirate."

Her father sighed. "I can't imagine what you mean by that."

"A good pirate finds treasure," said Hilary, "and a good pirate fights back."

THE FIRST STEP in fighting back, Hilary decided, was to alert Miss Pimm to her father's villainy. If anyone could capture Admiral Westfield and free the crew of the *Pigeon*, it was the Enchantress of the Northlands—even if she *was* retired. With Claire and the gargoyle by her side, and Fitzwilliam hovering anxiously over her head, Hilary rapped on the door to Miss Pimm's cabin.

The door swung open so suddenly that Hilary, Claire, the gargoyle, and Fitzwilliam all tumbled inside in a most uncivilized way. "My goodness," said Miss Pimm, "what a menagerie! Good afternoon, Miss Westfield, Miss Dupree, gargoyle." She looked up at Fitzwilliam. "Good afternoon, bird." collections of animals

Fitzwilliam squawked.

"This is most unusual." Miss Pimm shut the door and returned to the chair where she'd been working at embroidery. "Is there something I can do to help you all?"

"You can free my friends," said Hilary.

"And capture the villainous admiral," said Claire.

"And save the kingdom!" cried the gargoyle.

Miss Pimm frowned. "That does sound like quite a lot of work. Perhaps you'd better explain yourselves."

So Hilary did, accompanied by clarifications from the gargoyle and encouraging nods from Claire. But no matter what Hilary said to convince Miss Pimm that she had captured the wrong group of scallywags, Miss Pimm simply sighed and lifted her eyes toward the heavens. "Your father is an honorable gentleman," she said at last, "and a valued member of High Society. We have already captured the magic stealers and locked them belowdecks. I fear those villains have muddled your wits, my dear: I simply can't believe there's a bit of truth to your tale."

The gargoyle puffed out his chest. "Enchantress," he said, "do you mean to say that you don't believe your own gargoyle?"

"You were always fond of fanciful stories," said Miss Pimm. "This one is no different. My treasure has been perfectly safe for centuries, and I assure you all, there is no need to worry about it. This trip to Gunpowder Island has been rather exhausting, and I intend to deposit the villains in the Royal Dungeons and wash my hands of this nonsense once and for all." She peered at her embroidery and unpicked a thread. "I certainly don't intend to worry anymore about magic. I left the post of Enchantress long ago, and I have no wish to return to it."

"Well, that's just silly!" said Claire.

Miss Pimm arched an eyebrow.

"I'm terribly sorry," Claire hurried on, "but who wouldn't want to be an Enchantress? Traveling all through the kingdom, using magic, bossing people about—it sounds very grand."

Miss Pimm was silent for a moment. Then she put down her embroidery. "As you all are so fond of story-telling," she said, "I shall tell you a story of my own." She turned to Hilary. "It concerns a long-ago relation of yours, my dear."

Miss Pimm rummaged [searched] through her traveling trunk and pulled out a square object wrapped in purple silk. When she unwrapped the silk, Hilary saw it was the same silver-framed sketch Miss Pimm had kept in her office, the sketch of the old-fashioned gentleman in the balloon bas-ket. "Simon Westfield was a great explorer and a kind man. We were to be married—but this was all many years ago, of course."

The gargoyle sighed happily. "I love a good romance."

"I hardly think *good* is the proper word for it," said Miss Pimm. "I was very young when I first became the Enchant-ress, and even then, there were plenty of scoundrels like Mr. Fletcher. They wanted all the kingdom's treasure for themselves, and they certainly didn't want an Enchant-ress telling them what to do with it once they'd gotten it. When they realized that challenging me with magic was useless, they went after Simon instead." She looked down at the gargoyle. "I tried to protect him, of course, but Simon didn't care for magic. He thought it was unneces-sary. All he would allow me to do was carve a gargoyle for Westfield House, where Simon could ask him for protec-tion if he was ever in danger."

The gargoyle's ears perked up. "That's me!" ~~Made~~ *Made with magic*

Miss Pimm nodded. "But it didn't matter in the end—the scoundrels came for him when he was out in his balloon, with no protection to speak of. They conjured up a fearsome wind, and that was the end of it." She wrapped the purple silk around the frame once more. "After that, I wanted nothing more to do with magic. I couldn't tolerate being the Enchantress for another moment. But there was no one suitable to take my place, and I couldn't leave all the kingdom's magic sitting about without someone to look after it, so I gathered up as much as I could and hid it away." Miss Pimm tucked the picture of Simon Westfield back in her traveling trunk. "And I can't say I'm sorry. Magic has brought me nothing but misery, and we are all better off without it." *Sadness*

"I don't understand," said Hilary. "If you've washed your hands of magic, why do you give magic crochet hooks to all the girls at Miss Pimm's?"

Miss Pimm pursed her lips tightly, as though she wanted to keep the words inside from tumbling out. "If you must know," she said at last, "I am still searching for the next Enchantress. I'd like nothing more than to put magic aside, return to my home in the Northlands, and get a bit of rest, but I simply can't abandon my treasure until I'm sure it is in good hands. Being the Enchantress requires something of a knack for magic, you see. I felt sure that a High Society girl with that knack would pass

Ability

through my finishing school one day, and the responsibility for overseeing the kingdom's magic would fall to her. So far, however, I have been utterly disappointed. All my girls are more talented at crocheting than they are at enchanting." Miss Pimm smoothed her skirts and cleared her throat. "But I've said far too much. You girls mustn't start spreading any rumors, do you hear?"

Hilary and Claire nodded.

"And I do hope you'll forget this nonsense about my treasure being in danger. If I hear one more word about it, I shall have to speak quite strongly with your parents." Miss Pimm picked up her embroidery once more. "Now, I'd like to finish this pattern before the dinner bell rings, so I must wish you good day."

Residance hall

"BLAST!" SAID HILARY once they'd returned to the safety of the empty dormitory. "That didn't go well at all."

Claire pulled on her green woolen cardigan, which happened to be inside out. "At least we tried to warn her," she said. "We did the best we could."

"But it wasn't enough," said Hilary, "so we must be piratical about things."

Claire fumbled with the buttonholes on her cardigan. "Piratical?"

"Yes," said Hilary. "Father may not be the cleverest person in Augusta, but he is surprisingly skilled at villainy, and he'll tug Miss Pimm's treasure right out from under her feet. Unless I steal it first, of course."

"Oh, bother these buttons!" said Claire. "You don't really intend to *steal* the treasure, do you?"

"I do," said Hilary. "If we can't free Jasper from the Dungeons, I've got to be the Terror of the Southlands in his place. Jasper wanted to keep the magic safe from Father by handing it out to everyone in the kingdom, so that's what I must do."

"But you'll get expelled!" Claire bounced down on her bunk. "Don't you think there's a rule about not stealing things from the headmistress? Especially *magic* things? What if you're caught? Oh, Hilary, what if you're sent to the Dungeons forever and ever, and I'm not allowed to visit you, and you catch a terrible illness and you can't even *write* to me?" She clutched at her cardigan. "There's only one thing to do. I must be your (coconspirator) At least we'll be sent to the Dungeons together." Plunder

The gargoyle hopped across Hilary's bed and nestled himself on her pillow. "You're both getting worked up over nothing. We'll find the treasure, and we won't get caught."

"How can you be so sure?" said Claire.

"Well," said the gargoyle, "we're pirates, aren't we?"

Claire considered this for a moment. "Yes," she said finally. "I suppose we are."

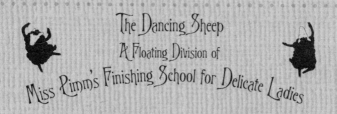

Dear Admiral Westfield,

Please forgive me for slipping this note under your door, but you seem to be out of your cabin at the moment. I am delighted to hear that you will be staying on in Pemberton for a few days when we reach the mainland. Of course you are eager to spend time with your daughter, and I appreciate your desire to learn more about our fine institution. I shall have a spare bedroom made up for you at Miss Pimm's when we arrive in a few hours' time.

I must admit that I have a delicate favor to ask of you in return. As you know, I intend to enroll the boy Charlie Dove at the Queensport Academy for Difficult Boys. However, I fear that it may be several days before the academy can find a place for him, and he cannot be allowed to spoil his own future by running away in the meantime. Would you be willing to watch over him at Miss Pimm's to ensure that he does not escape from the building or—good heavens!—wander the halls of the school?

I feel the boy could learn a great deal from your noble example. If you will allow him to share your accommodations, I will happily provide you with a lock and key.

Yours in gratitude,
Eugenia Pimm

Dear Hilary,

I hope this note finds you well. I regret that I was not able to say good-bye when we came ashore: the guards seemed rather insistent on dragging us away as hastily as possible. However, the Royal Dungeons are lovely at this time of year, and one guard was kind enough to bring me some writing paper. I have had to inscribe my own letterhead, of course, and I do wish I had my good fountain pen with me, but the guards assure me that criminals do not use fountain pens. As they are experts in criminal behavior and I am not, I have no choice but to believe them.

Are you enjoying Miss Pimm's? You must throw yourself into your studies and devote yourself to becoming a young lady of quality, for I would not want you to do anything rash and end up in the Dungeons. Not that the Dungeons are anything but pleasant—I have even befriended a small field mouse! We share the lump of cheese that I receive each day, and I have told him all about your courage and pluck. He sends his best regards.

Jasper occupies the cell adjoining mine, and he is just as cheerful as one might expect, given the circumstances. He has asked me to send you his good wishes, and he says that he hopes you are living up to your new title. I'm sure I don't know what he means by that.

We have been told that we may be given a trial if the royal judge is in the mood for one, but he is vacationing in his mountain lodge at the moment and cannot be reached. In any case, I hear that he is not too fond of pirates, so he shall probably send us straight back to the Dungeons. I have asked for some curtains and rag rugs to make my cell more welcoming. It is nothing like the bookshop I dreamed of having, but it makes one appreciate the simpler things in life, and I'm sure I will be a better person for it.

I must admit that I wish we were all back on the High Seas, but please, Hilary, do not turn to piracy in an attempt to rescue us! I know you never listen to a word I say, but you must understand that a few years of finishing school is highly preferable to a lifetime in the Dungeons.

With love,

Miss Greyson

CHAPTER SEVENTEEN

ALL THE LANTERNS at Miss Pimm's Finishing School for Delicate Ladies had been snuffed out hours before, but Hilary had no intention of sleeping. She paced the deck—or the floorboards, rather—of the room she shared with Claire. Then she folded and unfolded the letter she'd received from Miss Greyson in that evening's post. On the bookshelf above her bed, the gargoyle rested his snout on *Treasure Island* and grudgingly made space for Fitzwilliam, who had snuggled under the gargoyle's left wing.

"If you were the Enchantress," Hilary said, "where would you hide your treasure?"

Claire sat on the edge of her bed and poked at her guttering candle. "I suppose it could be anywhere in Augusta.

Oh dear; what shall we do if the treasure is buried up in the Northlands? We'll never find it then."

Hilary began to pace again. It made her feel a good deal more like the Terror of the Southlands, though she was fairly sure the previous Terror had never paced the decks in a white eyelet nightgown. "It simply can't be in the Northlands," she said after a while. "Father has decided to stay on in Pemberton, and I doubt he's making social calls. He must believe the treasure is somewhere nearby."

"Perhaps he's right," said Claire. "We're searching for the Enchantress's treasure, after all, and the Enchantress herself is right here." She wrinkled her nose. "What if it's in Miss Pimm's private rooms? What if it's in her *laundry*?"

"A pirate must consider every possibility," said Hilary, "no matter how terrifying."

Claire shuddered. "I believe I have a new respect for pirates."

On the bookshelf, the gargoyle sat upright so suddenly that he sent Fitzwilliam flying through the air. "Listen!" he said. "I hear footsteps!"

Hilary stopped pacing. Beyond the door, in the heavy hush of the dormitory staircase, someone's boots scraped up the steps. The gargoyle leaped off the bookshelf and dove into Hilary's blankets. "It's the ghost of Simon West-field," he cried, "come to seek his revenge!"

"Or Philomena," whispered Claire, "come to turn me into a fish stick."

"Or even worse," said Hilary, "it's Father."

The boots scraped closer. Then, just outside the door, they paused.

Claire gave a little shriek, and the door swung open.

"Oh, thank goodness." Hilary let out the breath she'd been holding. "It's only Charlie."

"*Only* Charlie!" Charlie blew out his candle and shut the door behind him. "I slip out from under the admiral's watchful eye, swipe a spare candle, wander the halls of this drafty mansion for nearly an hour, find my way to your room without stumbling over any sleeping schoolgirls, and I'm *only* Charlie? It hardly seems fair."

Hilary laughed and hugged him. "Whatever are you doing here? Shouldn't you run away before Miss Pimm sends you to that horrid academy?"

"I thought about it," said Charlie, "but I'm a pirate, and I can't abandon my crewmates. If Jasper wants us to find that treasure, I'll—" He stopped, and his smile slipped straight off his face. "Hilary," he said quietly, "did you know there's a finishing-school girl in here?"

"Oh! This is Claire. I suppose the two of you haven't met." Hilary turned to Claire, who was standing at the foot of her bed in her nightgown and robe. "Claire, this is my friend Charlie."

Claire curtsied. Then, for good measure, she took Charlie's hand and shook it heartily. "Hello," she said; "it's ever so lovely to meet you. Are you really a pirate? You're the third pirate I've met—after Hilary, of course, and the gargoyle. Hilary has told me all about your adventures on the *Pigeon*, and it's terribly kind of you to help us find the treasure. We don't *need* help, truly, but it will be pleasant to have company. I think Admiral Westfield is simply dreadful, don't you?"

Charlie turned to stare at Hilary. "What do I do?" he whispered.

"Why, Charlie Dove," said Hilary, "I do believe you're scared of finishing-school girls."

Charlie crossed his arms. "A pirate is never scared," he said. "It's . . . it's nice to meet you, Claire."

"How did you get away?" Hilary asked. "Isn't Father supposed to be keeping an eye on you?"

"Old Westfield crept out of the room long before I did, and he didn't bother to lock the door behind him. He had a spade tucked under his arm, so I think he's still hunting for the treasure."

"So he *does* think it's nearby." Hilary resumed her pacing. "But I suppose it could be anywhere in Pemberton. Do you know if Father left the building?"

"No idea," said Charlie. "I didn't follow him. I wasn't interested in getting myself run through."

"Ahem," said the gargoyle. He crawled out from Hilary's blankets and swished his tail. "I've been thinking about this treasure-hunting business, and I have an announcement. My ears feel funny."

Fitzwilliam rolled his eyes and cheeped. *Bird sound*

"No, it's not a private matter!" the gargoyle replied. "My ears tingle when there's magic around. And whenever I'm here at Miss Pimm's, they tingle like crazy."

Hilary stared at him. "Why didn't you mention that before?"

"I did," said the gargoyle. "Ages ago. But you told me I was just allergic to finishing school."

"Oh, gargoyle, I'm sorry. This is a wonderful clue." Hilary tipped an imaginary pirate hat to the gargoyle, and he tipped his own imaginary hat back. "But do you think you might be sensing the magic from the other girls' crochet hooks?"

"Well, I'm not quite sure," said the gargoyle, "but I think it must be more than that. Crochet hooks are little—compared to me, of course—and this feels big." The gargoyle's ears perked up. "Do you think the treasure might be other gargoyles?"

"I can't imagine that Miss Pimm would be silly enough to hide a community of gargoyles away for all eternity," said Claire. "Just think how cranky they'd get with no one to scratch their heads."

Hilary stopped pacing. "Hidden for eternity," she said. "Wasn't there something about that on the treasure map?"

Charlie nodded. "'May my treasure rest with me,'" he

said, "'hidden for eternity.' I suppose your Enchantress loves her rhymes."

"Well, that just proves it!" said Hilary. "If the treasure is resting with Miss Pimm, I'd bet anything that she's hidden it somewhere in this building."

Claire groaned. "I *knew* we'd have to sort through her laundry."

Hilary tugged a cardigan over her nightgown and pulled on her pirate boots. "This is no time to worry about laundry. I don't care if we have to take this school apart stone by stone: the treasure is here, and we're going to find it."

"Take that, Admiral Westfield!" cried the gargoyle. "Who's the pet rock now?"

FOR THREE NIGHTS they searched every inch of Miss Pimm's. On the first night, Charlie climbed to the cobwebbed rafters of the refectory, Claire dug up the gardening mistress's prize lilacs, and Hilary dove to the chilly depths of the swimming pool. By dawn they were dusty and dirt streaked and blue lipped, but they still had not found the treasure. Charlie hurried back to his room so Admiral Westfield would not notice his absence, and Claire and Hilary prepared themselves for a tedious day of waltzing and embroidering and fainting. Hilary would have preferred to abandon her lessons altogether—a few dozen absence notices were of no concern to the Terror of the Southlands—but she didn't dare give Miss Pimm any reason to be suspicious.

On the second night, the gargoyle hopped on every paving stone in the garden, but his ears refused to tingle. Fitzwilliam flew to the roof of Miss Pimm's and found nothing but an unfriendly flock of pigeons. Charlie nearly smothered himself in an avalanche of clean towels as he searched the housekeeping quarters. Claire peered inside all the cookery pots in the kitchen, and Hilary explored each of the fourteen powder rooms. The treasure was nowhere to be found. As Hilary and Claire made their way back to their bedroom at dawn, they caught sight of Admiral Westfield crossing the grounds, swinging his spade and looking rather grumpy.

"That's a bright spot, at least," said Hilary. "Father hasn't found the treasure yet, either."

Claire yawned and rubbed her eyes with a handkerchief. "I'm starting to think," she said, "that Miss Pimm has a summer house we don't know about, or a vault at the bank in Queensport, and the treasure is *miles* away, and we have absolutely no hope of sniffing it out."

"I'm sure that's not true," Hilary said, but she wasn't sure at all.

On the third night, the treasure hunters gathered up their courage and walked slowly past Miss Pimm's sleeping quarters. "Do you feel anything, gargoyle?" Charlie whispered. "Are your ears tingling yet?"

But the gargoyle shook his head. "Not any more than

usual," he said. "There's no magic here."

They trudged downstairs to the main hall, where they spent a good part of the night searching behind paintings and under carpets. The gargoyle even asked the stones in the walls for advice, but they didn't seem interested in making conversation.

"I had no idea piracy would be so exhausting," said Claire. She sat down on the floor to catch her breath. "If *I* had a treasure, I believe I'd hide it somewhere friendly and sensible. Under my bed, perhaps, or—oh, horsefeathers! Someone's coming!" She blew out her candle, and the hall was flooded with night.

As Hilary watched, a pinprick of lantern light traveled down the dormitory staircase, growing larger and brighter as it approached the main hall. The light paused in the doorway, and Hilary squinted into it.

"I thought I heard noises down here," said Philomena. She set down her lantern and sent shadows scurrying across the walls. "Miss Dupree and Miss Westfield, out of bed at a *most* unladylike hour. Well, I can't say I'm surprised—but who's this?" She jabbed her crochet hook in Charlie's direction. *Running quietly*

Charlie took a few steps backward. "That's none of your business."

"You're that pirate boy, aren't you? The one who's been stealing magic from your betters? No, don't move an inch." Philomena tapped her crochet hook against the palm of her hand "What do you think? Shall I stick you all to the floor until morning? It would make such a splendid surprise for the other girls at breakfast."

"You wouldn't dare," said Hilary. "If I had my sword, I'd run you through."

"Then you'd end up in the Dungeons," said Philomena, "with those dreadful damp pirates. I daresay you all would fit right in. But I shall be kind." She tucked her crochet hook back in her pocket. "I won't stick you to the floor this time. I will, however, report your misbehavior to Miss Pimm, and I expect she'll want to see you all in the morning." The lantern light faded as Philomena turned away. "And Miss Dupree," she said over her shoulder, "do stop trembling. I'm sure it won't hurt so very much when Miss Pimm takes your scholarship away."

MISS PIMM SUMMONED Hilary and Claire to her office before breakfast had even begun. As they walked through the echoing halls, Hilary dug a piece of hardtack out of her canvas bag and offered half to Claire, but Claire swore she was far too terrified to eat. "Do you think I've truly lost my scholarship?" she said. "My parents will be absolutely furious, and I'll never be allowed in High Society, and if I have to wrap up one more trout I think I shall scream!"

Hilary gave Claire a quick hug. "I suppose it could be worse," she said. "Miss Pimm could put all our heads on

her desk to gaze at Charlie—"it's clear that even Admiral Westfield is unable to control you. I simply cannot have pirate lads running loose in my school. Why, the thought is scandalous!" She dabbed at her forehead once more. "I've received word from the Queensport Academy for Difficult Boys that they have a place available for you, and you shall be on the first train to Queensport tomorrow morning."

Miss Pimm shooed away Charlie's protests and began to lecture Hilary about behavior befitting an admiral's daughter. Hilary groaned and slid down in her chair to give the lecture more space to soar over her head. She did not want to listen to Miss Pimm describe the glorious future of High Society balls, charitable works, and good manners that awaited her if only she would try a bit harder. Nor did she want to think about Claire, one slip away from being sent back to the fishmonger's, or Charlie, stuffed into that horrid suit and shipped off to a future far from the High Seas. What sort of pirate couldn't find treasure? What sort of pirate put her friends in danger? The temporary Terror of the Southlands had made a terrible mess of things.

Hilary couldn't meet Charlie's eyes, or Claire's, and she especially couldn't bear to look at Miss Pimm. Instead, she stared at the embroidered sampler on Miss Pimm's wall that warned her to *Beware the dangers of reverie.* She nearly laughed out loud. Villainous fathers and thoughtless Enchantresses seemed quite a bit more dangerous than reverie at the moment. Another motto assured her that *A lady never*

To much celebration

shrieks, but Hilary felt quite sure that she *would* shriek if Miss Pimm's lecture continued much longer. The most ridiculous sampler of all, however, was the one directly above Miss Pimm's head, with its rhyme embroidered in clumsy green thread on a stained square of fabric: *The greatest treasure in all the land—the delicate touch of a lady's hand.*

Hilary wished she could give the sampler a hearty kick. Who would have written such nonsense? It certainly wasn't the handiwork of a pirate: No pirate cared one bit for ladies' hands when there was a stockpile of magic to be found. And wasn't Miss Pimm the Enchantress? For goodness' sake, she *owned* the greatest treasure in all the land! She should have known better than anyone that the rhyme was absurd.

Hilary leaned forward to get a better look at the sampler. Embroidered at the bottom of the square, so stained it was hardly noticeable, was a small green figure eight.

"Miss Westfield?" said Miss Pimm. "Are you paying attention?"

Hilary nodded, but Miss Pimm's lecture had faded to a persistent buzz in the background. That hideous sampler must have been Miss Pimm's own work—or, more precisely, the work of the Enchantress. She enjoyed writing in rhyme, the figure eight was her signature, and the sampler mentioned treasure. It couldn't be a coincidence.

"'The delicate touch of a lady's hand,'" Hilary murmured. Was it truly nonsense? Or—she leaned forward so eagerly that she nearly toppled out of her chair—was it an instruction?

She could hardly sit still, but when the lecture ended at last, she tried her best to look solemn and sorry as she followed Claire and Charlie into the hallway. "I'll never be able to show my face on the High Seas again," Charlie was saying. "The Scourge of the Northlands wouldn't be caught dead in a starched shirt."

Claire covered her face with her hands. "And I'll be knee-deep in trout by autumn."

"No, you won't," said Hilary. "And Charlie, you won't have to go to that horrid school. By breakfast time tomorrow, we'll all be heroes."

Claire peered out from behind her hands. "Whatever do you mean?"

"I mean," said Hilary, "that I know where the Enchantress hid her treasure."

THE CLOCK IN Pemberton Square struck midnight as Hilary slipped out of bed, changed into her pirate clothes, and woke the gargoyle. He peered out from under the bedclothes, flapped his wings a few times, and yawned, showing his fearsome teeth. "Did I fall asleep?" he asked. "Did I miss the treasure?"

"You haven't missed a thing," said Hilary. Then she crossed the room to wake Claire. "You mustn't come with me if you don't want to," she whispered as Claire rubbed her eyes with the sleeves of her nightdress. "I won't have you getting expelled on my account."

Claire swung her legs out of bed. "How silly!" she said. "I've never had an adventure before—not a proper one, at least—and I don't intend to be left behind. Just think how thrilling it will be to find treasure! My sister, Violet, will seethe with jealousy."

Hilary picked up her candle in one hand and her gargoyle in the other, and Claire let Fitzwilliam settle on her shoulder. Then they slipped through the doorway without a sound.

The halls of Miss Pimm's were quite cold and dreary in the daytime, but at midnight they were positively chilling. Hilary's candle flickered in the drafty staircase, and the gargoyle jumped at every small sound that echoed through the school. At the bottom of the staircase, another candle flickered: Charlie was waiting for them.

"All's clear," he whispered as they walked through the main hall. "The admiral snuck out nearly an hour ago, and I followed him for a bit. I lost track of him when I came to meet you, but I think he's poking about in the library."

The gargoyle shivered in Hilary's arms. "Where are we going, anyway? You still haven't told me where the treasure is."

"I have a hunch that it's in Miss Pimm's office," said Hilary, "but I'll need you to feel around to be certain. Do you think you're up for it?"

"A gargoyle can overcome any obstacle, large or small," the gargoyle said. "But to tell you the truth, we're much better at overcoming the small ones."

The first small obstacle they faced was the lock on Miss Pimm's office door. From somewhere within the waves of hair piled on top of her head, Claire retrieved a hairpin, and Charlie used it to fiddle with the lock. After what seemed to Hilary like a great deal of experimentation, something clicked, and the door eased open.

The gargoyle looked around. He sniffed. Then he wiggled his ears. "I don't see the treasure," he said, "but I think my ears are tingling more than usual." Hilary set him on the floor, and he hopped to the far wall of Miss Pimm's office. "Yes," he said, "it's stronger over here. There's magic nearby, and lots of it!"

"Excellent," said Hilary. She placed the gargoyle on top of Miss Pimm's desk to give him a better view. Then she stood on her tiptoes until she could reach the sampler that hung in the center of the wall. Taking care to be as delicate as possible, she touched the sampler.

Nothing happened.

Charlie sighed, and Fitzwilliam let out what Hilary could only assume was a squawk of scorn.

She stomped her boots on the floor. "Oh, curses! I was sure that would work! To find the greatest treasure in all the land, you've got to apply the delicate touch of a lady's hand to the sampler."

"It makes perfect sense," Claire agreed. She hurried to the wall and touched the sampler herself, but the treasure refused to appear. Then Charlie touched the sampler, and then all three of them pressed their palms against it at once, but still nothing happened. "Perhaps we're simply not ladylike enough," Claire said at last.

"Oh, honestly!" Hilary stood on her toes again and snatched the sampler from its hook. "Maybe there's something we're missing."

"Like a big figure eight carved into the wall?" said the gargoyle.

"Yes, I suppose that would be convenient, but I hardly think—" Hilary broke off as she followed the gargoyle's gaze to the wall above her. In the space where the sampler had been, a large stone was marked quite distinctly with a figure eight.

"Well," said Charlie. "That looks awfully promising."

"Push it, then!" said the gargoyle. "I mean, be delicate about it and everything, but hurry up!"

Hilary took a deep breath. "Are you sure this is the right thing to do?"

"Yes!" said Claire and Charlie in unison.

"There's treasure behind that wall," the gargoyle added, "and you are a pirate. I don't think you have a choice."

"All right, then," said Hilary, and she touched the stone.

It wasn't a particularly ladylike touch—it was more of

a shove, really—but it seemed to do the trick. The stone sank back into the wall, and then, with a great rumbling noise, the entire wall slid away into the side of Miss Pimm's office. Framed embroidery crashed to the ground, sending bits of glass flying, and on Miss Pimm's desk, the portrait of Simon Westfield trembled.

Hilary held up her candle and stared. In front of her, in a room twice as large as Miss Pimm's office, piles upon piles of magic coins glinted golden in the candlelight. Stone shelves behind the coins were lined with rows of magical objects: carving knives and step stools, candlesticks and flowerpots, all quivering a bit from the surrounding magic. And a crate at the front of the room was stacked high with shimmering golden crochet hooks.

Charlie grinned, Claire gasped, and the gargoyle jumped up and down, making little dents in Miss Pimm's wooden desktop. "You've done it!" the gargoyle cried. "You've found the treasure! You're the Terror of the Southlands for sure—and *I* am your gargoyle!"

Charlie whistled. "I've never seen so much magic in one place before."

"No one has," said Hilary. "No one but the Enchantress." These coins and candlesticks must have belonged to her own great-great-grandparents, and to their friends, and to all the long-ago people of Augusta before Simon Westfield died and the Enchantress took their magic away.

Claire sank into Miss Pimm's chair and stared at the

magic. "It seems terribly unfair that it's been locked away all these years," she said. "I could have used a bit of magic at the fishmonger's."

"Well, it won't be locked away anymore," said Hilary. "Now, we've got to collect everything up and get out of here quickly, before Miss Pimm comes down to see what all the noise is about."

"It's too bad the *Pigeon* is still out in Gunpowder Bay," said Charlie. "We'll need a pirate ship to transport all of this magic."

It was true: The treasure was far too large for them to carry, and far too heavy, and far too *magical*. It was sure to draw the attention of anyone on the street who carried a magic coin or two. Hilary imagined pushing wheelbarrows full of golden crochet hooks through the streets of Pemberton. "I'm sure we'll think of something, but—"

Behind them, someone fumbled with the lock on Miss Pimm's office door. They stared at each other in horror.

"Open?" said the someone on the other side of the door. "Surely not! How convenient!"

Hilary had only enough time to reach for her sword— and remember, too late, that it wasn't there—before Admiral Westfield stood in front of her.

First, he stared at her. Then, he stared in turn at Charlie, Claire, the gargoyle, and Fitzwilliam. Finally, he stared past them at the gleaming piles of treasure. He crossed his arms over his belly and grinned. "Hilary, my dear girl," he said at last, "I must say I'm proud of you."

Whatever Hilary had expected her father to say, it certainly wasn't *that*. "You are?"

"Indeed," said Admiral Westfield. "You've found my treasure for me. Now, be a good little girl and let me have it."

an extract *From*
Treasure Hunting for Beginners:
THE OFFICIAL VNHLP GUIDE

IF YOU MUST **BETRAY** A FELLOW PIRATE:

Betrayal is a serious matter, and it must not be taken lightly. The VNHLP does not officially encourage betrayal, but we recognize that in certain situations, betrayal is necessary in order to save one's own life, obtain treasure for oneself, or achieve some other worthy goal.

When you are struck by the urge to betray someone, remember to STOP, THINK, and ACT:

First, STOP! Do not utter foolhardy phrases such as, "Ha! I have betrayed you!" before you are sure you have made the proper choice.

Next, THINK! Will betraying your fellow pirate cause more problems than it solves? Is the pirate likely to react with violence? Have you taken all necessary safety precautions?

Finally, ACT! Send the VNHLP a written request

for the necessary betrayal forms and complete these forms in triplicate. In these forms, you will be asked to provide the name of the pirate you are betraying, the reason for betrayal, and a description of the horrible fate you plan for the betrayed pirate. When the forms are received and approved by our head of Betrayal Services, you will receive a note permitting you to proceed with your betrayal.

Please note: All betrayals conducted without proper filing of betrayal forms are not considered official acts of the VNHLP, and the pirate responsible for the betrayal may lose his membership credentials.

CHAPTER EIGHTEEN

"N0," SAID HILARY. "I simply can't."

Admiral Westfield rubbed his ears, as though he hadn't heard Hilary properly. "What did you say, my dear?"

Charlie stepped forward before Hilary could stop him. "She won't let you have that treasure," he said, "and neither will I." He grabbed a porcelain-handled letter opener from Miss Pimm's desk and held it out like a sword as he approached Admiral Westfield. *Ceramic Glass*

Charlie was quick, but the admiral was quicker: He lunged forward and caught hold of Charlie's arm, twisting it backward and holding it there until Charlie yelped with pain. The letter opener clinked to the floor.

"Father!" cried Hilary. "Let him go at once!"

courage

Admiral Westfield sighed and let go of Charlie, who winced and dropped to the floor alongside the letter opener. "I admire your gumption, lad," he said, "but I've got no time for dueling." He reached into his pocket and pulled out a small golden coin that glinted in the candlelight. "Do you recognize this magic piece? I pinched it from your friend Jasper, and if you don't do exactly as I say, you'll wish you were in the Dungeons alongside him. Do you understand?"

Charlie rubbed his shoulder and nodded.

"You're a horrid beast, you know," said Claire, "threatening people with magic."

Admiral Westfield's eyes widened. "What's this? A little girl in a nightdress? Do you intend to attack me, too?"

Hilary turned to Claire. "Whatever are you doing?"

"Defending you, of course!" Claire smoothed the ruffles in her nightdress. "It's the only proper thing to do."

"But I don't need defending—"

Claire put her arm around Hilary's shoulder. "I'm sorry, Hilary, but I shall defend you whether you like it or not. Now, Admiral Westfield, I don't intend to attack you. I'm not very strong, if you must know, and I'm also not entirely featherbrained. But if you don't leave this building at once, I shall scream very loudly, and Miss Pimm shall come running. Surely she'll believe your villainy when she catches you trying to run off with her treasure." She cleared her throat. "I'll be screaming shortly, sir. And I

dumb

warn you, I'm rather good at it."

"Now, now, there's no need to be hasty." Admiral Westfield plucked an embroidery sampler from the floor, shook off the stray bits of glass, and mopped his brow with it. "A lady never shrieks. It says so right here on this hand-kerchief."

"Oh dear," said Claire. "I suppose that's another rule I'll be breaking, then." She smiled sweetly and took a deep breath.

Admiral Westfield made a fist around Jasper's coin. "Make that foolish little girl be quiet!" he said. "And make that pirate boy be quiet, too, while you're at it."

Claire opened her mouth, but no sound came out. She stood quite still for a moment, clenched her fists, and let loose a string of perfectly silent words that Hilary guessed were not at all complimentary to Admiral Westfield. On the floor by Miss Pimm's desk, Charlie was doing much the same thing.

The admiral dusted his hands together. "Terribly sorry about your friends," he said to Hilary, "but it will be much easier for us to talk now that everything is shipshape."

Hilary glared at him. "You don't care to magic me as well?" Organized

"Magic my own daughter?" The admiral looked scandalized by the thought. "It would hardly be proper, and after all, you're a reasonable girl. You understand, of course, that this treasure belongs to me. I have been searching for it for quite some time."

"So have I!"

"Ah, but there's a difference between us. This isn't a silly game for me. You can't possibly understand how important this treasure is."

Behind him, the gargoyle growled. "I want to pounce on him," he said. "Shall I pounce?"

"You'd better not." After the way Admiral Westfield had treated Charlie and Claire, Hilary couldn't bear to think what he might do to the gargoyle. "Father, I won't allow you to tyrannize the kingdom!"

Admiral Westfield folded the embroidery sampler he was holding into a neat square. "*Tyrannize*," he said, "is rather a strong term. I will simply be guiding the citizens of Augusta toward order and propriety." *doing the right thing*

"And throwing them in the Royal Dungeons if they prefer not to be guided?"

"Well, naturally. But I expect that my vast stores of magic will be enough to persuade even the most fearsome scallywags to do as I say." He smiled down at Charlie. "Isn't that right, lad?"

Charlie reached for the letter opener again, but Admiral Westfield tapped his forefinger against the magic coin, and Charlie punched the floor instead.

Admiral Westfield turned back to Hilary and put his

hands on her shoulders. "Now, tell me," he said. "What would you like?"

Hilary stared up at her father. He looked almost as she'd imagined him as a child, when he was away at sea and she was landlocked: tall and confident, and every inch a sailor, from the tips of his shiny boots all the way up to the beads of sweat on his brow. He dabbed at the beads with the embroidery sampler and gazed down at her. "I'll give you whatever you'd like," he said, "if you step aside and leave the treasure to me. I shall rule the kingdom soon, after all, and I want nothing but the best for my only daughter! Fine dresses—a whole new wardrobe, with those lace petticoats the girls like so much. Would that suit you? Or a sure-footed pony, shipped straight from the Northlands!" Admiral Westfield paused. "Of course; how foolish of me. Two ponies it shall be, and a new wardrobe besides."

The gargoyle snorted.

"Oh, for goodness' sake. I don't want ponies," said Hilary, "and I don't want a wardrobe." She removed her father's hands from her shoulders. Did he truly believe lace petticoats would do her a bit of good on the High Seas?

"Well, then, tell me what you want! I'll give you whatever your heart desires—anything at all, as long as you let me have that treasure."

Her father gave her a hopeful sort of look, and for once he showed no inclination to pat her on the head. They stood face to face, naval officer and pirate, and perhaps—just this once—the officer might respect the pirate's demands. Hilary hesitated. "Anything at all?"

Claire clapped her hands over her mouth, and Charlie shook his head furiously.

"You can't be taking him seriously," the gargoyle said.

"Will you let Claire and Charlie speak again?" said Hilary. She took a few steps backward. "And will you free my friends? Jasper and Miss Greyson—will you let them out of the Royal Dungeons immediately?"

Admiral Westfield wrinkled his brow. "Well, I suppose . . ."

"I'm not done yet." Hilary took another step away from her father. "Will you promise never to outlaw piracy? Will you ensure that the navy never attacks another pirate ship without reason?"

"My dear, I really can't . . ."

Hilary stepped backward once more. Out of the corner of her eye, she could see the crate of golden crochet hooks on the floor beside her.

"And if you truly want nothing but the best for me, Father," she said at last, "will you give me your finest ship for my very own, to captain as I see fit?"

Admiral Westfield stared at Hilary for a long moment. Then he burst out laughing.

"My finest ship! And you as captain? My dear, you had me quite convinced for a moment there; you gave me a terrible turn! Come now; be serious with me."

"I am *quite* serious," said Hilary. "Quite serious indeed." She spoke more loudly than she'd intended, and her voice sounded worryingly similar to Fitzwilliam's squawk, but she hardly cared now if she woke Miss Pimm. She'd wake the whole school and spend a lifetime in the Dungeons if it meant Admiral Westfield would be down there, too. Before he could do a thing to stop her, she bent down and gathered up a pile of golden crochet hooks in her arms. "Stay away from the treasure," she said, "and stay away from my friends."

Admiral Westfield clutched Jasper's magic piece, but Hilary shook her head. "That's no match for an armful of magic, and you know it. Put down the coin, Father, and back away at once!"

Strong!

The admiral placed Jasper's coin on the floor and took a careful step toward the doorway.

"Another step, now," said Hilary. "Go on."

He stepped back once more, shaking his head.

"You, my dear," he said, "are nothing but a pirate."

Then he turned, leaped onto Miss Pimm's desk, and snatched the gargoyle off it.

"Hello, my friend," he said to the gargoyle. "Perhaps I was wrong about you—you're very useful indeed. With your protection, I shall stroll up to the treasure and take it away one piece at a time."

The gargoyle shook like an earthquake. "But I don't

want to protect you!"

"That's a shame," said Admiral Westfield. "I don't believe, however, that you have any choice in the matter. You're working for me now, gargoyle—and don't any of you try to take him away from me." He glared at Charlie and then at Claire. "If you move so much as an inch, I'll make sure the gargoyle is nothing but rubble."

Hilary found herself gasping for breath, as though she'd been treading water for far too long and might sink to the ocean floor at any minute. "Please, Father, put him down! He can't stand to be used; it hurts him—"

"That's hardly my concern." Admiral Westfield looked down at the gargoyle. "You have to do as I wish, don't you?" He knocked his knuckles against the gargoyle's chest. "I imagine your precious heart won't let you do otherwise."

The gargoyle's ears drooped, and he nodded.

"Just as I thought." The admiral held the gargoyle firmly in both hands. "Now, then, gargoyle, I wish—"

"I shall be avenged!" cried the gargoyle, and he sank his teeth into Admiral Westfield's arm. "Hilary, quick! Avenge me!"

The golden crochet hooks clattered to the ground as Hilary dove headfirst into Admiral Westfield's legs. The admiral shouted and cursed, and the three of them crashed to the floor. Charlie pinned Admiral Westfield's feet down with his good arm, Claire grabbed Admiral Westfield's hands, and Fitzwilliam flew over them all, pecking at the admiral's shins. "I'll have that treasure," cried Admiral Westfield as he tried to squirm free, "and no half-grown pirates shall keep me from it!"

In the doorway, Miss Pimm gave a disapproving sigh. "Oh, James," she said. "I'm afraid I must disagree."

WRAPPED IN A paisley dressing gown, with her long white hair streaming down her back, Miss Pimm looked more than ever like an Enchantress. She set her lantern down on the floor, where it cast her shadow across the room and made Hilary feel quite small. She watched Miss Pimm examine the scene in her office: the broken glass, the stacks of papers knocked off the desk, the crochet hooks rolling about underfoot, and the vast array of treasure that shone behind it all.

"Eugenia," cried Admiral Westfield from the ground, "how fortunate you've come! These children were trying to steal your treasure, but I caught them in the act—"

Miss Pimm plucked a crochet hook from the floor and sat down in her chair. "Admiral Westfield, I believe you take me for a fool. Please be assured that I am not one— although I must admit I've given you far too much credit recently." She rolled her crochet hook between her palms. "I wish you wouldn't move an inch until I feel like removing you. You may let your father go now, Hilary; he won't be going anywhere but the Dungeons."

Sherif

In a matter of minutes, Miss Pimm had summoned the Pemberton Constable, and Admiral Westfield was escorted into a large black carriage, still fuming about That Meddling Old Biddy and That Treacherous Daughter. Hilary held the gargoyle close as they watched the constable's carriage squeak away into the night.

Claire rested her chin on Hilary's shoulder. Miss Pimm had restored her voice and Charlie's, but both of them still sounded a bit scratchy. "Will you be all right?" she asked.

Hilary didn't answer, but Charlie thumped her on the back. "Of course she will," he said. "Pirates always come out all right in the end."

Miss Pimm closed the heavy front door and bolted it shut. "Miss Westfield," she said, "I owe you an apology. It seems I captured the wrong villains after all. And Miss Dupree, Mr. Dove—please forgive me for the lecture I gave you this morning. Thank you all for defending my treasure."

"We were trying to steal it, actually," Charlie murmured.

Hilary nudged him in the side. "So Claire won't lose her scholarship? And Charlie won't be sent to that awful school?"

"That's correct," said Miss Pimm. "In the morning, I shall send a letter to the queen explaining the entire muddle, and I'm sure she will release your companions from the Dungeons at once."

"Thank you," said Hilary. "I swear they're not villain-ous." Then she thought of Jasper's reputation; he might never forgive her for damaging it. "Except for Jasper Fletcher, of course; he's terribly fearsome."

The clock in Pemberton Square chimed the hour, and Miss Pimm clapped her hands together. "You'd bet-ter hurry along to bed," she said, "or the dawn shall take us all by surprise. Now, if you'll excuse me, I must get my treasure in order before some other villain attempts to plunder it."

"Wait!"

Miss Pimm turned back to Hilary. "Yes?"

"Do you mean you'll simply lock up that treasure behind your wall again? The coins and the crochet hooks and everything?"

"Of course." Miss Pimm's eyes narrowed. "What else would you have me do?"

"Return it, of course," said Hilary. "Give it back to everyone in the kingdom who hasn't got any, so they can defend themselves from scoundrels." Robinhood

"It's out of the question," said Miss Pimm. "I told you before that Augusta is well rid of magic, and I meant every word of it."

"But we're *not* rid of it, don't you see?" said Claire. "Those grand High Society families still have a bit of magic, and most of them are awfully unpleasant about it." She hesitated. "I know you took all that magic away to stop people from being horrid, Miss Pimm—but plenty of people are still horrid anyway."

"And I can't bite them all," said the gargoyle. "I've only got so many teeth."

Miss Pimm tapped her fingers together. "I still don't see how setting all my magic loose upon the kingdom would improve matters."

Dueling with Miss Pimm, thought Hilary, was far more exhausting than any sword fight. "Think of Simon Westfield!" she cried.

The silence in the hall pressed like a blade at Hilary's throat.

"I assure you," said Miss Pimm at last, "that I think of him daily."

"If he'd had a bit of magic in that balloon with him," said Hilary, "perhaps he would have survived."

Miss Pimm pressed her mouth into a sharp line. She didn't say anything at all.

Then a familiar lantern light appeared on the dormitory staircase. In a flurry of pink nightdress ribbons, Philomena stomped down the stairs and straight across the hall. She clutched her lantern in one hand and her crochet hook in the other. "Just as I thought!" she cried. "Out of bed again. I warned you three last night that I'd stick you to the floor, and this time I shall do it."

Behind Philomena, Miss Pimm cleared her throat, but

Philomena didn't seem to notice. "Or perhaps," she said, "I shall give you all hives. It would be rather pleasant to watch you itch. Which do you prefer, Miss Dupree? Shall it be hives after all?"

Rash

"I don't think hives would be at all agreeable," said Claire, "but thank you ever so much for asking."

Disagreeable

"Don't be impertinent," Philomena snapped, "or I'll think of something quite a bit nastier than hives." She raised her crochet hook above her head.

"Philomena Tilbury!" Miss Pimm's voice filled the hall to its rafters. "Lower your hook at once!"

Philomena froze. Then she turned, set down her lantern, and dropped into a curtsy. "Oh, Miss Pimm," she said, "I didn't realize——"

"No, you didn't," said Miss Pimm, "and neither did I." She walked up to Philomena and removed the golden crochet hook from her hand. "Your behavior has been quite illuminating. I expected far better from my girls—but perhaps I was wrong to do so. You shall have your magic back, Miss Tilbury, when you learn how to use it in a manner befitting a young lady."

Philomena stared at Miss Pimm. She stamped her foot. "I shall tell my mother about this at once!" she said. "All of High Society shall be scandalized."

"Quite probably," said Miss Pimm.

"And I don't need your silly little crochet hook, anyway." With a sniff, Philomena retrieved her lantern from the ground and marched away in a pink-ribboned rage.

"Oh, dear," said Miss Pimm. She rolled Philomena's crochet hook from one hand to the other. "Perhaps I was too hasty after Simon's death," she said after a while. "I simply didn't want anyone else to be hurt."

"Giving magic to Philomena was a bit of a mistake, then," said Charlie.

"It seems I've made a number of them lately." The candlelight flickered across her face, and for a moment, she looked nothing like an Enchantress; she simply looked tired. "I suppose I must do what I can to set things right."

"Then you'll return the treasure?" said Hilary

Miss Pimm closed her eyes. "I will," she said at last. "A bit at a time, but I'll do it. Sending magic into the kingdom may help me locate the next Enchantress, and then I might have some rest at last."

The gargoyle hopped down the hall to Miss Pimm, pressed his ears against his head, and bowed. "Thank you, Enchantress," he said.

"Yes," said Hilary, and she bowed to Miss Pimm as well. "The Terror of the Southlands thanks you, too."

ROYAL NAVY ADMIRAL ARRESTED IN MAGIC THEFTS

PEMBERTON, AUGUSTA—High Society is simply abuzz! In a shocking turn of events last night, James Westfield, former admiral of the Augusta Royal Navy, was taken into custody in connection with the string of magic thefts that has plagued Augusta for months. As this fine publication previously reported, two pirates were arrested for this crime only last week. However, it now appears that these individuals—while they are surely rapscallions of the highest degree—had nothing to do with the thefts in question, and they have been released from the Royal Dungeons.

"We have Pirate Hilary Westfield and her fine crew to thank for this change in our fortunes," said Jasper Fletcher, one of the innocent victims of a wrongful accusation. "Pirate Westfield is the Terror of the Southlands, you know—bringing villains to justice and all that. And she's got quite good aim with a tin of beets. Any ship on the High Seas that stands in her way should be shivering its timbers. If the VNHLP knows what's good for them, they'll accept her as a member on the spot, before she hunts them down and feeds them to the sea monsters."

A spokespirate from the VNHLP could not be reached for comment.

In a related incident, a young naval apprentice named Oliver Sanderson was ~~apprehended~~ captured last night in a bungalow in Wimbly-on-the-Marsh. Mr. Sanderson was attempting to break into the bungalow while carrying a large sack of stolen magical items when he was noticed and chased by a band of ~~irate~~ angry pirates. "Aye, we captured the bilge rat," said one gentleman who identified himself as Cannonball Jack. "I respect a good plunderin' as much as the next fellow, but leavin' yer treasure at a pirate's house? That's just bad form." The items in Mr. Sanderson's possession are believed to match some of the items recently stolen from noble houses in Queensport, and they shall be returned to their owners in short order. Mr. Westfield and Mr. Sanderson refuse to say where the rest of the stolen items are located, however, and the queen's inspectors are still searching for this stash of magic. The inspectors also hope to determine whether Mr. Westfield and Mr. Sanderson were assisted by additional villains.

Mr. Sanderson will be sent without delay to the Queensport Academy for Difficult Boys. Mr. Westfield currently resides in the Royal Dungeons, where he is said to be healthy but rather damp.

THE ENCHANTRESS OF THE NORTHLANDS
ROYAL OFFICE OF MAGIC REGULATION
PEMBERTON, AUGUSTA

Dear Citizen of Augusta,

It is my duty to inform you that our kingdom's long-lost collection of magic has recently been located by an astute individual. Regretfully, this astute individual has also located me and persuaded me to write this letter. Do not think, Citizen of Augusta, that you shall receive correspondence from me on a regular basis. I assure you—we shall not be pen friends.

In the coming months, you will receive a small portion of the recovered magic, along with instructions for its use. All individuals, regardless of status, will receive equal shares, each equivalent to ten (10) magic coins or two (2) crochet hooks. The notable freelance pirate Jasper Fletcher has kindly volunteered his services to this office, and he shall be traveling throughout the kingdom on his ship, the Pigeon, to deliver this share of magic to

you personally. I shall oversee all magic use in Augusta from this moment onward, and I shall have no patience with those who use magic unwisely, so I presume, Citizen of Augusta, that you will behave yourself.

When everyone has received a share of magic, I shall begin a kingdom-wide search for the next Enchantress. If you observe a particular knack for magic in your friends or relatives, or if you possess such a knack yourself, please contact me at once so that I may set aside this nonsense once and for all. I may be reached in my permanent position as headmistress of Miss Pimm's Finishing School for Delicate Ladies, Pemberton.

Sincerely yours,
Eugenia Pimm
Enchantress of the Northlands

CHAPTER NINETEEN

AT ONE END of the small room above the empty bookshop, a round glass window looked out over Queensport Harbor. Its curved edge nearly touched the floor, allowing Hilary to lie on her stomach and watch the ships sail into port, load their decks with cargo and sailors, and ride the gray waves out again. In the distance, a naval ship sailed past, but it was hardly as quick or as grand as the *Augusta Belle*, and it was hardly as interesting as the hulking galleon that had just arrived in the harbor, with billowing black sails and polished brass cannons. Large Ship

Hilary watched a group of three men lower themselves from the galleon, row to shore, and disappear somewhere in the streets under the bookshop. A few moments later,

Miss Greyson hurried up the stairs.

"Hilary," she said, "there are some—well, some *elaborate* visitors here to see you."

"Elaborate? It's not Mother, is it?"

"No, I'm afraid not." Mrs. Westfield had refused to come out of her bedroom since her husband's arrest, and upon discovering that her daughter was the pirate responsible for his capture, she had fallen into a swoon finer than that of any Miss Pimm's student. Hilary and the gargoyle had thought it wisest to stay with Miss Greyson until Hilary's mother no longer spent a good portion of her day locked in her wardrobe. "I'd put on a pot of tea," said Miss Greyson, "but I don't think these callers are the tea-drinking type. I may have a bottle of grog in one of these boxes, though."

Hilary hurried downstairs and opened the door to find three elegant and imposing pirates lined up on the front step. The one on the left sported a peg leg, the one on the right an eye patch. The one in the center, who managed to look every inch a pirate without any of the traditional accessories, bowed to Hilary.

"Hilary Westfield, I presume?" he said with a twirl of his hand.

"Yes," said Hilary. "Who are you?"

"I," said the center pirate, "am Captain Rupert Blacktooth, and these are my colleagues, Hugo St. Augustine and One-Legged Jones."

"From the VNHLP," said Hilary. "Of course. Mr. Jones, I believe we've corresponded in the past."

One-Legged Jones looked down at his peg leg and murmured that perhaps they had.

"Won't you come in, gentlemen?" Hilary was not entirely sure how Miss Greyson felt about having strange pirates in the house, but she guessed that it would not be proper to leave them standing in the chilly sea breeze. "I'm afraid we don't have any furniture yet. The floor's quite comfortable, though, if you'd like to take a seat."

But the pirates declined. "We've only stopped by for a moment," said Captain Blacktooth, "on our way to a dueling exhibition on the other side of the harbor. Hugo, the trunk?"

The pirate named Hugo reached behind him and heaved an enormous wooden trunk into the bookshop. He handed Hilary the key to its gleaming silver lock. "On behalf of the VNHLP," he said, "with our most humble apologies."

"Yes," said Captain Blacktooth. "We hear that we have you to thank for the preservation of piracy, and we regret any, ah, miscommunication that may have taken place between us. Don't we, Jones?"

One-Legged Jones shifted his weight to his good leg. "Oh, yes. Absolutely." Thankfulness

"As a symbol of our gratitude," Captain Blacktooth continued, "we shall open membership in our organization to all qualified pirates. We'd hate to get on the wrong side of your cutlass, Pirate Westfield; we've heard some dreadful things about the pain you've caused your enemies."

Hilary thanked the captain, although she suspected that most of the pain her enemies had suffered had come from the gargoyle's jaws. When the pirates had departed, she unlocked the trunk and swung back its heavy lid.

The gargoyle peered down from a bookshelf high on the wall. "Now *that*," he said, "is a sword."

A shiny, curved cutlass with a golden hilt rested on top of a pile of brocaded pirate coats, balloon-sleeved cotton shirts, and sturdy sailor's breeches. A separate compartment in the trunk held a soft pair of leather boots and a fine black three-cornered hat, with six different colored feathers to tuck into its brim. And at the very bottom of the trunk lay a small printed card:

THIS DOCUMENT CERTIFIES THAT

PIRATE HILARY WESTFIELD

IS A FULL MEMBER IN GOOD
STANDING OF THE

VERY NEARLY HONORABLE
LEAGUE OF PIRATES

Miss Greyson rushed downstairs and exclaimed over every item Hilary pulled out of the trunk, and when everything was laid out on the bookshop floor, she uncorked her bottle of grog, pouring a glass for herself and a few sips for Hilary. "It's not fair, though," said the gargoyle as he munched on a celebratory spider. "*I* bit Admiral Westfield twice, but do *I* get a hat? No, not the gargoyle!"

"It does seem rather unjust," said Miss Greyson. "Perhaps I shall sew you a hat myself, if I can find a pattern that leaves room for your ears." She sipped her grog and looked around at the empty shelves surrounding them.

"It's a lovely bookshop," said Hilary. "Is it just how you dreamed it would be?"

"It is indeed. But now that I'm here at last, I can't help but feel that something is missing."

"No kidding," said the gargoyle. "You don't have any books. Do you want to borrow *Treasure Island*?"

Miss Greyson laughed. "It's not just that. I wonder," she said to Hilary, "what people would think of a floating bookshop?"

Hilary imagined Miss Greyson in her bathing costume, bobbing in the waves and handing out sea-soaked novels to passing fish. But no, Miss Greyson was far too practical for such things. "Would the bookshop be on a ship?"

"Precisely! I could sail from town to town, and I could advertise to pirates and naval officers who get bored on the High Seas."

"I think it sounds lovely," said Hilary, "but I suppose you'll need a ship, and someone to sail it."

Miss Greyson flushed again. Perhaps her stay in the Royal Dungeons had made her more sensitive, for she seemed to flush quite a lot these days. "I thought," she said after a while, "that the *Pigeon* might do."

"Well, yes, but then you'd have to sail about with Jasper. . . ." Hilary stared at her governess, who was now entirely pink. "You're marrying Jasper! Miss Greyson, you are positively scandalous!" Hilary leaped to her feet and hugged Miss Greyson. "However did he convince you? It was the Dungeons, wasn't it?"

"It was quite a bleak moment in my life," Miss Greyson agreed, "but I was ever so grateful to have Jasper in the next cell. It seems we've grown rather attached to each other."

"I bet they held hands through the bars," said the gargoyle.

Miss Greyson would neither confirm nor deny this. "I believe a pirate may be good for me," she said.

"You'll make a wonderful team," said Hilary. "Just think—you can torture his enemies with hours of lessons! But I do have one concern."

Miss Greyson clutched Hilary's hand. "What is it?"

"I don't think I'll be able to call you Mrs. Fletcher. It's not a particularly dashing name for a pirate's wife."

"Ah. It shall have to be Eloise then. Although," she whispered, "I won't mind if you call me Miss Greyson."

THE WEDDING OF a former governess to a freelance pirate proved to be a much grander affair than anyone had anticipated. Jasper and Miss Greyson had planned to be married in Jasper's vegetable garden in Wimbly-on-the-Marsh, but word spread quickly that Pirate Hilary Westfield and her friends would be in attendance. Soon, scourges and scallywags from across the kingdom were clamoring [gathering] for an invitation and a chance to meet the heroes who'd found the Enchantress's treasure and bested [won] the pirate-loathing admiral. It became clear that such a crush of pirates could never fit in Jasper's garden without tromping all over the beans and popping tomatoes under their boots.

When Mrs. Westfield finally emerged from her wardrobe, Hilary hurried up to Westfield House to meet her. "Please, Mother," she said, nearly knocking over Mrs. Westfield's best china teapot in her enthusiasm, "you've just got to let Miss Greyson get married here. No other lawn in the kingdom is large enough to hold all the pirates."

Mrs. Westfield nibbled on a cucumber sandwich and closed her eyes. "Pirates on the lawn of Westfield House," she murmured to herself. "No, I couldn't bear it. Pirates are far too violent. Besides, they'd trample the peonies."

"We'll ask them to step lightly, then," Hilary pleaded, "and they can leave their swords at home. Just think, Mother: the wedding is sure to be the buzz of Augusta. Wouldn't it be a grand thing to be its hostess? I'm sure pirate weddings will be all the fashion next season."

Mrs. Westfield looked up from her sandwich. She was still very pale from her time in the wardrobe, and Hilary had not seen her smile since Admiral Westfield had been taken to the Dungeons. Now, however, the corners of her mouth turned up ever so slightly. "Thanks to your father's villainy," she said at last, "this family's honor has been badly damaged, and your scandalous behavior hasn't helped matters one bit. To lose my reputation as the kingdom's finest hostess, however, would be the final blow. *Someone* has got to keep the Westfield name afloat." She shook her head. "All right, I'll allow it—but if there is even a hint of a duel on my lawn, I shall return to the wardrobe at once."

On the day of the wedding, Hilary stood in her old bedroom and adjusted her pirate coat in front of the mirror. She had chosen a red one to match Miss Greyson's bouquet of Gunpowder Island roses, with a lovely hem that billowed out behind her when she turned. "What do you think?" she asked the gargoyle, who had returned temporarily to his perch above her bedroom door.

"Not bad," said the gargoyle. "But it will be better when you put on your hat."

"Oh! I almost forgot—Miss Greyson sent you a present." Hilary dug in her trunk until she found a small box wrapped with ribbon. "She says you've got to look dapper if you're going to be Best Gargoyle."

Stylish

The gargoyle squirmed as Hilary tugged on the ribbon. "Do you think? Oh, could it be? It *is*!" he cried as Hilary pulled out a gargoyle-sized pirate hat, perfectly black and pointy, with an elegant white feather on top. "It really is! Get me down from here so I can try it on."

Hilary and the gargoyle were admiring their hats in the mirror when Charlie knocked on the door. Captain Blacktooth must have paid him a visit as well, for he was decked out in new pirate finery of his own. "You look quite fearsome," said Hilary. "It's exactly what the Scourge of the Northlands would wear."

Charlie grinned. "You think so?" He tugged at his breeches, which were rolled up above his knees. "Jasper says I'm supposed to grow into them. In the meantime, though, we're wanted on the lawn." completely

Hilary followed Charlie and the gargoyle down the hall, past the stained-glass heroes of history. She tipped her hat to Simon Westfield, who looked thoroughly impressed to see her in such a state. And she laughed out loud when she passed the Enchantress of the Northlands' window. Miss Pimm herself had stood in front of the window a few hours before and pronounced it terribly unflattering, although she admitted that at least the smile was accurate.

Just beyond the Enchantress's window was a small door leading out to the lawn, and just in front of the door stood Miss Greyson, looking a bit seasick. "I'd rather face a boatful of bloodthirsty naval officers," she whispered to

Hilary. "I don't believe I've ever seen so many pirates in my life!" But the pirates were jolly, and they cheered as the wedding party paraded across the grass. The gargoyle, at the head of the procession, kept the pace to a slow hop, so Hilary had plenty of time to study the faces in the crowd: A pirate she recognized from Gunpowder Island chatted with one of Miss Greyson's friends from finishing school, and Miss Pimm appeared to be getting along remarkably well with Cannonball Jack. And there in the very front row was Claire, beaming and waving as Hilary passed by. Hilary beamed and waved back. Then she took her place next to Jasper, who seemed to be nearly as seasick as Miss Greyson. Fitzwilliam sat on his shoulder, resplendent in a parrot-sized bow tie. Glorious

The musicians broke into a rollicking sea chantey as Miss Greyson walked across the lawn to Jasper. By the time they were standing next to each other, both of them had turned a good deal less green. "You've kept me waiting for nearly ten minutes, my dear," Jasper murmured. "I was beginning to worry a sea monster had gotten you. Is this the first time in your life that you've been anything but prompt?" On time

Miss Greyson smiled. "Mr. Fletcher," she replied, "in the pirate community, it's quite the thing to be fashionably late."

Jasper burst out laughing and took Miss Greyson's hand. Then they pledged to love each other through mutinies and treasure raids, and to always be practical. Claire bawled when they were pronounced pirate and bookshop keeper, and even the gargoyle dabbed at his eyes with a handkerchief attached to his tail.

Then the grog was uncorked and there was a great deal of celebrating. Hilary danced with Claire and Charlie and Cannonball Jack and the gargoyle, but between all the guests congratulating her on her piracy and all the guests congratulating the newlyweds, she couldn't push through the crowd to Jasper and Miss Greyson. Before she knew it, the sun was setting and the wedding guests were making their way through the streets to Queensport Harbor, where the *Pigeon* waited.

Jasper and Miss Greyson climbed onto the deck of the *Pigeon* and waved to their friends on shore. Hilary was usually very good at waving from the docks—she had gotten a good deal of practice waving to her father's ships, after all—but this time she nearly tripped on the cobblestones, and she had to borrow the gargoyle's handkerchief. Perhaps the salt spray from the water had stung her eyes, for she knew perfectly well that a pirate never cries. Now Jasper was checking the sails, and now the pirates on the docks were casting off the ship's ropes—

"Wait a moment, me hearties!" cried Jasper. "Where's my crew?"

Hilary looked up from her handkerchief.

Jasper waved his arms in her direction. "Hilary! Get up

here at once! Bring Charlie and the gargoyle, too."

Hilary blinked. "You want me to come with you?"

"I have several tons of magic to pass out to the good people of Augusta," said Jasper, "and with Eloise selling books all day, I'll need the finest pirates in the kingdom to help me. I may be the former Terror of the Southlands, but I can't do it alone." He held out a hand to Hilary and pulled her up onto the *Pigeon.* "You'd like to join us, wouldn't you?"

Hilary grinned and hugged him, not caring for an instant that pirates hardly ever embraced their captains. Jasper seemed to be unaware of this rule, for he hugged her back. "I assume this means you'll be joining us," he said.

"Of course it does," said Hilary. "But if you'll excuse me for a moment, I have to assist the gargoyle."

She settled the gargoyle into his Nest at the bow of the ship and made sure his hat was attached securely over his ears. "Anchors aweigh!" the gargoyle cried. "We're off to have an adventure!" He sighed happily. "I love adventure."

"So do I," said Hilary. "It's because we're pirates, you know."

She waved good-bye to the crowd on shore and to Claire, who jumped up and down and promised to write. Then a fine breeze caught in the *Pigeon*'s mainsail, Hilary hoisted the Jolly Roger, and waves parted to let the pirates pass as they sailed toward the High Seas.

ACKNOWLEDGMENTS

MARTINE LEAVITT WAS Hilary's first fan and her greatest champion. Thank you, Martine, for everything.

At HarperCollins, my wonderful editor, Toni Markiet, asked the perfect questions and turned this book into the story it was always meant to be. Rachel Abrams was wise enough to poke holes in the plot and kind enough to help me stitch them up again. Thanks also to Phoebe Yeh and the rest of the brilliant team at HarperCollins Children's. At Simon & Schuster UK, special thanks are due to Venetia Gosling and Jane Griffiths, and to Julia Churchill for putting this story in their hands.

Thanks to my agent, Sarah Davies, who works magic in her own right.

Thanks to the faculty, staff, students, and alumni of Vermont College of Fine Arts, particularly Julie Larios, Franny Billingsley, Sharon Darrow, the League of Extraordinary Cheese Sandwiches, and all the writers who saw the earliest pages of this book and wanted to know what happened next.

Melanie Crowder, Anna Drury, Hannah Moderow, and Meg Wiviott read early drafts and gave invaluable feedback and support. Amy Rose Capetta, Jonathan Carlson, Alison Cherry, Debbie Cohen, Kelsey Hersh, Eric Pinder, Emma Schroeder, and Kathleen Wilson bravely read various incarnations of Hilary's adventures. Thanks to the Lucky 13s for their friendship and advice, and thanks to Sarah Prineas for showing me how it's done.

My parents, Jane and Chris Carlson, taught me to love books and supported me in every way when I decided I wanted to write them.

And thanks to my husband, Zach Pezzementi, who stands by me through mutinies and treasure raids and who always believed.

THE VERY NEARLY HONORABLE
LEAGUE OF PIRATES

Magic Marks the Spot

**The Very Nearly Honorable League of Pirates
Membership Application**

A Conversation with the Gargoyle

**Read an excerpt from *The Terror of the Southlands*,
the second book in the series!**

THE VERY NEARLY HONORABLE LEAGUE OF PIRATES
Servin' the High Seas for 152 Years
MEMBERSHIP APPLICATION

Attention, young scallywags!

Would you like to join the Very Nearly Honorable League of Pirates as a pirate apprentice? Simply copy the sample application below on a clean sheet of parchment, substituting your own answers for the ones shown here. Completed applications may be delivered by postal courier or floating bottle to:

VNHLP Headquarters

16 Whiteknuckle Lane

Gunpowder Island, The Northlands.

Aspiring pirates who do not reside in the Kingdom of Augusta may submit their applications to our representative, author Caroline Carlson, through electronic post at caroline@carolinecarlsonbooks.com. If your application is exemplary, it may be shared with other pirate apprentices on Ms. Carlson's website.

Model

Name: *Hilary Westfield*

Desired piratical nickname: *The Steadfast Scoundrel*

Age: *13*

Home port: *Queensport Harbor*

Talents (check all that apply):

[x] knot-tying [x] sailing [ ] swordsmanship

[x] chantey singing [ ] parrot maintenance

[ ] mapmaking [x] digging [ ] cannon-firing

[ ] magic use [x] shouting [x] swimming

[x] ruthlessness

Can you tread water? [x] yes, for <u>37</u> minutes [ ] no

Are you allergic to parrots? [ ] yes [x] no

Name three items a pirate must never be without: *a cutlass, a fancy hat, and a fearsome reputation*

List three places suitable for hiding a treasure: *a desert island, a hollow tree, and an abandoned shipwreck*

Who is your favorite pirate from history or literature? *Long John Silver*

According to pirate lore, what is one of Augusta's famous long-lost treasures? *The toothbrush collection of Blackjaw Hawkins*

What is your opinion of the Augusta Royal Navy? *Their admiral seems quite unpleasant.*

Why do you want to become a pirate? *I simply can't imagine doing anything else.*

Thank you for your application!

The VNHLP looks forward to seeing you soon on the High Seas.

A Conversation with the Gargoyle

Daring, clever, and remarkably handsome, the gargoyle is a hero whose adventures on the High Seas have won him legions of admirers throughout the kingdom of Augusta. Earlier this year, the gargoyle sat down with author Caroline Carlson for an exclusive interview.

Hello, gargoyle. I'm so glad you agreed to speak with me today.
It's my pleasure. I wouldn't want to disappoint my fans.

Now, gargoyle—may I call you Garg for short?
I'd really prefer it if you didn't.

Oh. Sorry about that. If you don't mind my asking, why don't you have a name?
You humans are awfully fascinated with names, aren't you? I suppose it makes sense, since there are so many of you. If you didn't have names, you'd get yourselves all mixed up. I, however, am the only gargoyle of my acquaintance. For me, a name is as unnecessary as a bathing cap.

Do you mean that you've never met any other gargoyles?
Well, not *magical* ones. I've seen a few pleasant-looking fellows carved into the walls of churches, of course, but they're not very talkative. They usually just stare down at you without blinking, and they never even bother to compliment your hat.

Yes, I've noticed that. I think your hat looks very nice, by the way.
It does, doesn't it? Thank you for noticing.

You're welcome. Now, there's something else I'm curious about. How did you feel when you found out that your story was going to become a book?

Oh, I was very happy. As you know, I love all sorts of books, and I'm pleased that I finally get to star in one.

Well, Hilary's really the star of the book.

Are you sure? Maybe you made some mistakes while you were writing it. You might want to fix those the next time around.

No, I'm pretty sure—

And while we're on the subject, do you mind if I suggest a change to the title? *Magic Marks the Spot* is good enough, I suppose, but what do you think about *The Magnificent Gargoyle*? Or how about *The Generous but Humble Gargoyle*? Yes, that has a nice ring to it.

Um . . .

You should also add in some more romantic bits. The part about the wedding is pretty good, but Jasper and Miss Greyson don't even kiss! If you'd spent as much time with them as I have, you'd know they smooch all the time.

I guess I can talk to my editor about it. Other than the romantic bits, what's your favorite part of the book?

The part where I bite Admiral Westfield, of course!

I like that part too. How did he taste?

Sort of like mothballs mixed with sausage. I don't recommend the combination.

And what was your least favorite part?

I really didn't enjoy being carried through the waves on the way to Gunpowder Island. Water can be terribly treacherous for gargoyles. Luckily, my trusty assistant, Hilary, was able to keep me from sinking into the sea. She's very good at things like that.

Can you tell your fans what you've been up to lately?

Having adventures, of course! I've been sailing the High Seas, keeping watch from my Nest, and confronting all sorts of nefarious villains. We locked Admiral Westfield away in the Royal Dungeons, but his unsavory friends have been keeping my hands full, figuratively speaking. There's been a kidnapping, plenty of battles, a few magical explosions, and some very bumpy carriage rides—but it's all in a day's work, beloved fans. A gargoyle's job is never done.

**Turn the page for a peek at
Hilary's next very nearly honorable
adventure (gargoyle included).**

CHAPTER ONE

THE *RENEGADE* ARRIVED just after breakfast.

Hilary had been waiting for it, and she spotted it first. From where she stood on the deck of the *Pigeon*, the distant ship resembled nothing more than a small black smudge against the horizon, but when Hilary raised her spyglass to her eye, the smudge resolved itself into the billowing black sails and flaming torches of an impressive pirate galleon. "Isn't the *Renegade* grand?" she said, holding up the spyglass so the gargoyle could peer through it. "Doesn't it make your spine tingle?"

The gargoyle shrugged as well as he could without arms. "I don't know about that," he said, "but it does look a lot like a squashed spider." He drew back from the spyglass and gave the galleon an approving nod. "Now, back to business. Which do you think sounds better: *courageous* gargoyle or *intrepid* gargoyle?"

Hilary sighed. She was becoming rather used to this sort of question, for a few months ago the gargoyle had decided to write an account of his thrilling adventures on the High Seas. After several ink-splattered attempts to hold a pen in his mouth, however, he had asked for Hilary's assistance, and now she was spending a perfectly good morning taking dictation instead of sailing off on a thrilling adventure of her own. To be fair, it had been quite a while since any sort of adventure had crossed Hilary's path, and the commonplace tasks of life on a pirate ship—deck swabbing, sword polishing, and cannon dusting—were starting to make her feet fairly itch in their boots. But now Captain Blacktooth was coming to see her for a most important meeting, and wherever Blacktooth sailed, wasn't adventure sure to follow? Hilary looked out over the sea at the *Renegade* and willed it to hurry along.

The gargoyle nudged her with the end of his tail.

"Sorry!" said Hilary. With a good deal of effort, she turned her attention from the galleon to the parchment in front of her. "*Intrepid* has a nice ring to it, but you've called yourself intrepid five times on this page alone."

"That," said the gargoyle, "is because I am."

Hilary laughed and scribbled a few words on the parchment. "What do you think Captain Blacktooth wants to discuss?" she said. "He hardly ever pays personal calls." In fact, she had met him only once before, when he had arrived on her doorstep a year earlier to thank her for finding the kingdom's long-lost trove of magical treasure. It had been a most piratical accomplishment indeed, but surely Blacktooth wasn't sailing halfway around Augusta just to congratulate her again. "Do you think he might be planning to promote me? Or to send me on an important mission for the League?"

"Maybe he'll give you a medal for your bravery on the High Seas," said the gargoyle. "And maybe I could share it."

Hour by hour, the *Renegade* drew closer. By eleven o'clock, Hilary could count its sails. By one o'clock, she could smell the smoke from its torches. And at half past three, it sailed into the harbor a few yards away from the spot where the *Pigeon* had dropped anchor. Hilary woke the gargoyle from his nap and hurried to rub an errant scuff from the toe of her boot. "Captain Blacktooth has arrived!" she called, hardly caring that most of her mates weren't close enough to hear. Jasper Fletcher, freelance pirate and captain of the *Pigeon*, was ashore in the village of Otterpool, distributing bits of magical treasure to the townspeople. His first mate, Charlie Dove, was out in the dinghy, rowing piles of magic from the ship's treasure storeroom to the Otterpool shore.

And Jasper's wife, Eloise Greyson, was busy at the stern of the ship, where she ran Augusta's only floating bookshop. It was a shame they wouldn't get a chance to climb aboard the most magnificent pirate galleon in the kingdom, but Hilary was determined to memorize the *Renegade*'s every detail and tell them all about it when she returned from her meeting.

A pirate in a tattered striped shirt lowered a small boat from the *Renegade*'s deck, and he rowed across the harbor until, with an unceremonious jolt, he crashed into the side of the *Pigeon*. "Ahoy!" he cried. "I'm here to pick up Pirate Hilary Westfield. She's to have a word with my captain, and he won't have any arguin'."

Miss Greyson poked her head out of the bookshop. "What in the world was that bump?" she said. "It nearly sent all the detective novels crashing down on me."

"Ahoy!" cried the pirate again. "Are you Pirate Hilary Westfield, ma'am? You're much grumpier than I expected."

Miss Greyson pursed her lips to prevent a scolding from flying out, and Hilary waved her arms in the pirate's direction. "I'm Pirate Westfield," she said. "Are you Captain Blacktooth's mate?"

The pirate gave her a golden-toothed grin. "That's right. The name's Twigget."

"Well, it's lovely to meet you, Mr. Twigget." Hilary tucked the gargoyle into her canvas bag, slung the bag over her shoulder, and hung a rope over the side of the ship.

"And I certainly don't intend to argue with you. I know the captain is eager to see me, and I'm rather eager to see him as well."

Miss Greyson looked on with her arms crossed as Hilary lowered herself and the gargoyle into the rowboat. "Be home by suppertime, please," Miss Greyson said, "and remember to mind your manners."

"She used to be my governess," Hilary confided to Mr. Twigget, "and I'm afraid there's still a bit of governess left in her." She waved to Miss Greyson and promised to be home in time for supper—or, at the very least, in time for dessert.

Then Mr. Twigget tugged on the oars, and the rowboat squeaked and groaned its way across the harbor, bumping into the *Renegade* with a crash that nearly sent Hilary toppling overboard. When she had recovered her balance, Mr. Twigget led her up a wobbly rope ladder to the galleon's deck. "If you don't mind takin' your boots off," he said, "the captain likes to keep a tidy ship." He gestured to a large wooden crate, upon which the word *BOOTS* was written in red paint. "And we'll be needin' your sword as well." He pointed to the wooden crate that said *SWORDS*.

Hilary hesitated. She had polished her boots especially for this occasion, after all, and it was thoroughly unpiratical to give up one's sword to another scallywag. Still, this was Captain Blacktooth's ship, and it didn't seem wise to disobey his orders. "I'll get it back, won't I?" she asked as she slid the cutlass off her belt.

"Aye, of course—if you make it back alive." Mr. Twigget chuckled and slapped her on the back. "Just a little pirate humor, Miss Westfield."

"That's Pirate Westfield, thank you," said Hilary. She wasn't sure she cared much for Mr. Twigget's sort of humor, and she stood up a little straighter to make up for the lack of boots. "Would you be kind enough to direct me to Captain Blacktooth's quarters?"

"Oh, you won't find the captain in his quarters, matey." Mr. Twigget looked up into the *Renegade*'s billowing sails and pointed. "He's up in the crow's nest."

"And he won't come down to speak with me?"

Mr. Twigget shook his head. "He likes a good view, does Captain Blacktooth. You'd better hurry up and get climbin', for he's not too fond of waitin' around."

Hilary supposed there was no use in protesting; she wasn't eager to get into an argument with Mr. Twigget without her cutlass by her side. "Very well, then," she said, giving a brisk nod to Twigget. "If Captain Blacktooth prefers to stay in the crow's nest, that's where my gargoyle and I shall go."

The other pirates on the *Renegade*'s crew, who had been hauling grog barrels up from the galley and polishing the great brass cannons that stood at both port and starboard, stopped their chores and stared at Hilary as she crossed the deck. All of them were barefoot as well, but they had not been asked to relinquish their swords. "That's the pirate who's the Terror of the Southlands," someone in the crowd called to his mates. "I didn't reckon she'd be such a pipsqueak."

Hilary dug her fingernails into her palms but didn't say a word. A true pirate would never let such an ignorant scallywag bother her—though when the gargoyle stuck his head out of his bag and snarled at the *Renegade*'s crew, she didn't bother to scold him. "I would have bitten them, too," the gargoyle said, "if you'd let me get closer."

"That's very kind of you," said Hilary. She stared up into the ship's black sails and swallowed. "The crow's nest is certainly a long way up."

"Do we really have to go up there?" the gargoyle asked. "It seems like an awfully strange way for Blacktooth to give us a medal for our bravery."

"There's something rather strange about this whole meeting," Hilary agreed. But perhaps this was Blacktooth's idea of a test. Well, if that was the case, she had no intention of failing it. Charlie had taught her ages ago how to scramble to the crow's nest on the *Pigeon*, and when her father had been admiral of Augusta's Royal Navy, she'd swung from the ropes of his ships whenever he wasn't paying attention to her, which was often. "You'd better not look down," she said to the gargoyle as she pulled herself up into the rigging. "I know you don't like heights."

"It's not the heights I mind," the gargoyle replied from deep inside the bag. "It's the falling from them."

"In that case, you've got nothing to worry about. I'm going to show Blacktooth and his crew what I'm made of."

"If you splatter all over the deck, they'll see *exactly* what you're made of," said the gargoyle cheerfully. "And it won't be pretty."

Captain Blacktooth's crew had gathered below her by now, and they all stared up, tapping their peg legs impatiently and raising their eye patches to get a better view. Hilary clenched her teeth and climbed until the curious pirates were hardly more than small splotches beneath her feet. She climbed until she could see the *Pigeon* bobbing like a toy in the harbor below her, until the clouds were closer than they had any right to be. Why in the world did the *Renegade* have to be so absurdly tall? And why did her shoulders dare to ache so ferociously? When she reached the crow's nest at last, she hauled herself up and landed on the seat of her breeches, directly in front of a pair of polished black boots.

"Pirate Westfield," said Captain Blacktooth (for he was the owner of the boots). "My goodness. I was beginning to think you'd never arrive."

Hilary scrambled to her feet, set her bag down, and held out a sore hand for Blacktooth to shake. "I'm terribly sorry, sir. I thought most pirates preferred to be fashionably late."

"They do," said Captain Blacktooth, "but it's not a fashion I care for." He took her hand in a hearty grip, and Hilary did her best not to wince. It was peculiar, she thought, that the president of the Very Nearly Honorable League of Pirates didn't look the slightest bit fearsome— at least, not at first. He didn't have an eye patch or a peg leg or a hook, and the wrinkles at the corners of his eyes made Hilary suspect that every so often, when no one was watching, he allowed himself to smile. Still, he managed to seem more thoroughly piratical than all of his crew-mates combined. Perhaps it was because he was the only one allowed to wear boots.

"I see you've brought your gargoyle along." Captain Blacktooth raised an eyebrow at the gargoyle, who had hopped out of Hilary's bag. Then he rubbed his chin and leaned toward Hilary. "Are you sure it's wise to keep a gar-goyle as a pet? Don't you think a parrot would be more suitable?"

The gargoyle gasped in horror.

"He's not a pet, sir," Hilary said. "He's a friend of mine, and a pirate as well."

"That's right," said the gargoyle. "I've got a hat and everything."

"Ah. So you do." Captain Blacktooth pulled a pair of spectacles from his pocket and balanced them on his nose. "But Pirate Westfield and I have more pressing issues to discuss. Do you know why I've called you here?"

"For a medal?" the gargoyle said hopefully.

Captain Blacktooth frowned.

"I've been told that you want to discuss a matter of great importance, sir," said Hilary, "but I'm afraid I don't know what matter you mean."

"What I mean," said Captain Blacktooth, "is this." He reached inside the folds of his pirate coat and retrieved a thin slip of paper, which he passed to Hilary.

⊡ NOTICE OF UNPIRATICAL BEHAVIOR ⊡

This notice certifies that

Pirate Hilary Westfield

stands accused of violating the
Very Nearly Honorable League of Pirates
Rules of Conduct
and of behaving in a most unsuitable fashion.

This is your

[x] first warning [ ] second warning [ ] third warning

THE SWASHBUCKLING ADVENTURES CONTINUE!

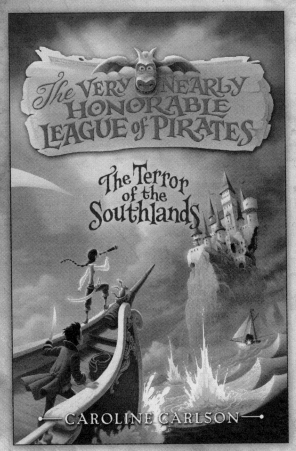

THE VERY NEARLY HONORABLE LEAGUE of PIRATES

The Terror of the Southlands

CAROLINE CARLSON

Sail the high seas in this
piratical sequel!

HARPER
print of HarperCollinsPublishers

www.harpercollinschildrens.com

What Pirates Would
Oo/not do

Pg. 84   Pg. 107

Pg. 177   Pg. 74

Pg. 142   Pg. ~~maybe~~ 17

Pg. 183   Pg. 26

Pg. 165   Pg. 67

Pg. 49   Pg. 200